Memory and Straw

By the same author:

The Greatest Gift, Fountain Publishing, 1992
Cairteal gu Meadhan-Latha, Acair Publishing, 1992
One Road, Fountain Publishing, 1994
Gealach an Abachaidh, Acair Publishing, 1998
Motair-baidhsagal agus Sgàthan, Acair Publishing, 2000
Lagan A' Bhàigh, Acair Publishing, 2002
An Siopsaidh agus an t-Aingeal, Acair Publishing, 2002
An Oidhche Mus Do Sheòl Sinn, Clàr Publishing, 2003
Là a' Dèanamh Sgèil Do Là, Clàr Publishing, 2004
Invisible Islands, Otago Publishing, 2006
An Taigh-Samhraidh, Clàr Publishing, 2007
Meas air Chrannaibh/ Fruit on Branches, Acair Publishing, 2007
Tilleadh Dhachaigh, Clàr Publishing, 2009
Suas gu Deas, Islands Book Trust, 2009
Archie and the North Wind, Luath Press, 2010
Aibisidh, Polygon, 2011
An t-Eilean: Taking a Line for a Walk, Islands Book Trust, 2012
Fuaran Ceann an t-Saoghail, Clàr Publishing, 2012
An Nighean Air An Aiseag, Luath Press, 2013
The Girl on the Ferryboat, Luath Press, 2013

Memory and Straw

ANGUS PETER CAMPBELL

Luath Press Limited

EDINBURGH

www.luath.co.uk

First published 2017

ISBN: 978-1-912147-08-3

The author's right to be identified as author of this book
under the Copyright, Designs and Patents Act 1988 has been asserted.

The paper used in this book is recyclable. It is made
from low chlorine pulps produced in a low energy,
low emission manner from renewable forests.

Printed and bound by TJ International, Padstow

Typeset in 11 point Sabon by Main Point Books, Edinburgh

For Linzi

I

EMMA IS PLAYING the piano.

The notes rise sporadically, as if they have no connection with each other. There is no obvious pattern. C. Ten seconds elapse and she touches D. Fifteen seconds this time. Twenty. Then E and F in quick succession, as if the order of time has been disturbed. She never practises her scales or arpeggios.

As a child I learned that time was fixed. Wake up. Brush your teeth. Wash yourself. Put your clothes on. Have breakfast. Cereal at the weekends. Bells rang throughout the day telling you that Maths was over and that now you should go to Room Fourteen for French. Then at eleven fifteen a longer bell sounded and you could play. Boys' games. Throwing or kicking a ball in the winter, hitting it with a bat in the summer.

The periods lasted forty-five minutes and the longest bell of all rang at four pm. The bus arrived at four ten and by four thirty we were home. Half an hour was given for play and at five o'clock we went into the study for an hour's revision. Dinner at six o'clock. Grampa sat in the old wooden chair at the head of the table. Granma moved between her chair and the kitchen. My sister Aoife sat to my left and I sat at the other end of the table, directly in line with Grampa. It was pleasant enough to be told what to do. I could then think of other things.

Aoife and I were not allowed to touch our knives and forks until Granny and Grampa lifted theirs. We were careful not to eat too fast, so as not to overtake the grown-ups. We would allow them to have two mouthfuls, then we'd take one. It was agony at first, but after a while we became used to it: eating carefully, like an adult.

After dinner, practice time. Aoife played the violin. I played the cello. I loved the deep sound it made, like a tiger growling in the dark, and spent my hours making animal noises with it. Depending on how you held the bow, you could be a lion or a mouse. A tiny frightened squeal at the top of the strings and a deep threatening roar down near the base. If you quickly rat-a-tat-tatted across the strings near the top you had a whole field full of rabbits running towards their burrows, and if you caressed the bottom ones it felt like Primrose the cat cuddling into your neck. Because I spent my practice time playing these games I never made any progress, while Aoife practised her scales and exercises diligently and played for the National Youth Orchestra.

From that, I learned that progress is always specific, never haphazard. If you want to reach a goal, you set targets. I could have been a decent cellist if I'd practised more efficiently. However, when I gave it up, in sixth year, my teacher Mr Henderson said, 'Your problem is that you don't love the cello.'

Emma loves the piano. Not for the sound it makes, but for the sounds it doesn't make. 'What fascinates me', she says, 'are the intervals. The spaces in between the notes.'

We'd just met. It was Maundy Thursday morning, and we went for a spin in the car down to Epping Forest. The sun was shining as we walked through the oak trees. I was telling her that May the 29th used to be celebrated in England as Oak Apple Day when she suddenly stopped and looked up.

'See.'

I looked. The sun's rays were shining through the leaves.

'See.'

'Yes?'

'The way the light catches the space between the leaves.

Isn't it gorgeous?'

A light wind was blowing the leaves, enlarging and diminishing the spaces.

She is now playing Gymnopédies, which I like. Things can be irregular, yet have a beautiful pattern.

Clouds for example. What I can't stand is disorder. The way she leaves her clothes strewn all over the place. It's not as if we don't have shelves and dressers and hangers and cupboards for them. I built them myself, from rescued wood from an old school they were demolishing: beautiful old pine which I scraped and smoothed and oiled. The little labelled cupboards I made from stained glass.

They are clearly marked, so really there's no excuse. Socks. Underwear. Jerseys. Blouses. Scarves. Handkerchiefs. When the sun shines through the roof windows the clothes glitter behind the patterned glass. And then there are the pictures, which she hangs haphazardly on the walls. As if a Picasso could hang beside a Rembrandt. They are of a different order.

'You're a bit OCD,' she says when I raise the issue, so I try not to. Instead, she gave me permission to put things in whichever order I liked, as if it didn't really bother her.

I spend time going through the house, tidying up her life – moving blouses to where they ought to be, putting the books back on the shelves in alphabetical order, so that next time we can find Graham Greene where he should be, sitting between Robert Graves and the Grimms.

'It's displacement,' she said. 'External order for internal chaos. The truth, Gav, is that your life is without emotional architecture. Like a room hanging in mid-air. It needs a structure. How do you get to it? Or from it? By stairs? By flying? And anyway, what do you do in that room?' She spoke like a lecturer.

I used to have a box. A simple cardboard shoe-box which my grandfather Magnus gave me. It was filled with old photographs and scraps of paper. I'd look at them now and again: black and white pictures from another time and place, and all kinds of hand-written notes about gardening and fishing. I had it stored beneath the shoe-rack at the bottom of the cupboard, but one day I returned home and it was gone.

'I needed a box just that size to send some manuscripts in the post,' Emma said. 'I put the stuff that was in it in the drawer.'

As if the box itself didn't matter.

I'm currently reading Hobbes, who also argued for order. I try to stop myself from quoting him when I speak to Emma, but I can't help myself. He puts things so well in the midst of chaos. At breakfast, for example, she put the honey spoon into the marmalade jar. I just looked at her and she immediately said, 'You're angry, Gav.'

There's nothing I dislike more than when she is reasonable.

'It's courage,' I said. 'Hobbes said that sudden courage is anger.'

'Fuck Hobbes,' she said.

It's Saturday, so after lunch we go to the beach, where order is always restored. The waves lap on to the sand and you can watch the rising tide-line until it can go no further. Then it recedes. It takes four hours to come in, and four hours to go out. It's just science: because the Earth spins on its own axis, ocean water is kept at equal levels around the planet by the Earth's gravity pulling inward and centrifugal force pushing outward. There's nothing mystical about it. One thing leads to another. It's like birdsong: the chaffinch sings the same song eternally.

The beach is quiet. One of the many little coves in the area. An hour's drive from the town, so hardly anyone ever there.

We have it to ourselves again. Emma is getting ready to swim. She has a wonderful way of undressing. I need to stand up to take my clothes off, but she does it all in one elegant movement standing, sitting, or lying down. It's childlike in its liberty. As usual, she flings her clothes on the sand. I resist the temptation to tidy them up. Her skin glistens.

'Swim? Go on, Gav.'

She knows I prefer to lie in the sand sunbathing. She takes my hand and I undress in my usual awkward standing-on-one-leg way at the edge of the sea. We swim out as far as the inner light. She leads the way with strong steady strokes and I follow with equal measures. The initial chill has gone and the further out we swim the warmer it seems to get.

'The sand bank,' she calls out. 'Makes it warmer out here.'

Warm enough to float easily on our backs gazing at the sky. We are weightless, like birds. Perhaps if we remain here, afloat, we will live forever. As the water moves, our bodies occasionally touch. A hand, a foot, the sharp contours of our hips. For a moment she seems like the best evidence for God in the universe. When we touch one another it confirms the fact. We kiss the salt off each other's lips. Her hands are smooth and the soft down on her arms reminds me of the first time we lay down in the woods, afraid. The moss beneath us was like velvet, and as we looked up we saw a tree as we ought to have seen a tree, for the first time. It got thinner the higher it climbed, until the branches became part of the blue sky.

She suddenly dives into the water and I count. It's our game: how long she can stay submerged for, and the longer she stays the more difficult it is for me to guess where she'll surface. I reach ninety and see a stirring in the waters about a hundred metres to my left. She emerges ten seconds later a hundred metres to my right, her hand raised in a victory sign. She has a dazzling smile.

We go home. We usually have a shower then and go for a walk. Down by the boulevard and on to the coastal path that takes you right along the side of the golf course. There are several resting-places along the route, each with its own view. By the edge of the fifth tee you can see all the way out beyond the lighthouse and watch the oil-tankers glide north and south, to and from the terminal. The next bench is at the corner of the twelfth fairway, where we look west towards the low-lying undulating hills which never harness any clouds. And the final resting place is down from the eighteenth green where you have the best view of the town itself, with its splendid spires. We then walk back the same way, sometimes stopping for a beer at one of the beach café-bars, before getting dressed for dinner.

Enrique knows we always arrive there at six, so everything is ready. We have our own corner table. The simple red and white checked table cloth, the single white rose and the solitary iris, a plate of unseeded Greek olives and bread fresh from the oven. And we like the music he plays, which makes you feel as if it will always be like this. My Granma used to say that if you wished for something hard enough then it would happen.

We smile and play the game of choices. When the menu arrives we extend the game by taking ages to go through every option, discussing the possibilities. Too warm for soup of course, so we have the usual discussion as to whether to have a starter and main course or opt out and go for a sweet afterwards. We vowed years ago never to have the three courses except when there are friends there and we extend the meal for hours.

This time we choose a mussel and calamari salad for starters, followed by sea bass for me and quail for her. Each and every morsel of each dish is delicious. The mussels and calamari are just the right textures – firm, but moist and delicate – and the bass and quail perfect. We have our usual light-hearted discussion about the wine, finally choosing the Leflaive, which tastes like nectar. We linger over coffee, watching the evening lovers stroll down the sea side of the street where all the vendors are trading.

We join them for our own stroll. I buy Emma a gardenia which she carefully places in her hair, and she buys me a decorative pop-up striped mini umbrella which I play with as we walk along, singing in the rain, though the sun is setting orange in the west and not a drop of rain has been felt here in months. We end up on the main beach itself amongst the others, sitting on sailcloth chairs which Jamie hires out at ten dollars a time. The sea laps round the edges of the leisure boats which adorn the harbour.

'What is it?' she asks.

'Nothing.'

'Nothing?'

'It's a big word.'

So big I have no words for it.

'It's just…'

'Yes?'

Tiny beads of perspiration glisten on her upper lip.

'Shall we walk?' I suggest. 'Along to the pier? We'll get something of a breeze along there.'

She slips her arm into mine and we walk along the wooden decking towards the quay. We stand near the edge gazing at the green light blinking to our left and the red light answering to the right.

'For those in peril on the sea,' I sing quietly.

'Oh, hear us when we cry to thee,' she whispers in response.

This is it. It will never get better than this.

The breeze is warm on our faces. The best bench, the green one with the comfortable arm rests, is empty so we sit there, side by side. Her finger traces some kind of outline on the back of my right hand which rests on my knee.

'What are you thinking?' she asks.

I hedge again.

'Was that a map?' I ask. 'On the back of my hand.'

She laughs.

'A map? *Boy's Own* stuff. Everything's a map. Don't fudge things, Gav. What is it?'

What is it? We have settled here, that's all. After all that. In this beautiful weekend port on Martha's Vineyard, where the sea is so blue, the sky so clear. It was like coming up for air after holding your breath underwater for days. Like emerging into a sunlit meadow after being trapped in the undergrowth for years. It was a necessary heaven, gifted to us by Fitzgerald.

We'd always dreamed of it. This place beyond chaos, where the headland erases memory, where the permanent lapping of the sea reassures you that everything is in order. Things which seemed miraculous have become commonplace, while the things which were commonplace are now miraculous. We listen, and sometimes hear each other speak.

I remember the first time we flew into the Vineyard with Cape Cod glittering below, so near that you could almost touch it. Like everyone else, I suppose we'd brought our dream with us, but despite that foolishness it did not disappoint. We played Joni Mitchell tracks and danced. It may just be the million to one chance, but I think it was more. I think it was that inevitable thing, where the dream fitted the reality, rather than the other way round. Like when as a child the bit of wood found down by the stream really became the cricket bat which scored all those sixes. Aoife would bowl and I would always ask her to throw the ball gently so that I could hit it over the other side of the river.

It's always so difficult to cross the river. So damn difficult. For how do you get the fox and the goat and the hay all across safely? The ferryman can only take one across at a time. And, if left alone, the fox will eat the goat, and the goat will eat the hay.

'So how did he manage it?'

Emma looked at me.

'He took the goat over first, and left the fox with the hay.'

'And?'

'And then he returned for the fox.'

'And?'

'And, having ferried it across, he then took the goat back, and left it.'

'And he then ferried the hay across, which he left with the fox, and returned for the goat.'

'And took him across?'

'Correct.'

There was always a solution.

'What's higher than mountains, deeper than sea, sharper than blackthorn and sweeter than honey?' she asked in return.

'Love.'

2

IT STARTED SIMPLY as part of my work. Technology has developed so rapidly that it's difficult to remember we grew up without any of this assistance. My dad used to take me fishing, and the best thing was simply making the rods: gathering fallen bits of branches from the forest, then whittling them down by the stove on the Friday evening.

'Splice forwards,' he'd say, holding my hand steady as I cut the knife through the wood. 'And always go with the grain.'

Hazel was best. It was pliable, yet firm. After a while it moulded into the shape of your hand.

I now know that my ancestors had other means of moving through time and space, and the more I visit there the simpler it becomes. For who would not want to fly across the world on a wisp of straw, and make love to a fairy woman with hair as red as the sunset?

The more I discover, the more I like the precision of their world: to dream of your future husband, you pluck a few ears of corn with the stalk and place them with your right hand under the left side of your pillow. Threshed corn will not do. Exactitude is important. Otherwise, the magic won't work. If you made a clay corpse it had to be in the image of the person you wanted to harm. You pierced the body exactly where you wanted the ailment to strike. Curses, just like blessings, were specific. Once extracted from their native heath and time they don't work.

I work in nanotechnology, which is where my drive for precision found its home. There is no room here for approximation. As the old divines would have put it, things are either right or wrong. One binary digit equals the value of zero or one, and so eight bits equal one byte and one thousand and twenty-four bytes equal one kilobyte and so on up to my good friend the petabyte which equals 1,125,899,906,842,624. None of it ever varies or hesitates with doubt. It is perfect music.

Over the past two years I've been the lead engineer on masking for the care industry. The franchise is owned by a Japanese company, but they've subcontracted the work out to our branch here in New York. It's a growing industry simply because people get older by the day.

I won't tire you with the statistics, but the demographics look good. In the next decade alone the number of over eighties is due to quadruple throughout the world, with the biggest market developing in the far east itself. My job is to put a human face on the robots who will care for that generation. As a mark of respect for the great man, we call the central machine Albert.

Despite all our technology, humans cling on to their traditions. Old people especially like the familiar. They like routine, a safe process which keeps death at bay for a while longer. Even though our robots can run every care home far more efficiently that any nurse or carer, the residents still want to see a human face in the morning serving them breakfast, and last thing at night tucking them into bed. So we've made our robots human; have developed lifelike masks which have deceived even the young in experiments. If something looks human, it is human.

My line manager Hiroaki Nagano put it straight to me the very first day.

'We're doing these guys a favour. It's dangerous out there in the world for them, so far better they never leave their homes. Most of them don't want to anyway, and the rest would be better not to. Safe from muggings, assault, robberies, terrorism. They're old, and will never need to leave their houses again. We'll provide them with the tireless companion who will meet their every need. A cyborg friend who won't complain, demand better wages or conditions, speak back or abuse them. A win-win for everyone, Gavin.'

It's not just an engineering problem. The real challenge is aesthetic. Creating mask-bots which are not only lifelike, but lifelike in a familiar, flawed way. For beauty is in the eye of the beholder. Apart from a few perverts and perfectionists, most of the old people we cater for prefer carers as fragile as themselves. If you really study the human face you'll discover that it's perfectly imbalanced. Most folk imagine that the nose is halfway down the face: in fact the eyes are the halfway point. What comforts us is human imperfection. A face is nothing without its history.

As a team, we spent some considerable time studying facial characteristics across the world, because the market is now multicultural and global. You'd be surprised how racist many old people still are. Here in the United States, many of the older residents feel more comfortable being cared for by masks of their own colour, though they are happy enough to see black or Mexican faces making their beds or cleaning the floors. Old habits die hard. Our target is to make a composite face which will be universally acceptable.

I stumbled across my own genealogy while doing this research. Because there's such a big Irish diaspora over here I was tasked with the job of studying Celtic features. I resisted for a while because I knew the word was meaningless – where would I begin or end? In 200BC in Thrace or in 2000AD in Scotland? I recognised the moral uncertainty that ran through the whole project, filtering individual human characteristics and histories down to general traits. But I wasn't Mengele. At the end of the day, the project was designed to help people, and if some generic features made old vulnerable people feel safe, then surely all to the good? The ends always justify the means.

The clearest lesson I learned during my research was that features on faces are earned, not given. The age lines, the wrinkles, the curve of the mouth, the light – or darkness – in the eyes. These are the consequences of lived lives, not just the DNA. Hurt, pain and joy experienced are all etched there, as if Rembrandt had suddenly caught the moment when joy or sorrow had called.

I stripped naked and looked at myself in the mirror: the slight middle-aged paunch, the stoop of the shoulders, the face that reminded me of a boy I knew once upon a time.

I probably broke some unwritten rule that you never complicate your research with your personal life, but one day as I was idling at the computer I entered my father and my mother's name, and the day disappeared leafing through their history. Or at least the history that was recorded there, for like all histories, most lay unrecorded. Like those gaps which Emma saw between the leaves, I suppose.

The internet is such a recent phenomenon, but nevertheless it has already harvested the work of centuries, so it wasn't that difficult to scour genealogical and historic sites. The photographs were particularly fascinating: the further back I went the more difficult it was to find images of my own ancestors, but there were so many historical society sites that it was easy enough to get a sense of the times and places they lived in.

Old men with beards and old women with long black skirts outside stone houses. Sometimes children playing in black and white, with toy wooden boats or prams. Horses and dogs and carts carrying luggage. Hundreds of faces looking down as the ship left the quay.

I showed some of the material to Emma that evening. She didn't seem greatly interested.

'Isn't that what people of a certain age do for a hobby? Start finding their roots?'

'Well, I never really fancied stamp-collecting.'

I told her a bit about my family tree.

'You should go to a séance. You could meet them there,' she said.

What fascinated me immediately were the objects my ancestors had. Ploughs and hand-made saws, clay pots and spindles: things you could see in such fine detail once you digitised the old photographs. Sometime later, on one of Grandfather Magnus's shelves I found a family photograph of my great-grandmother's cottage with a bogle leaning against the thatched roof. The bogle was the slim stem of a dead fir, devoid of branches except at the top which was dressed, like a scarecrow, with a white cap and an old jacket. It was set on the ground leaning against the wall and roof overnight, and shifted every morning from one side of the doorway to the other to protect the house and the inmates from harm by the witch.

It was magic. Images were totems which brought blessings or curses. You could sail to success or starvation. I studied the photograph of the people on the emigrant ship. They were of all ages, from babes on the breast to old women in shawls. None of the faces wore masks – fear and hope, sadness and joy were etched on all the faces. I realised that making masks for care work was essentially about tracing these emotions into the contours. The more I understood these emotions, the more effective these masks would be. More people would buy and use them.

I decided to make a test case of myself. To discover how my face worked – what had left it the shape it was, with all the anxieties and hopes that made it more than a fixed mask. The face that I was, beyond DNA, uniquely sprung from all the faces that had been. I travelled. Read. Remembered. Visited ruins and homes. Talked to relatives. Found Grampa's notes in his old shed, studied the local papers in the Inverness Library Archive, met Ruairidh on the old bridge that takes you to Tomnahurich. Borrowed, plagiarised, and invented things.

'Will you come with me?' I asked Emma. But she had her reasons.

'I'm working on a new composition. And there's a deadline, Gav. You know that.'

'The real answer is that you don't want to go.'

These are the stories I rescued out of the infinity that opened up before me, beginning with my great-great-grandmother, Elizabeth.

3

SHE LAY THERE. The first twenty minutes always gave her a chance. To listen. To the sound of the night fading away, or to the river outside. Time to put things in order. First the fire, then the porridge, then the milking and the children. For once he turned over, that was it, and some sweet sleep would come.

Strange how you could see things with your eyes closed. There was Maisie the cow grazing, and when you stood on the distant headland at Rubh' an Òrdaig you could watch the porpoises dancing far out in the bay. They were there even when she was not. She could conjure them up with a thought. Even things that she'd never seen or heard. Gorgeous plumed birds and spokes that moved and children that grew fat on laughter. You didn't need to see things to know they were there. They were inside you, like clouds becoming sudden shapes in a dark blue sky.

Sometimes Elizabeth dreamt. Of silk and white brocade and a brooch like Lady MacLeod wore the day she came to the funeral service. Everyone was surprised to see her, but the minister pointed out it was a great honour to the deceased that Her Ladyship was in attendance. Old Morag had, after all, attended to her every need since she'd been a child, and she was now returning the compliment at the last. The brooch was silver and glinted in the pale afternoon sun which shone in over and across the coffin through the church window. Morag's husband John had made the coffin himself out of driftwood saved for this inevitable moment.

These were daydreams. At night it was just the deep dreamless sleep of exhaustion, until one of the cockerels woke her. There were three of them. Old Thomas, who crawed at the most unlikely hours, having lost all sense of day and night. And the two younger ones, Red and Flash, at the peak of their powers crowing just as the sun rose, summer and winter, spring and autumn. They had instinctive precision, as if the sun rose at their behest and not the other way round. Every morning they heralded the dawn of a new day into this rolling world divided into quarters. For there was east and west and north and south, spring and summer and autumn and winter. Each morning – each season – was like a fresh loaf of bread out of the oven. You couldn't eat it all at once. You had to keep some for the afternoon. For supper. For tomorrow, just in case. You never knew. Anything could happen, even as the sun shone and while the crops grew.

Calum built the bed so that it was easier for her to slide out first, nearest the door. She could do it all noiselessly, almost invisibly. In one movement, pulling on the woollens before her stockinged feet hit the sandy floor. The latch raised and lowered quietly so that he could sleep on, and the bairns all piled together in the other room. Even the cows at the other end of the house had learned to slumber until everything was ready, warming the whole house with their rich slow breath.

A winter's morning. She kindled the fire and added the peat and boiled the pan. Outside, the stars twinkled in the frost. She did her morning's business in the hollow down by the back of the byre. She could hear him coughing as he rose. The damp would be the death of him. He was a good man, though as light-headed as the lark. If it wasn't for providence they would all have died years ago. As she strained, she minded the day he came to ask for her, going through the ritual of asking for her sisters first, before she was given as the finest filly in the parish.

'I'm looking for a big horse,' was Calum's opening line,

and her father told him that the biggest horse was already given to the young minister.

'Well, in that case, the chestnut mare will do,' and again how her father told him that Morag, with the beautiful red hair, was already promised to Seonaidh the Miller, and how they eventually agreed on her as the bride.

'I suppose, then, that the pony will do.'

You never married beneath yourself.

He was sitting by the fire stirring the porridge pot when she came back in.

'There you are,' he said.

'Aye.'

They ate the porridge silently, then Calum put on his big woollen coat and bunnet as she poured out another six plates for the children. The ones who had survived: Donald and Iain and Neil and Mary and Catrìona and Joan. Angus was in the Crimea.

They entered in twos. The eldest, Donald, with the youngest, Joan. Iain with Catrìona. Mary leading Neil by the hand. Poor Neil who'd fallen in the rock pool and damaged his leg. As always, they gave him the warmest stool nearest the fire. They ate quickly and noisily, except for Neil who ate slowly and silently.

Their father was gone. They could hear him coughing outside in the chill of the morning as he tied the cart to the little pony. And then the soft thuds of the pony's hooves and the thumps of the wheels as father led the horse and cart across the stones by the midden's edge. The sun would rise shortly. Already, the eastern sky was pink and the stars beginning to fade. Where did they go when the light came and they stopped blinking at one another? One by one they petered out like tallow candles.

He walked westwards, leading the pony by the old heather and marram-grass rope he'd made the year they'd married. One strand of grass to every three of heather, bound so tight that it would last as long as he lived. The animal wanted to graze, but Calum dragged it along. It would get enough grazing later on, once he started on the kelp. Even though it was just after St Bride's, it was surprising how much the pony would find to eat. Especially if he spoke the charm on the way. *Mathas mara dhuit, mathas talamh dhuit, càl is iasg, connlach is feur dhuit. Goodness of sea be thine, goodness of earth be thine, kale and fish, straw and grass be thine.* He left the pony and cart in a sandy hollow where there was some grazing and carried the creel on his back down to the shoreline for the day's work – cutting the kelp and gathering the tangle which would fertilise his small patch of ground.

Inside, Elizabeth was nursing Neil. She prepared the daily poultice to set on his crippled leg. It was basically a cabbage and oatmeal mixture she boiled every morning and then wrapped in an old nightshirt that Angus had brought back from Egypt. It eased the swelling and brought some colour to his cheeks, though the real healing for him was in her touch. For there was so little contact in winter, everyone swaddled in layers of wool all day and all night as the bitter winds swept in from the east. You couldn't expose yourself to the devouring world. And the miracle of seeing in the smoky dark. You were born into it, accustomed to hearing things before seeing them, so that by the time you were two you could see things before they happened. You acquired second sight. The horse neighing outside was a stranger on the horizon; a thunderstorm the wrath of God. That cough was your father dying.

The blacksmith could see the future, though he said it was just the past.

'I see time differently,' he once claimed. 'You all see it going forward. The only difference is that I see it going backwards. It's just a different way of looking at things. It's like sailing from Seal Point to the Stac, instead of sailing from the Stac to Seal Point. You see the same things, but the other way round.'

The children went about their daily tasks. Donald and Joan milking the cow. Iain carrying the water home from the well. Catrìona already sewing in the corner. Mary had gone out to herd the goats. The whey from goats' milk was the secret to eternal life. They drank it every day.

Elizabeth raked the fire, adding a few bits of peat. She had two kinds of peat: the small hard black stuff from the hill, which burned hot, and the larger softer turf from the corner of the field. That lasted longer, but gave less heat. At this morning time she was economical. The pots merely needed to cook slowly. One filled with clothes, the other with broth and the ever-present kettle on at the back.

The responsibilities were hers. These dear children she'd brought into the world with no real thought of the future but that God would provide from the bounty of the sun and sea and earth. She earned grace with the sweat of her brow.

Donald and Joan returned with the milk and the making of crowdie and cheese began. It began to snow. Neil crouched by the tiny window, absorbed by the silence of the fall. He watched it closely. The flakes tumbled down, twirled, then piled on top of each other like little children. So, that's how snow was made: one flake on top of the other. If things clung together they made a crowd. He'd once placed a stone on top of a stone next to a stone and before he knew it he'd built a small wall. Everything turned white outside: the byre, the hens' midden, the rocks, the hill and the distant sky. A blackbird sat on the small stone wall that separated the byre from the house. Its yellow beak opened and closed, as if trying to catch the falling snowflakes. What kept him on that stone wall and not on the birch tree next to it?

'And isn't it strange,' said Neil, though no-one answered him, 'that when Donald and Joan and Iain and Mary and Catrìona and I all stood round the tree in a circle looking at it, we all saw a different tree?'

He knew birds in all their fragility. Their diminishing evening vespers and their glorious morning angelus, and the idea behind their ever-repeating songs. The idea that to be alive was to sing and that by the time the second song was sung the first had been utterly forgotten.

And then the sky darkened, there was a flash of lightning and they all held their breath waiting for the thunderclap which came at the count of seven, deep and strong from the north-west. The heavens opened and it began to pour, and in moments little rivers began to stream down the open chimney and through the closed door and mother asked everyone to heap the sand from the kist into all the little crevices.

What fascinating things crevices were. Secret little beasts lived there, whispering and scratching in their own occult language. Insects no bigger than dust and odd occasional noises which reminded you that everything was alive and spoke. The wind rose, first like a child whimpering, then like a woman crying, and finally like an angry man. He shouted and hit and thumped and uprooted things, but mother stirred the broth and sang and despite all his yelling and he caused them no harm. He remained outside.

Down on the shore Calum found shelter underground. Where the little people lived. The horse with the small cart was sheltered in a cave. Calum crouched beneath the earth in the old broch, hearing nothing of the hurricane outside. He heard no voices. Nothing stirred. There was no point in speaking, for no-one would listen. The wind could be sold to mariners: it was enclosed in three knots. Undoing the first brought a moderate wind, the second half a gale, the third a hurricane. Calum loosened the thong that tied his boots together. Would it work in reverse? He tied two knots and left the third undone.

Up above, the gale quietened. The pony gazed out at the softening sea and whinnied, but remained where she was inside the cave. Calum sat in the dark, in the silence. Fairyland was a noiseless environment. Free from all human strife and racket. The din of women and children, the clamour of the horse-fair and the sheep-market, the rising tide of the sermon. It was a place of condensed air, a pendulous state. Time was suspended there.

Iain was crying, claiming that Donald had hit him. Elizabeth separated them, scolding them for being children.

'Anyone would think you were cats in a cot. Look at you! At your age!'

And Donald, at thirteen years of age and on the dawn of manhood, blushed. Next year he would join Angus in the Crimea. He would. One day he'd lift the big stone, put on a cap, and be a man.

'Look,' she said, 'the storm has passed. And the byre needs to be cleaned.'

And they both went out, taking their wooden spades with them from behind the door.

The spinning-wheel was set and she began to work. Neil carded the wool and passed it to her. She spun it carefully through the spindle. It whirred, like the sound the corncrake made in the evening in the early spring. All the birds spoke, for there is nothing better in a bird's mind than its song. How wonderful it would be when spring came, with the sound of the cuckoo and the curlew and the lambs bleating in the fields and the cows with their bonnie calves and the children all running round barefoot and whistling and whooping and singing. And Calum himself, with his hands on the plough and old Ned pulling it along nice and slow, and how she herself would follow, flinging the seed from the sling over her shoulder in arcs of goodness. I will go out to sow the seed in name of Him who gave it growth, I will place my front in the wind and throw a gracious handful on high. Should a grain fall on a bare rock it shall have no soil on which to grow, as much as falls into the earth, the dew will make it to be full.

Work was a beautiful thing. You ploughed and the earth parted. You turned the spindle and cloth appeared. You lowered the bucket into the well and clean clear water emerged.

They were evicted on the worst of days. A Friday. A bonnie autumn day it was too, with the heather still in full bloom and the Michaelmas rental set aside. Not that any of that mattered. Kennedy the factor was dispatched by His Lordship to break the news and they received it in silence. To say anything was merely to ensure that the few things they had would be torched along with the thatch. And they weren't alone: everyone in the settlement was told to move by the time the sun set, and make their way east where they could find some land amongst the rocky skerries. These things were like the elements. Beyond their power, and all they could do was pity those who were inflicting such cruelty.

Kennedy had a wife and children to look after too. He wasn't really to blame. No-one was. And to whom could you complain anyway? The queen herself? God would deal with them. Calum put the bed on his back and Elizabeth the few household goods they had, and the children carried the pots and pans and kettles and scythe and spade and churns. It took three journeys there and back across the long stretch of moor, finally taking the single cow and the five goats and the horse and Neil on his stretcher over the hill.

They moved physically only ten miles, from the inner green strath to the rocky eastern peninsula, yet it was as if they'd moved to the other side of the world. They'd heard fabulous tales about a land called America, where the trees touched the sky. Old Catrìona could look into a seashell and see it all: lights and noise.

'Beyond the stream, over the hills and far away, city lights flare up,' she said. 'They are turning orange, changing the colour of the moon. None of them will ever find their way home, because the moon is gone.'

The great Robert Kirk, in *Secret Commonwealth of Elves, Fauns and Fairies,* reports that all uncouth sights enfeeble the seer: 'Several did see the second sight when in the Highlands or Isles, yet when transported to live in other countries, especially in America, they quite lose this quality, as was told me by a gentleman who knew some of them in Barbados who did see no vision there, although he knew them to be seers when they lived in the Isles of Scotland.' For dreams have a tide line too, where the ocean ceases and comes no further.

But maybe it was a matter of distance. Visions could stretch for ten miles but not for ten thousand. The map had limits. The horizons of the hills on one side, the sea on the other. Old Joan refused to move, crying that to move an inch was to emigrate forever. She died before sunset in her own bed and her soul was seen rising into the skies in the shape of a butterfly.

They sheltered in a cave down by the shore, living on shellfish. Three of the little ones almost died that first winter. They were all in rags by the time spring came, bringing with it a bounty on the tide: the contents of some great ship which must have sunk somewhere out in the Atlantic. A mast floated in, and days after that the ship's canvas, and then the planks and several chests full of hammers and chisels and nails and clothing. Heaven came to earth. Providence gave them the beginnings of a new home.

That first spring they gathered stones to build a house. A place for the cow at one end, then enough space for all of them at the other, and the roof held up by the grand oak beams from the wrecked ship. Elizabeth washed all the clothing and made it into shirts and trousers for the boys and into dresses and headscarves for the girls. Pride of place went to a shawl she made out of a rescued portion of embroidered woven silk, which had green curlicues at the fringes. One day she would wear it in public.

So they became a new community, the displaced. George and June MacDonald and their children down by the cliff edge. The MacPherson family halfway up the cliff. The MacMillans on the incline beneath the steeple rock, the MacIsaacs next to them, and the aged couple, Ebenezer and Agnes MacRae, in a hut in the gully. The MacInneses set up home over by the stream, and Calum and herself and the children in the shelter of the old temple mound where others had worshipped once upon a time. The place was said to be haunted, but then so was everywhere, and it was only said by those who'd never actually stayed there. Those who lived on hearsay and rumour, imagining things about remote places which soughed and became inaccessible in the winter wind and darkness. Once you lived there it was no more haunted than your childhood cot or the womb in which you'd been born.

Others, evicted from different villages, set up sporadic settlements in the next glen and in the next and the next. Tracks opened up, and within a generation new borders were established. This village became known as Baile; that other one as Clachan. Here they fished, there they farmed. Here they sang, there they told stories. MacPherson was the seer, and the seventh son of the seventh son too. Elizabeth thought he spoke nonsense. Calum believed him. Hadn't he said years ago that when a Kennedy reigned the people would suffer? And hadn't he said that one day men would speak and be heard thousands of miles away? That the message would arrive before the messenger. As if that was anything new. Hadn't they always heard things in the wind, and what about that time the raven croaked outside old Flora's house, and the next morning she was found dead, covered in feathers?

You couldn't manage it one day at a time. You had to

believe it mattered more than that. That one thing could lead to another. Day after day, the relentless grind, the poverty, the rain, the darkness, the sheep huddled against the walls, the cow bellowing at the other end of the house, the distemper and illnesses. Calum's dreams and the hopelessness of ever fulfilling any of them. And the smoke coming from the big house yonder a perpetual reminder of finer things: tailored clothes, a doctor, venison on the table, napkins, decanters, candles as a decoration. When you passed the house in the morning you could smell perfume, and whisky in the evening. They had leisure. Were all able to sit around for hours during the day doing nothing.

You could only survive by treating life seasonally. That way you could hope. If something didn't work today it might work in better weather, when the sun shone, or the wind changed direction, when the cold receded back into its cave. When something happened. The belief that spring would follow winter, that summer and harvest would follow. Whether you were here or not. Whoever was or wasn't. You could only plant and work and hope that the corn and the potatoes would grow. How long was it now since the blight and the famine that had taken Christina and Iain and Seumas? You looked forward. Lived in certainty. Jesus would welcome you home. The mackerel-clouded sky was a good sign: it would be a fine day tomorrow. If you reached the city, you could make your fortune.

She ladled out the broth into their wooden plates. And a full cogeen for Calum. Donald would take that down to the shore for him, along with a cask of milk. The broth warmed them all up. Enough to remove the shawl and the outer stockings. How rarely she touched her skin nowadays. The simple pleasure of being naked in bed or in water. Stroking a knee, her thighs, the curve of her breast.

As a child she remembered spending a summer with her grandmother in the valley of the primroses. They grew in little clumps all over the place, adorning all the little crevices where the good people stayed. If you put your ear to the cleft you could hear them chattering or singing or dancing. The place was full of streams with soft verges of grass on every bank and she would strip naked and plunge into the small pools where all the world's fishes lived. Tiny little creatures which glistened silver as they passed her in their hundreds and thousands, which splashed like thrown rocks when they decided to leap for air. She would lie ages in the little pools watching the water ebbing and flowing over her. Tiny insects danced on the surface. How was it possible for spiders to walk on water? What she would do too if she had eight legs. Run. And there was a waterfall as well where you could stand and let the jets pour down your hair and face and neck and breasts and tummy and legs and watch the little rivulets between your toes then run down to join the stream which then became a river and eventually the loch. One thing turned into another.

Since then she felt her life was layering one thing on top of another until nothing bare could be felt. These thick long woollen stockings which were necessary to keep out the cold. The woollen vest and knickers which kept the chill from her bones. The full tweed skirt and the thick tweed jumper and the bobbly shawl which kept the wind and rain out as she carried the peats home in the creel and washed the blankets in the tub and birthed the calves and lambs in the spring. You had to be encased to survive.

There was a time of passion and touch all right, some years ago. The initial fumblings behind the peat stack and the exploration of strange things, like crossing the moor on a dark night, with the heather catching your knees and the ever-present danger of bogs and holes and ditches. Strange how the world had been on fire within you all the time, so unlike everything that grew and grazed and moved outside. It wasn't a cow, more like music. It made you tingle. And sometimes you'd hear a cough right behind you and run all the way home reassuring yourself it was only a sheep with the flux, though you knew fine it was the ghost of a lost sailor yearning for home. This hovel, this castle, of mine. Home. There's me and Calum and Donald and Iain and Neil and Mary and Catrìona and Joan. And Angus even though he's in the Crimea, and Isabel and Margaret and Oighrig in heaven.

And every other evening at this time of year the neighbours would all come for a ceilidh at her house – the MacDonalds, the MacPhersons, the MacMillans, the MacIsaacs and the MacRaes – and the marvel was that they brought with them hundreds of the dead and the long gone, from Fionn MacCumhaill himself to the King of Lochlann's three daughters, who would all sit there by the fire with their lustrous cheeks and their swift sharp swords cutting through the smoke and gloom. What a joy it was to have the travellers from Greece and Ireland playing dice on the marbled floor. Old Ebenezer would light his pipe and sit closest to the fire where the flames lit up his hollowed face which was so like the cliffs of Dun Mòr, where all the puffins and the kittiwakes flew and screeched their own stories.

After a while he would nod off, and Agnes would gently take his pipe from his mouth. Elizabeth thought then he was the best story in the house, far away in a disconnected place. His mouth would drool with memories of the retreat from Corunna and the quenching of the Irish Rebellion, and he occasionally smiled in his sleep, once again hearing the castanets and seeing the Red Contessa dancing in Barcelona. Time and space really were fluid when Napoleon sat there jawing with Maghach Colgar and Alexander the Great dealing aces with the blind man who could play cards that didn't exist. Ace after ace after ace. It was as if stories brought people they had never seen and were long dead back to life. And old Seumas could send a spit flying right into the ashes from the other side of the room.

Then you could forget it all. That life was really all about enduring. Staying warm and dry. Having some kind of roof over your head. Some kind of man, or woman, beside you in bed. Some kind of food on the table. Fish. Meat. Shellfish and boiled cabbage if needed. Seaweed itself when the going got tough. Keeping the cailleach at bay. That hellish cold. The frost in your bones. The chill in your blood. The infant's cough. Poor Neil's gammy leg. Calum's wheeze deep in the chest. Her own pain deep in her bowels. And the distance things were at night, so far away from everyone over bog and moor in the dark. Sometimes candle lights flickered in the dark to tell you that you hadn't died.

It was good to believe in God. The One who made Heaven and Earth, and all things Visible and Invisible as the Maighistir Alasdair never tired of saying when he managed to visit their remote hamlet, once a month or so. It was no easier for him, poor man, having to tolerate His Lordship and Her Ladyship up there in the big house and meantime care for all the pastoral needs of all these scattered children of Israel cleared and evicted by their Majesties from every green glen and strath out into all the rocky crevices that God too had made in His great provision.

He was a good man the Reverend Alexander. The Reverend Alexander MacKenzie, a scion of the great Seaforth Clan who had won famous victories at the Battle of Bealach nam Bròg and at Sauchieburn and were valiant at the Battle of the Boyne and died courageously by the score too on the bloody field of Culloden.

Young Alexander could have chosen the heroic path also, but was eventually converted in the Second Great Awakening under the fiery preaching of Robert Murray McCheyne. Alexander, who was already an ordained Establishment minister of Moderate persuasion happened to be in Dundee when McCheyne was holding one of his outdoor meetings and went there out of curiosity, but as he listened to the impassioned young preacher his heart burned within him with shame about his own softness. He was only a minister because he had taken professional steps towards a career, not because he believed in anything. He hadn't risked anything.

'God risked everything,' McCheyne preached. 'O, there are some who argue that everything was certain, but the God of love is the God of risk. He risked everything for you, trusting Jesus to deliver. Most of you have risked nothing. Especially those of you who purport to be ministers of the Gospel. For in Christ even your human doubts can fortify rather than weaken your faith.'

Alexander MacKenzie thought McCheyne was speaking only to him amongst the thousands. That God Himself was speaking to him, alone. Saying that only love, not elegance, could cover a multitude of sins.

'Safe in your glebes and in your respected positions. Safe behind your orthodox theologies and rituals. What have you, you supposed ministers of the Gospel, risked for Christ? Nothing. Go and sell everything you have and give to the poor, go risk all your securities, for the Redeemer of Calvary. You are God's enemies not by nature, but by will. You sin because your understanding is finite, but your liberty is infinite. So choose differently,' preached McCheyne, and MacKenzie fell on his knees, put his head on the grass and rose a converted man. For to confess Christ is to be changed.

Alexander MacKenzie became an evangelical without formally joining the evangelicals. He wanted to risk even that. He concluded that God's way for him was to labour in the poor vineyard in which he'd been set, and decided not to join the newly established Free Church when it was founded that famous day in Edinburgh. Instead, MacKenzie stayed to fight the battle within.

He travelled north by foot, carrying his worldly possessions on his back like a hobo, camping with tramps and tinkers and hawkers on the way. He read portions from the Bible and *The Pilgrim's Progress* to anyone who listened. He had nothing to prove, because everything was sealed already. God was not to be discovered, like America, but to be found, like the orchid in the roadside ditch.

He fasted for days and stepped out of time.

He met a man sitting on a stone by the roadside looking at pictures in a little box he held in the palm of his hand. The pictures were moving.

'Good morning, Sir,' said Alexander MacKenzie.

'Hi,' said the man.

'Bonny morning.'

The man looked up at him. 'Not everywhere.'

MacKenzie knew that. He looked at the thing the man held in his hand. Stormy waves were lashing against a beach. The man rubbed his thumb against the object and naked men and women appeared, fornicating. They were like the animals in heat he saw in the fields, thrusting and jabbing at one another, though they took much longer about it than John Campbell's stallion. It was a breach of all the commandments, not just the seventh. Man as beast. When it was all over the man turned the abomination off and looked up at MacKenzie and at the thing he held in his hand.

'What's that?' he asked.

'The word of God.'

'People call things all kinds of things.'

'And what's that you're sitting on?' asked MacKenzie.

'A stone.'

'And if I called it a feather,' said MacKenzie, 'would it still be a stone?'

'It is what people call it,' the man said.

The preacher stood up.

'How chained you are by your time. Let that thing go and be free.'

It was May-time with all the birds of the air talking to him all the way home. The starlings and all their husbands and wives wheeling ahead of him all the way. Here a thrush laughing its heart out. There a sparrow cleaning his feathers. An owl yawned in a tree above him as he slept by the roadside at night. He rolled out his blanket by the loch another evening and stayed awake all night watching all the little stars fall into the loch. It reminded him of the little woodland lake of Nemi he'd seen in a painting in the din of London years before.

He'd been a scholar, and spent the first ten years of his moderate ministry writing down the songs and stories of his parishioners. Those foolish things that were like the bread of life to them. In that time of vanity, the tale of Cuchullin was better than the story of Abraham, but this time on his journey north he was of a different conviction. Poetry had been made flesh. All tales revolved round the Christ, who spoke in parables and loved the poor and died for the sins of the world. There was no bigger Fingalian hero than the Christ, no songs greater than the psalms of David, no story more important than that of the Incarnate Redeemer and the Risen Saviour. 'The Lord is my Shepherd', he sang all the way north, not unaware that all the glens and straths he passed through had been emptied of men to make way for sheep. Men could perform wonders, but they didn't know which wonders to perform.

When he returned to the extended scattered parish, the people noted his new fervour. He still asked after them and still sat for hours by the fire or outside by the grassy knolls on the bright summer days writing down all their old lore, but treated these now as pagan treasures to be classified rather than as living codes by which to behave. Instead of turning away from old traditions, Reverend Alexander MacKenzie knew that by acknowledging them he would unveil them and so take all their superstitious sting away. For when things are invisible they have power over us. He weighed words carefully, knew that each one hauled a universe behind it.

And he had the power of words, for he could do something that no-one else in the community could. Read and write. He would take their stories and songs and ancient remedies and put them down in a big lined book, and if anyone asked to see what he had written he would patiently show them the symbols and take them through each magic word repeating back, syllable by syllable, what they had said. Even though he realised that by setting down a single word he had already changed its meaning.

At first they found it strange that their words were that particular shape, but when they heard them spoken back they believed they were the same words that they had spoken to him. So words were just pictures after all. A was the roof of the byre with the spar across it where the hens slept. C was the shape of the curved river that ran through the glen. O was everyone's favourite letter for it was the full moon. But he encouraged them all.

'For after all,' he said to them, 'you can read the land and the sea and the sky far better than I can.'

He was teaching them that the medium was the message. That you understand the world only through the means you have. A people surrounded by water fear and worship sea gods, he said. Those living on the edge of forests the nymphs of the grove. The secret was to keep your eye on the moon, to remind you of how small a great thing looks. And the birds – look! God has given them different gifts – the gifts of flight, of feathers and of songs. 'Never confuse the name of a thing with the thing itself,' he said to them. 'A stone is much more than a stone, and all of you are much more than your names or *sloinneadh*, your genealogy. You are all made in the image of God, who is greater than anything you can ever begin to think or imagine.'

Alexander MacKenzie knew that when the people themselves

could read, the story would need to change. And how strange the words sounded from the page, as if the writing itself was telling the story and not the minister. During the service later on, he would open the big book himself, turning the pages with loving care and reading, emphasising certain words and phrases like the people themselves did when talking. Even though he came from a different district than themselves and thus spoke the words strangely, they all listened with keen ears, hearing the nuances of the drama and the unexpected turn of impossibilities, where the poor were loved and won. When you have nothing, heaven has everything. It thrilled their hearts to see such results. The blind could see. The deaf would hear. The dead will rise.

Then spring came and Calum returned from the shore. The seas calmed and he fixed up the cobble-boat once more and rowed out to the headland where the fish were plentiful. Small things began to grow out of the earth: tiny leaves and flowers and roots for which only the very old now had names. Burdock and skirrets and fucus and vetch, which if you boiled and then swallowed whilst walking three times sunwise round the old temple would cure you of jaundice. Gorse juice would fix a cough. Most things you could boil and eat, though there were a few things you could only admire. The beautiful crimson foxglove which guarded the way to the cemetery, but which also opened the doors to other imaginary worlds if you used it wisely. Nothing ever changed until it changed suddenly.

This was the time to clean things. Elizabeth removed all the tweed blankets from the bed and washed them in the river, laying them out on the rocks to dry. Then she removed all the children's winter clothing and washed these in the soapy upper pool, hanging them on branches of trees and on the jutting pinnacles. From now on until Michaelmas they would all go barefoot. Feel the grass on their skin, become once again accustomed to the sharpness of stones, the softness of moss.

They fetched out the turning-spades and began to plough the earth. MacPherson was the seed-man and Calum went there to barter. A bag of oat seed for a tub of mackerel and two days' labour. A bag of seed potatoes for five tubs of herring and five days' labour. Everything was provisional.

MacPherson was the Lady's man, and hoped one day to get a proper house himself. The fool, thinking he could ever aspire to such grandeur. He used to spy on the Lady, watching her through the window as she played the piano on wintry afternoons. He was fascinated by the whiteness of her fingers which had never been spoilt by earth or potatoes or fish, but were beautifully sculptured and refined, like the long blue shells of the razor-fish on the strand. He would stand outside in the dark not hearing a word of the music, but absorbed by the beauty of her fingers gliding across the piano keys. What it would be to be caressed by these slim hands making music across his broad back. A broad back earned by such hard work on her behalf, building that road up the hillside to her summer lodge. For which she rewarded him with a summer picnic outside the lodge when he was given fruit in a glass bowl and allowed to kiss her gloved hand.

'Thank you,' he stammered.

She peered down at the crown of his head.

'Private and public decencies should always be observed,' she announced.

Calum and Elizabeth and the children planted the oats and the potatoes. The oats here on the bit of sloped grass between their house and the river, where the sun was best; the potatoes there on the lower slope, where the wind was less severe. It was splendid weather that year: long dry sunny days, then showers of rain overnight, ensuring that nothing dried out or withered. Calum was good, cutting peats or thatching or gathering wood from the shore or hoeing or harrowing during the day, then out fishing with Donald and Iain every evening. Elizabeth and the girls knitted and spun and gathered crotal and herded, while Neil carved himself a new future.

As a cripple, he was destined to become a tailor, but instead became absorbed in making things out of wood and straw. He began with whistles and chanters made out of dark rushes with the reeds made out of barley stalks, but then stumbled on a way to make a living by making cane fishing-rods which he showed to MacPherson who of course showed it to her Ladyship who showed it to her husband who showed it to his fishing friends when they came north for the salmon, so that by the time he died, Neil – the most unlikely Victorian entrepreneur – had built a little lodge of his own down by the salmon stream. Angus came home from the Crimea with a Turkish Crimea Medal on his lapel, but promptly left again and emigrated to Canada and was never heard of again. They say his ghost built a cabin in the Rockies, near Mount Robson.

The oats grew buds and flourished and the potato stalks sprouted all green and healthy, and the children ran about in the sun browned and happy. It made you glad to be alive. They even managed to go all together to the annual tinker fair over in Druimbuck, everyone walking, except Neil who sat in the cart hauled by Ned.

And what a day it was, of horse-trading and drinking and card-playing for the men, with the women and girls chumming each other to all the cart-stalls where you could buy handkerchiefs, pots and pans, brooches, pins, mirrors and feathers, and have your fortune told by a red-haired Irishwoman called Nell. Some would travel far and strangers would enter their lives, some would live long and into happy old age, and some would have troubled times ahead. But these wouldn't last.

A handsome looking traveller beckoned them over to his cart covered in ribbons. He held a beautiful oval mirror in the palm of his hand. Some small strange fruit on a tree was carved round the edges.

'Only tuppence. You can see the past and future in it.'

He had a beautiful smile. Lying bastard. Though time proved him right.

So Elizabeth bought the little looking-glass where she saw her own image properly for the first time, rather than in the rippling waters of the river where nothing was ever fixed and where a fly landing on the water could make you dissolve. All the children wanted turns looking into it and smiled and pulled faces and stuck out their tongues and watched with delight and laughed as they looked at themselves looking back at themselves. There was even a dance on that evening, down in the grove by the well, and Calum, fired up by a dram or three taken during the day insisted that they all stay on, for it would be such a grand occasion and a rare opportunity to enjoy themselves.

'We can walk home by moonlight,' he said to Elizabeth, as if that were an added attraction. And stay they did, to the great delight of the children, who could have lived there forever. And who wouldn't, amidst such colour and laughter and life? For look – there's Big Sam Stewart hurling fists at Jimmy MacTavish and over yonder a young gypsy girl dancing on top of a spinning horse.

The dance lasted all night, beneath the moonlight. Jigs and strathspeys and reels from Jimmy MacPhee on the pipes and a small dark tinker from Speyside, Hamish MacPherson, on the fiddle, and an Irishman, O'Toole, on a red melodeon. The O'Rourkes fought the MacGurks and the Kellys the Flannigans. Some old clan skirmishes were re-fought as well, with the MacKays and the Camerons pelting each other down by the river. But the young danced, in what looked like improvised jumping but was really years-old rituals. To and fro, me to you, touch your toe, I love you! Calum fell asleep eventually and they managed to haul him on to the cart where he lay snoring beside poor Neil all the way home as Ned led them across the moorland. It was a joy to be alive trying to count the stars. A new one was born every minute. They looked as if they had been scattered across the inky sky solely for her benefit.

What it would be to live like a tinker, under the blanket of the stars, mending pots and pans and drinking and fighting and dancing and telling stories and moving from place to place as the fancy took you without some clan chief or landlord or Her Ladyship telling you where to live and what to do. Though, God only knows, they had their own travails, surviving under canvas in the winter storms and being hounded from place to place by fear and anger and hatred and disdain. What was it that made us as we were? Or left us as we are. Wanting this, that, and the other and always ending up at the bottom of the pile.

O, she kent fine how Mr Alexander explained it, and believed every faithful word he spoke. How everything was made by God and how everything he made was good, but that Eve was then tempted by the serpent and ate the fruit and everything fell apart. It was like when she baked a perfect loaf and went outside to see if the clothes were dry and by the time she came back in Calum or one of the children had already taken a bite out of the bread.

'You should have left it,' she'd say, 'to settle. It's always better left for half-an-hour or so.'

But the temptation was always too much, for there is nothing under heaven as sweet and tasty as barley bread steaming fresh from the oven.

A shooting star fell from east to west, trailing a long silver spray behind it, like a salmon leaping the Corran Falls. The old people claimed it signified a death in that village to the west, though Elizabeth refused to believe that such a light could bring any darkness. Others claimed that the falling stars were homeless angels caught halfway between Heaven and Earth when Satan was expelled from heaven from having become too proud. Those that fall safely all the way to earth become fairies. Others smash against the earth when they land and their blood can still be seen as red crotal clinging to the rocks.

A crescent moon hung low in the north-east lighting the way home. She looked at Calum, lying there like a newborn babe curled up in a blanket in the corner of the cart with Neil fast asleep, resting his hand on his father's shoulder. The other children, still exalted from the dance, ran and skipped ahead of the cart. All those poor innocent bairns of hers, with the whole world ahead of them. What on earth was to become of them? She prayed. May God keep them. May all of them have the grace of the swan and the likeness of the Lord. May yours be the best hour of the day, the best day of the week, the best week of the year, the best year in the Son of God's domain.

She prayed for their daily bread, knowing what it was not to have it, and that the potatoes would grow well and be gathered like manna, and all her prayers were so selfless that they were guaranteed to be heard and answered. And there, already, was their home, the turf falling in at one end and the goats and sheep having pushed open the door, and she would now need to light the fire again, and clean everything up, and make the porridge while they all slept the sleep of the ever blessed.

4

IT SEEMED AS if the mirror was the only thing that had survived the past twenty years, for every time she looked into it she could still see her own face as it was that first time, bonny enough and freckled in the summer sun, and the young faces of the children before they had all gone. Donald joined the Cameron Highlanders and came back after five years to tell about his adventures in India. He then returned after another five years to tell about different places, Bhutan and Abyssinia, which were so hot that your eyes blistered and your shoes melted. Though they hadn't heard from him since.

Iain sailed to the seasonal herring fishing and met and married a lassie from Wick and made his home there, while Catrìona, Mary and Joan all went into domestic service in Glasgow. Neil was already thriving in his rod-making and instrument-making business and well on his way uphill to the lodge. The girls were the best, faithfully sending money home to their parents each quarter from their own meagre wages: a few pounds each, which made all the difference to Calum and Elizabeth between mere grinding subsistence and the luxury of being able to buy things from the travelling pedlar when he came on his rounds. Laces and thimbles and knives and stuff.

The last time he'd called, he had with him some beautiful silk coverings from India, and she spent the girls' gifts on a brocade covering for her bed. He talked of a new sewing machine that was coming his way, which he'd bring sometime if he could get hold of one for her. For things were improving bit by bit. There was even talk now of the Irish coming over and helping them get some bits of land for themselves.

The little mirror from the tinkers' fair had taken on almost magical properties in the intervening years. It was never used to admire herself. Folk lived in it, as in a little village. She had no photographs by which to remember any of her children, except those pictures stored away in her heart. But the mirror contained them all.

In the mornings now when Calum was off by himself up the moor herding or down the shore gathering sticks and remnants, she would fetch the mirror out from under the mattress and sit by the fire where the glow was best and look into it and relive that fantastic day in Druimbuck. She smiled, watching Tam Stewart once more leathering the living daylights out of MacTavish, and that beautiful ringleted gypsy girl pirouetting on white horse, and Catrìona and Mary and Joan dancing with the lads, under her watchful eye.

Calum had his own mirror, out on the moors and down by the shore, where he saw all kinds of fancies and wonders as the clouds scudded east in a gale or as the rain teemed down or as the wind blew its cheeks out and tried to lower every raised thing on earth.

He knew each inch of his world. Where the cattle would graze and where the sheep could crop, where the rabbits could be caught and the crotal could be found growing on the rocks, where the best place was to lie and stare up at the eternally blue sky when a summer's day finally arrived without a single passing cloud spoiling the view. Everything had a place and a name. The hills knew their own height, the rocks their own weight.

The first time he saw the fairies was on an early autumn evening just after the harvest. He'd been out cutting the hay all day with Elizabeth and she had then gone on ahead to prepare the dinner while he tidied up the stooks in the field. He sat down on a rock and took out his whetting stone and began to sharpen the scythe. The wheesh of the stone on the downwards stroke then the sweesh on the way back up, and every time the blade glinting brighter and brighter in the amber evening sun. Occasionally a corncrake called or a dog barked in the far distance, but the day was settling into a kind of slumber, even the sun herself yawning in the reddening western sky, her toes stretching down into the water.

Out of the corner of his eye he caught a glimpse of movement, like a rag waving in the wind. He looked, and there was nothing there. A few final strokes from the whetting stone would do it, and just as he finished with a downward flourish he saw the glimmer again, this time on the other side, to his left, on the slope of the brae. She was wearing a green cap with a beautiful tuft of silver feathers waving from its crown and a short blue skirt, but he blinked and the vision was gone and when he stood where she'd been nothing could be seen or heard, though a sweet perfume filled the air. Do we imagine things? He looked behind the stones and rocks and in the hollows, but all was empty, and after a while even the fragrance was gone.

Would he tell Elizabeth? Could he? Och, she would just laugh at him. Call him daft. And maybe he was, even thinking about believing in all that nonsense. Hadn't he laughed himself at old Bella who claimed that the gulls flying about her house were witches and that MacDonald's wife down the glen was a seal under spell, considering the amount of time she spent down at the shore paddling about barefoot in the sea? Fools who believed what their eyes saw.

'*Do you know what I saw today?*'

And they would glance at you.

And what could you say? '*The sun dancing in the sky?*'

'*Oh? But did you remember to bring home the oatmeal?*'
So he decided not to tell her. Not yet anyway.

They had their supper. Herring and potatoes, in the usual silence. The time of eating was not the time of talking. You had enough to concentrate on enjoying every morsel of the rare, good food on the table. The herring was salty and a bit fleshy, but all the better for that, rather than the thin early season herring which just melted in your mouth and didn't satisfy. And the potatoes were good this year – nice and dry, so much better since they'd moved the patch a bit further uphill where the drainage was better. The skins were best, peeling off in your hand like shreds of tobacco. Which reminded him to light his pipe.

As he smoked beside the fire he gazed into the peat flames which formed story patterns through the smoke. Curls and lines and circles and puffs. It was said that if you looked long enough you could learn to read the smoke, in the same way as the Reverend Alexander read the books. A curled haze of smoke meant complications, while the smoke going in a straight line up the chimney meant that things would work out smoothly, just fine and dandy. The smoke tonight was in circles, which brought him back to the fairy woman he'd seen, for she seemed to move in circles, going round clockwise, which was a good sign. Green and silver and blue she was. Her bare arms dripping wet and glistening.

It was dark outside. Every evening at this point they went to bed. What else would you do between sunset and sunrise? Which was now a fraction later every day. But unexpectedly, Calum rose and said he was going out, 'To see if the sheep are fine.'

Elizabeth looked at him and said, 'It's dark.'

'I know,' he replied. 'I'll take a kindling from the fire to light the way.'

And he put a glowing peat in a tin and set off into the night.

She was nowhere to be seen. The wind rose and fanned the kindling in the tin, turning the world orange. Shadows moved everywhere: his own shape illuminated on the big rock, and the lantern enlarged like a fiery furnace. He went over to the big waterfall and watched it pouring down over the rocks in spurts and leaps and jumps and streams. Nothing hindered it. It could do what it pleased. The water rose like an arc then descended like a flood.

He heard things. Otters scuffling about in their burrows, an owl somewhere folding his wings, a dog barking, a sound like a hammer striking an anvil. Which couldn't be, because old MacLeod would by now have laid his tools aside and be snoring in his bed. And then Calum's lamp went out and it was completely dark.

During the day he had no power. Lady MacLeod and her factor kept their eyes on everything. You couldn't till beyond your patch. You couldn't fish south of the skerry. And the Reverend Alexander had given them several commandments. Thou shalt not commit adultery. And there were other communal commandments. Things you couldn't do. Such as lying out in the field during broad daylight doing nothing but gazing up at the blue sky. Dreaming when you ought to be working. In the twilight these ordinances dissolved and he could, at last, do what he liked. The darkness gave him courage to disobey. To tell fearful stories, lie all night on top of Elizabeth and, if need be, wander the dark moors where anything was possible. Though even there customs and boundaries had to be carefully observed.

He heard stories. Listened to them. The *ùruisg* and the *taibhs* and the *manadh* and the *each-uisge*, the water-horse in all its lying beauty. He tried to remember the rules, to remember the grace, not to speak and – now he felt for it in his pocket – always to carry iron. There it was, the small knife he always carried with him. He'd be safe and fine as he walked back across the moor, safe because he knew where each hollow and ditch and hole and bog lay. Heart-sore, because she had not appeared again with those gorgeous feathers and that bonny skirt above the pale shining skin. He ran with his heart in his mouth, hoping she would catch up.

Elizabeth was preparing for bed. Combing her hair, which had grown so grey. Auburn hair was best, like the rowans. She minded that first time she'd met Calum, on the way to the church. He lived over the hill in the next glen and these Sabbath days were a wonder as folk converged from all around to walk down towards the kirk, which stood in splendid isolation at the bottom of the strath, half a mile from the manse and the dairy where the Laird's fine-looking cows grazed in the lush fields, even on the Sunday.

She was sixteen then, and only afterwards realised that Calum was a year younger, though he seemed older and more mature with his height and his strong shoulders and long loping walk. She'd never seen him before, because he'd just come to live with his grandparents, having been brought up over on the far coast with his parents, who had died of some fever. He was dark and quiet. Neither of them spoke as they walked with her parents and his grandparents down through the ferns towards the church. But she could see that he admired her bonny auburn hair blowing in the breeze beneath her Sabbath bunnet. He too was wearing a cap, which of course he removed when he neared the kirk gate.

She sat with her parents in their usual pew at the back to the right, whilst Calum sat beside his grandparents further up and to the left. This was in the old days, before the Reverend Alexander arrived, when the people still suffered the ramblings of old MacCuish who was as likely to talk about the moods of the weather as he was of the miracles of Christ. Once, Elizabeth looked up and glanced over where Calum was and caught him looking round at her; she lowered her eyes and he smiled, glad that she had seen. Afterwards they all walked back together over the hill, ever so slowly because his grandparents were old, and nothing suited Elizabeth and Calum better than the eternal slowness of the walk in keeping with such a fine sultry Sabbath day. It was as if the eternal ordinance had been made just for them.

'You young people should run ahead,' Calum's grandfather said, remembering that furnace he'd felt himself when courting Jessie centuries ago. How you could neither listen to a sermon properly, nor shear a sheep right, or even walk uphill without thinking of how much better it would be to be running downhill to meet Jessie by the dairy doors. So Calum and Elizabeth moved ahead, and he let her walk ever so slightly in front of him so that he could admire her auburn hair moving in the wind. It was curled and reached down beyond the nape of her neck and God only knew how far it would reach if she took that bonnet off and let it flow free. It looked soft and thick, unlike his grandfather's horse's mane which was thin and straggly and felt like old broken pieces of string when you put your hand through it to calm him down.

And she combed the long grey strands which he had now not touched for so long. And not just her hair, but those slouched shoulders and her loose breasts which had nursed everyone, and the rest which needed to stay eternally warm in the permanent damp and wind. Every time she passed the comb through her hair a few strands would fall out and she was superstitious enough to put every strand into the fire. Otherwise they would meet her feet in the dark and make her stumble. It instantly burned. At least she would not drown.

She smoored the fire and went to bed just before Calum returned. She heard him say something outside, but could not make out what, except that it contained the word 'nothing'. Maybe that thing the Reverend Alexander had said about

God making the whole world out of nothing, but more likely he was just muttering that nothing mattered or that they had nothing to worry about. Which they didn't. What was the point of worrying about things beyond your control, from the weather to the mood of Her Ladyship, from what had happened to Angus to Calum's state of mind?

Which of course didn't prevent her from worrying, endlessly and without ceasing. How the poor girls were, all on their own down there in Glasgow, and not a sign or a word of any of them marrying yet, even though that too would just be something else to worry about. Best to leave it all in the hands of providence. She wondered about the Reverend Alexander and why he had to make everything so complicated and unnatural when it was really all so simple. There was nothing really difficult at all about what he called the supernatural – didn't the sun rise every morning in the east and set every evening in the west, and no matter how huge and angry the waves were they had never yet risen above the low sand. Did you need faith for that? For Elizabeth, miracles were a simple matter. They happened every day. They had food on the table and a fire in the stove and a roof over their heads.

Calum climbed into bed beside her fully clothed, except for the outdoor oilskins and boots, which he left drying by the fire. He took her hand and squeezed it as if to tell her that he loved her, then buried his head on the back of her shoulder and tried to sleep. She smelt of peat. Earthy and familiar. That hint of fairy cloth blowing in the wind kept returning to him. Who was she? Maybe she was young and as pretty as the May wind and had auburn hair, or maybe she was an old crone in disguise. He had to be careful. Desire is dangerous. But no matter how hard he tried to envisage her face and form he could not, for the fairies, as everyone knows, never come bidden. They have to reveal themselves. They find you.

And then Elizabeth made an unexpected move. She turned towards him in the bed and he could feel her breath on his face; memories stirred and he too minded that day when they first walked through the glen and how her gorgeous auburn hair had blown in the breeze and he responded despite the barriers of clothing, finding his way through the thickets to where she was somewhere beneath the clouds of tweed where the fairies lived, singing and dancing and drinking wine from golden goblets which sparkled in the magic light which only daylight itself could extinguish. Put out the lights, put out the lights that I might see the world, he cried, and whatever you do don't speak in the brugh or you get trapped there forever.

And he lay there, blinded, but was given the gift of music as recompense, and sang sweet nothings into her ear, all night long until morning came, with the cockerel crowing once more outside and the hens scratching at the door and the birds singing, because they had just woken and it was a new day, and who knew if they had any memory of yesterday or the day before, or of anything except their song and their next meal.

In the morning, Elizabeth knew she was pregnant again, after all these years. Not that it was a miracle, for she was not that old. Not even fifty, as far as she knew. It didn't take long for word to get round. Not that it was really word, just looks and glances, because these old women knew. They knew the signs, that look in her eyes, as if she had more important things to think about than whether the bucket of water was properly full, or whether the hens had laid a dozen eggs.

They knew everything, these old women, from why men were the way they were to what needed to be done if a cow stopped giving milk. It was the evil eye of course, and wasn't Elizabeth aware – and her a woman of her age who had already borne, how many children was it again, six, nine?

– that her condition was dangerous? You could see it in her frame. That tendency to thinness, her lack of bulk. And what was it that had happened to poor Neil again? Then there was Mary Cuagach, who had withered away to nothing while her neighbour's cows had grown fat though not being fed a single morsel by that old witch MacKay. And poor Effie, whose skin erupted in ever more pestilences the more cats old MacAskill acquired. She eventually died and one by one they slunk away out into the hills where the whole neighbourhood could hear them wailing in the dark.

Elizabeth did her best to avoid their company, though it was next to impossible as she had to go out to the well daily, and to the fields. They would wander out with their buckets and hoes as if the moment had been accidental, and though she averted her eyes she could feel them already healing all sorts of imaginary ailments. Winding bits of thread round their wrinkled fingers so that the child within would not be born deformed, and muttering incantations to prevent blindness and deafness and epilepsy and God only knows what. Stealing her joy with their ancient superstitions.

In the midst of it all the Irishmen came, preaching revolution and the rights of man. A big white-bearded fellow by the name of Shaughnessy and his small dark-haired accomplice called O'Riata. Shaughnessy was the more powerful speaker. His big booming voice echoed across the hills and glens when he held his open-air meetings, while O'Riata did the leg work, going from house to house taking names for a petition to parliament while, at the same time, gathering volunteers who would join him at night in damaging some of the Laird's property, which he called 'the restitution of rights'.

'Stop looking inwards and upwards for faults and solutions,' he declared. 'Seek happiness not in a future heaven but in a fairer earth, here, right here where you are. Religion is fine for prayer, but for those of us seeking justice the answer is to be found in politics.'

Nevertheless, he sounded like the Reverend Alexander: 'The keys to the kingdom are not distant and far away, but are firmly in your own hands. Use them.' It was so much easier to preach the big things rather than the little things. Sometimes when people spoke anything seemed possible.

Shaughnessy was persuasive, though a bit vague at times. His basic message was that the earth beneath the people's feet belonged to them as much as the common air they breathed or the rain that fell on them all, and that no person anywhere had any right to call the earth his personal property or wall it off like they'd done up at the big house.

'There is no such thing as private property,' he proclaimed.

Which confused all of them, whose only possessions were the hovels they stayed in, which they'd carried stone by stone from the hills and thatched with the rushes from the hillsides. Was he going to take that away from them as well? Did that too belong to everyone?

But he sounded grand and seemed to be great friends with a whole number of people, including Abraham who had nothing when he was promised descendants as numerous as the stars in the sky, and Finn MacCumhaill who fought the powerful people of his day, and Marks who had told him that the people had nothing to lose but their chains, when they only really had home-made ropes for the cow and to tie the boat up, and someone called Proud Horn who was an anarchist, which meant that everyone was free to do what they liked, which sounded like a wonderful thing if you didn't have to work all day and all night just to eat, as even the Redeemer and Saviour Himself, Christ Jesus, had to who was born in a byre and had nowhere to lay his head and had to work as a humble carpenter, not to mention all these disciples of his who were fishermen. They would certainly have given him what they had, even if it had only been a few potatoes mashed in milk, and what could be better anyway in the whole wide world?

Young Angus Morrison and Donald MacDonald and Archie MacColl joined O'Riata in a couple of his night-time skirmishes but were caught red-handed and the constabulary arrived to cart them off to Inverness. Isn't it strange how everyone agrees that the thing that happens is for the best? For with that, the whole rebellion petered out and the revolution came to naught. The leaflets which O'Toole had left in every house proclaiming *Workers of the World Unite! You have nothing to lose but your chains! Property is Theft!* disappeared within days, used to light fires or as toilet paper because the words were printed on such lovely soft material.

Elizabeth listened carefully to Shaughnessy. His Irish accent confused her at first, but once she tuned in to the lilt of it she understood everything he was saying about how unjust everything was and how much better things could be if the people had power. Only they did here already, she thought, and all that had caused her lately was grief, with their comments and suggestions and treatments. She often cried as she listened to Shaughnessy out in the open air and she wasn't the only one. They would all cry together and laugh together and clap and applaud. It put her in mind of the twice-yearly communal fanks when they all sheared the sheep together, or when they'd gather to share a miraculous catch of herring, or to distribute the last peats of the season out to the widowed and the lame and the bedridden, and everyone felt that the world was at long last right and fair.

But Shaughnessy went on too long and the people got fed-up. And anyway, Elizabeth had a thousand and one other things to do, what with young Joan teething and the old ewe dying from flux and the burn overflowing and half-running through the house and the thatch needing to be repaired. With the weather closing in, if Calum didn't get that cobble out soon they'd starve, no matter how well Shaughnessy spoke, he who had such a fine round belly that he could last for months even if no herring were ever landed again until next century. He was a strange one, even proclaiming the loveliness of nature. 'The hills and moors and seas are there for your joy and delight' he preached. 'Things of beauty for you to behold.'

As if they had time to stand and stare. Nature was not there to be admired, but to be endured.

Everyone reduced the universe to size. For Shaughnessy, nothing seemed to matter but politics, even though every sentence he spoke was laced with the guilt of having left fourteen illegitimate children scattered throughout every parish in Ireland, for what else could explain the anger and regret with which he spoke? Whilst for old Morag at the bottom of the glen, nothing mattered except singing her endless collection of ancient songs because her heart was thrice-broken by lovers who had promised so much and then left. For Hamish nothing seemed to matter except his annual crop of carrots though he'd never recovered from the death of his three young children in the fever of fifty-five. As if life was just politics, or music, or a tallow candle, while billions of stars glittered in the sky.

Elizabeth lit the candle beside the bed and watched the light flicker yellow, then steady to a single white glow.

5

THE MOST POWERFUL person in the community was the Reverend Alexander MacKenzie. He taught people how to think. Not to steal. Not to envy. Not to bear false witness against their neighbour. Yet folk lived in the gaps between these commandments. Forever gossiping, quietly slandering, envying each other.

'Did you hear what Archie did yesterday?'

'What a nerve she had. Taking it. Just like that.'

'The whore.'

'Honestly, you can't believe a word he says.'

Then the Reverend Alexander MacKenzie had a dream. All the rocks melted and turned into waterfalls which flowed down in streams and rivers into the sea. And he was sitting on a straw riding the waves, navigating the spaces between the rocks, sailing round all the obstacles that lay between the high cliffs and the wide ocean. It meant that his life had to be lived in the gaps. In the spaces between solid things, where men and women lived and died. Where they sang their songs, told their stories, saw their imaginary fairies. Where God also reigned.

It meant that the most solid of things liquefied and that he should forthwith forsake all things – the stone manse, the regular services, the rigid Westminster Confession of Faith – for serving the poor. Every stream had to run into the ocean.

He was done with signs. No longer would he consider words as clues from God, because He did not need to give clues. The world was not a puzzle to be worked out. It was not a maze to be navigated. Knowledge, after all, wasn't some kind of reminiscent vision. For everything was as it was, and his job was just to deal with it. To lift a fallen thing if he saw it. To mourn with those who mourned. To rejoice with those who rejoiced. To do something. Anything. And it came to him as a revelation: that his work was just to love everything, because then he would love and know God. Without knowing it, he took up Wycliffe's position, that property is the result of sin and that since Christ and the Apostles had no property, the clergy ought to have none. He wanted to be so unburdened of things that he could move in an instant as the Holy Ghost led him.

He looked out the window and saw an old woman leading a cow on a rope. Jessie Cameron was her name, the widow of John Cameron. She would drag the beast some yards, then the cow would lie down and refuse to move. Jessie hauled at the rope and the beast struggled to its feet and walked for a while before lying down again.

Alexander MacKenzie left the manse and walked downhill towards the woman.

'She's in heat,' the woman said, 'and been bellowing all night. Yet refuses to go where she needs to go.'

'Why don't we take the bull here instead?' MacKenzie said. 'Now that there are two of us.'

So the woman stayed with the cow and the Reverend MacKenzie walked towards the field near the river, where the bull was. When he arrived the bull was pawing at the ground, desperate to get to the cow. MacKenzie opened the gate, and the bull ran, so that by the time he got back to the woman and the cow the whole business was done. MacKenzie led the meek bull back to his field while the woman led the quietened cow back home in the opposite direction.

God, thought MacKenzie, is like this bull. Far more willing to come to us than we are to him, despite all our crying and bellowing. Nothing was a sacrifice if you had nothing. Once MacKenzie gave everything away he would have nothing to surrender. So he praised God for his health, put a few things into a bag, closed the manse door behind him and stepped out when the first rays of light filtered through the window-panes. He put on his best shoes, for a good pair of boots is the business. The dew still beatified the morning. His manse was on the high ground, and he could see for miles in every direction. The morning stars were still visible. The mountains were beginning to stretch, but still lay half-asleep to the east. An early morning mist covered the great sea to the south. The west too was still slumbering, while a brightness shone in the north, forecasting a sunny day. For Alexander was a man of the soil and knew all the weather signs. Nature never lied, once you'd reached an agreement. The fine day was a gift from God. When the Lord blesses, He blesses forever.

He thought briefly of places beyond these visible horizons which he would likely now never see again. The tall grey spires of Edinburgh and the foul-smelling closes of Glasgow; the great city of London where he had once dined with the Lord Mayor, one Thomas Challis. They had eaten venison and drunk port and had then talked all evening about the poetry of Walter Raleigh.

An eagle flew high overhead. *They that wait upon the Lord shall renew their strength, they shall mount up with wings as eagles, they shall run and not be weary, and they shall walk and not faint.* He set forth praying as he went that God would be gracious unto the nation and that the leaders of the nation, both spiritual and political, would repent of their ways and return unto their God and Maker.

He prayed for the queen and for the government that they would rule with wisdom, but that God Himself would over-rule their wrong decisions. And he prayed for the city of London that it would be unlike Babylon and repent in sackcloth and ashes. He pictured Challis as a little child seeking the face of Jesus, for He said, *Verily I say unto ye, unless ye be converted, and become as little children, ye shall not enter into the Kingdom of Heaven.* What a bonny morning it was. Creation sang. A sudden shower of rain fell, dampening the waiting earth. Then a covenant rainbow embraced the sky from north to south.

The Reverend Alexander walked the glens and dales and hills and scattered hamlets for months, staying where he could, listening, preaching the word, ministering to the sick, encouraging the weak, warning the strong, baptising, marrying, burying. The story of the children of Israel, their kings and prophets, the acts of the Apostles, and the redeeming works of Christ were the only stories he treasured in his heart or read on the page or spoke to the people. For life was too short and eternity too long to be concerned any more with superstition, with trivial things and rubbish – what the Apostle Paul himself had called dung. He didn't want to spend eternity damned because he had sat in an easy-chair by the fire reading a book. He heard voices, but the only voice that mattered was the voice of God. His lips formed the words and the hills listened silently.

Beware of dogs, beware of evil workers, beware of the concision. For we are the circumcision, which worship God in the spirit, and rejoice in Christ Jesus, and have no confidence in the flesh. Though I might also have confidence in the flesh. If any other man thinketh that he hath whereof he might trust in the flesh, I more: Circumcised the eighth day, of the stock of Israel, of the tribe of Benjamin, an Hebrew of the Hebrews; as touching the law, a Pharisee; Concerning zeal, persecuting the church; touching the righteousness which is in the law, blameless. But what things were gain to me, those I counted loss for Christ.

He knew it all by heart, for how else was anything to be known and believed and lived but by heart? The song had wonderful authority. And was he himself not like Paul – born into the aristocracy, the great MacKenzies of Seaforth, royal agents to the kings and with an empire of castles that stretched hundreds of miles from east to west and whose crest proudly proclaimed 'Luceo non uro'? The great clan which had won all its prestige on the battlefield. Had earned it with their lives. Though that was like hoarding dust in a sieve. All of it dross. For all the MacKenzie land gained by violence was forever stained by blood, since the end was forever condemned by the means. He truly believed that nothing could be earned, only given.

So he came to the decision to burn all that rubbish he'd helped gather over the years – those pagan stories and myths which kept the people in worldly bondage and hindered them on the road to salvation. He would burn them all in a quiet hill-fire of vanities. They were tares amongst the wheat, jagged stones in the way of the blind, a babel of noise blocking up the ears of the deaf. *Daughters of Jerusalem, weep not for me, but weep for yourselves, and for your children.*

And hadn't he wept? There was a girl who had melted his heart like the summer snow. Jenny Gunn from Caithness. He was a student. He was walking down through the Grassmarket after a lecture when he heard a disturbance in one of the closes. A woman came running out and fled down the street towards Tollcross, where he happened to have lodgings. She disappeared through the West Port, but he found her minutes later slumped by the dairy wall at Fountainbridge. He knelt down and asked her if he could help. She tried to usher him away, but he persisted. As soon as she spoke he knew that she too was a Gaelic speaker.

'*Bana-Ghàidheal?*' he asked.

She looked up at him. And was the most beautiful woman he'd ever seen. A girl, really. Sixteen. Maybe seventeen.

'*An toir mi...*' he began... 'will I take you to the hospital?'

'No. No. There's no need for that. I'll be fine.'

He gave her a hand and when she stood up towered over him by inches. She had seemed so small when running and crouching.

'Alasdair,' he said. 'Alasdair MacCoinnich. Alexander MacKenzie.'

She inclined her head a fraction.

'*Sìneag*. I... Jenny Gunn.'

'*Gunna*? *Gallaibh, an e*? Gunn? Then you'll be from Caithness?'

'I am, Sir.'

'Please...'

The absurdity of being called Sir. For he was just eighteen himself.

And so they walked out, as the phrase went at the time.

'Where do you...?'

'O, with an aunt, down by the Canongate,' she said, and he asked if she minded if he accompanied her safely back home. No, she didn't mind.

'It might be safer, Sir.'

'Please...'

And it was the last time she used the word.

Maybe it was grace. Maybe it was shyness, but he never asked what had happened. For surely it was hers to tell? And she never did.

He left her outside her aunt's house, but not before they'd arranged to meet again. On the Wednesday night at the castle walls. And they walked. And walked and walked. Down the Royal Mile and round by Calton Hill and on towards the New Town, where they sat for a while side by side in the gardens and admired the trees and the buildings that were being built all around them. The blossom was in full bloom.

'They smell like crushed roses,' Jenny said. 'Granny grows them. Then at the end of every autumn when the petals fade she brings them into the house and puts them in hot water which she keeps boiling for days, then pours the perfume into little bowls which waves all through the house when the frosts come.'

It was the moment he kissed her for the first time. The first moment he'd ever kissed anyone. And she too was like a rose. Her lips opened like a petal and even in his awkwardness he knew that this was the sweetest thing he would ever taste. It poured through him. He thanked God he had a coat on.

They walked back over George Street and on to Princes Street. The gloomy castle was covered in clouds high above them as they walked up the Mound. It was getting chilly and Jenny put her gloves on. Fox-skin.

They paused by St Giles.

'I'm leaving,' she said. 'Next month. For America.'

He was so shocked that he almost blurted out the Lord's name, in vain.

'America?'

'Yes. A place called Philadelphia. I'm going into service. With Mr Ritchie, the banker.'

And she explained how it was. That she'd served Mr Ritchie and his wife now for a year, but that they were returning back home and wanted to take her with them.

'There are prospects,' she said. 'They have some property in New York City as well, where Mr Ritchie works for half the year and they'd like for me to look after them as they move around the place.'

'Maybe...'

'No' she said quickly. 'It's best you stay here. It's... it's impossible. There are... there are circumstances.'

'Circumstances?'

But she turned away, and he didn't want to press.

'You have your own future.'

Oh, he wanted to pour it out. That there was no future without her. That he would do anything. Sail to America after her. Swim there. But her face forbade it.

'So what if there are circumstances,' he said. 'God's grace is sufficient for all circumstances. His strength is made perfect in weakness.'

She stretched out her gloved hand and stroked his cheek.

'Dear boy, dear man,' she said, wiping away the tears that were streaming down his cheeks.

'Write to me,' he said. 'Please. Please write to me and when…'

'Shush, shush, shush,' she whispered. 'Of course I will. Of course I'll write.'

She never did.

Jenny who had sailed to America. Bonnie Jenny, who could sing the birds into silence and stop the sun in its tracks. No wonder he had entered the ministry, wounded and seeking solace. But praise be to God for His grace and favour, who turns all things to the good, for even out of that poor, selfish reason – Jenny's rejection of him – He could bear fruit. For we know that all things work together for good to them that love God, to them who are the called according to his purpose.

As he was about to burn the stories, a bird sang. Alexander looked up. A robin was sitting on a bough made gold by the evening sun. It was singing in Gaelic. It said, *Bìg, bìg bigein, cò chreach mo neadan? Mas e gille beag e, cuiridh mi ri creig e; mas e gille mòr e, cuiridh mi le lòn e; ach mas fear beag gun chèill e, gun glèidheadh Dia d'a mhàthair fhèin e.* Chirp, chirp, chirp, who robbed my nest? If he's a small boy, I'll throw him off a rock; if he's a big boy, I'll fling him in a pond; but if he's a little senseless boy, may God protect him for his mother.

So birds also proclaimed the Gospel. And if birds were angels, so was Jenny. Because she loved to sing. She must have. She must have loved to sing. And he suddenly remembered how tender she'd been with him. Despite her decisiveness she had been as tender as a lamb, stroking his cheek. And for the first time in twenty years he caressed his face, feeling each and every hollow, the shape of his nose, and the curve of his brow, and the bristle of his stubble, which he would now grow without cutting ever again. He sang. *I will build my love a tower by yon clear crystal fountain and on it I will pile all the wild flowers o' the mountain.* Like the Lord Himself. And so songs and stories and fiddles and pipes were also means of redemption. Nothing was vanity, and that day nothing was burnt. For to destroy anything was to destroy God. Paradise lost could never be regained but it could be made new every morning.

And as he walked from village to village and from hamlet to hamlet, the Reverend Alexander met shepherds and prayed with them, met maidens out herding the cows and blessed them, met children begging for bread by the roadside and gave them every morsel he had. He became acutely aware how everyone made decisions, if that was the right word, and stayed with these decisions for the rest of their lives. How essentially conservative humankind was, how unwilling to change.

He would suggest more efficient ways to till the ground and people would listen and then return to their old ways, saying to themselves that there was nothing wrong with the way their fathers and their forefathers had tilled, and who was he anyway to tell them how to dig the ground? Let him keep to his speciality, and they would keep to theirs.

'This was the way my mother made the bread.'

'This is where the cow always slept.'

'That's what my father said.'

And the even more powerful collective.

'They always used to wash wounds with gannet oil.'

'This is the way they always did it.'

'That's what they said anyway.'

Whoever 'they' were. The massed host of spirits who

hovered at every corner telling the living to walk this way, to avoid travelling that way, instructing them not to open that furrow up for it contained the bones of the dead, not to bury that child in consecrated ground because she had been born out of wedlock, not to buy that horse because it was under a spell.

And the Reverend Alexander MacKenzie also knew full well how contingent and haphazard these 'decisions' were, though they had such eternal consequences. He met a man out on the moor who lived in a turf hovel and when MacKenzie asked him why one half of his dwelling was boarded off he said that was for the cow.

'But you don't have a cow,' said MacKenzie, and the man replied, 'But my father and my grandfather did and that's how they built their little houses.'

MacKenzie advised him to build a wee byre in case he ever got a cow and the man agreed but as soon as MacKenzie left, muttered to himself about the folly of the gentry.

MacKenzie knew fine, from his own aristocratic upbringing, that the gentry were exactly the same: living by habit, guided by their own ghosts. Living beyond their means, not because they could afford it, but because that was the way their people always lived. Why change anything as long as it made an impression? For the impression itself was what mattered and gave prestige. And prestige was power. Fine wines in the cellars and enormous bank loans while their peasants laboured down on the shore cutting kelp for them, and anyway what would these poor people do without the glory of the big house, and the deeds of their heroic ancestors? They would have nothing to talk about.

He knew the chains of habit in his own life. He'd buried Annie. Buried human love and desire away deep in his heart for a quarter of a century without confessing its hold, its liberating power. It was fine to have been young, and in love, and heartbroken, so it must be fine too to be old, and believing and grieving.

In his lonely walks over the moors MacKenzie meditated long and hard on the contingencies which left Lady MacLeod in her manor and old Seumas in his hovel. How could one ever understand the other, when they lived worlds apart, in different universes only a few miles from each other? Proximity didn't guarantee anything. Neither friendship nor enmity. Weren't the fiercest battles fought at the hearth, not on the heath?

And why should they understand each other when they had no need to? Old Seumas there in his guttural Gaelic and Lady MacLeod in her refined English and he himself in the fortunate, or tragic, position of being a bridge between the two, fluent in both. But wasn't his Saviour fluent in both – in the languages of heaven and of hell? Wasn't that why He came to earth: the word become flesh, so that the two could be reconciled, so that both the Lady and the tramp could be saved?

And saved from what? MacKenzie asked himself. Sin, of course, was the right answer, but what did that mean? From themselves. From privilege. From the habits and desires that left her Ladyship thirled to the fine bottles of Bordeaux wine she quaffed daily and left Seumas bound to his poverty, like the crippled man who lay for decades by the pool of Bethesda and when asked by Jesus if he wanted to get well poured out a long litany of excuses and reasons, that others always got to the healing wells first, that others were always faster and stronger, that he was bound by his ailments. By his excuses, his reasons. By everything that keeps us from dancing. Everything that keeps us from singing. The sin that so easily entangles. It was as if life itself could deliver you from all sin. Perish the pagan thought, but what beauty there was all around. The waterfalls teeming with light, the rivers full and flowing, all the birds of the air singing their hosannas: it would make a dead man rise.

He was sitting on a knoll halfway up the hillside. All of a sudden he saw an eagle swoop down from over the high cliffs and make for a lamb grazing down in the glen. The great wings were silent as the bird arrowed down and he watched in awe as the eagle picked up the lamb in its talons and flew off towards its lair. That too was election. What choice did the lamb have? Or the hungry eagle for that matter, following its instinct. For Alexander MacKenzie, the countryman, knew that no eagle would attack a lamb except when in great need of food. He was led like a lamb to the slaughter. Behold the Lamb of God! Feed my lambs, feed my sheep. He knew all the metaphors off by heart. *What man of you, having an hundred sheep, if he lose one of them, doth not leave the ninety and nine in the wilderness, and go after that which is lost, until he find it?* His work was to find the lost sheep, not to choose them.

How valuable sheep were. Each lamb could become a meal or a mother or, one day, a coat. He'd already seen the great cotton mills at work during his visit to Manchester, and before his conversion had a dream that one day a cotton mill would be established up here in the glens, where the wool was so plentiful and the workers so hardy and honest. And he used to make little speeches to himself that he never got the opportunity to share.

'Imagine', he would tell the gathered peasants 'having your own factory here. Instead of sending your wool down south for the profit of others, having a mill which would belong to yourselves. The fruit of your labours, the produce of your fields, the works of your hands as a holy, and profitable, offering unto the Lord.'

For he had seen the brutal conditions in the factories and knew them to be the work of Satan. Had he lived, he would have established the New Jerusalem in the glen and given the keys to the people, as part of the promise that they would inherit the earth.

The heather was in full bloom, and as the Reverend MacKenzie walked, ticks began to cling to his skin. You never notice ticks at first. Only after a while, when you feel the itch on your leg or in your crotch or somewhere where the flesh is soft and juicy and the blood good for them to suck. They eventually kill you if left there, infecting your whole body. Alexander was meticulous at removing them, inspecting his skin closely at the close of every day and removing ticks with the pincers he had in his bag. They were like sin: not to be tolerated. To be removed. Yet despite his care, a tiny tick evaded him in the end. He felt the itch during the day and sat down by the river in the evening to remove it, but his homemade pincers broke and left a trail of black so tiny as to be almost invisible.

It did its work quietly, secretly. It weakened him. He wondered whether one day men would not believe in God at all and consider his work of mercy as a primitive vanity.

He stood up, looking down towards the glens and hills where smoke curled from a thousand chimneys. All the glens he knew so well, where the cows grazed by the streams and where the pigs grunted in the fields and where the dear people lived and moved and had their being. With their lovely stories and songs and hopes and dreams and fears and failures. The wretched of the earth who were more loved in God's sight than Herod the mighty King or even her Ladyship up in the manor, and may the Lord forgive me for judging her, who needs as much mercy as the biggest sinner in the universe, whether that be Paul or myself. *O wretched man that I am! Who shall deliver me from the body of this death?* And he walked down the glen where an old widow beckoned him into her hovel and gave him milk and bread and some broth made of fish heads. It was the sweetest and best food he'd ever tasted, with the grace being in the giving and eating rather than in the quiet words of thanks.

That too was the year of the great fever which swept through the district like a muir fire. A fever which was so contagious that to breathe the same air as a person who'd caught it was to be guaranteed death. They died in their thousands throughout the whole countryside, from the infants on the breast to the aged stooped by the fires. All neighbourliness vanished because folk were terrified to go near each other or each other's houses and fields, so the sick were left to die in their hovels and the dead left where they had fallen, inside and out. Nobody was buried, for to contemplate going near or touching a corpse was to ensure your own death, and those family members who survived would try and fling a rope around the dead and if they were lucky catch a hand or a foot or a head and haul them out like horses.

And the only saint under the heavens was Alexander MacKenzie who fearlessly, for his earthly life hardly mattered except in so far as he could live the Gospel, entered every house and brought out the sick and the suffering and the dying and dead and cleaned them and cared for them and baptised and buried them, until he too caught the fever which took him to his Master, on a bonny autumn afternoon in the year of our Lord 1876, just when the harvest would normally have been brought in, had there been enough harvesters to go out into the empty fields.

6

AS A CHILD, Calum was attracted by movement: how wisps of straw caught by the wind would fly, how the clouds in the heavens changed shape, how the small hole in the rock from which a trickle of water flowed became a stream, then a river, then the ocean.

He said he remembered waking up as a baby and watching the atoms of dust moving through the air as the sun streamed in through the open door, and as he watched the motes of dust dancing his mother was singing. He discovered that things were adjustable. If he cried, his mother would come to him.

Later on as a young boy he would go out late at night to pee and stand amazed as the moon raced beneath the clouds, its pale light first on the hill, then on the loch, then on the byre before another cloud raced by and shadows came, then darkness. And when his father died he minded how everyone carried him in his coffin on their shoulders across the hills to the cemetery, the men all taking turns in groups of four in moving him from the land of the living to the land of the dead. Calum was six at the time.

Calum knew fine what attracted him to the fairy people: their lightness of being. They lived on the margins where risk was rewarded, in a place where things appeared the moment they were desired. Wish for a jug of whisky and there it was. Wish for a beautiful woman and she was yours. Wish for a good harvest and there instantly was a field of golden corn. He yearned for the airiness of their existence. Anything to take him away from the dull and heavy daily grind of turfing the earth and cutting tangle and heaving things across the sodden moors.

The fairies are bodies of condensed air, and those who have seen them repeatedly say they are as air 'somewhere of the nature of a condensed cloud and best seen in twilight', according to Kirk. The Gaelic-speaking people called them *Sluagh Math*, 'Good People'. They were known not by their appearance but by their powers.

They are flimsy, brittle things, easily destroyed by sudden human movements and discourtesies. Nothing is rigid. Their existence is as fragile as a child's breath. And it was that very flimsiness, that sense of something ephemeral, glanced, passing, which caught Calum's attention in the first place: the cloth's delicacy, that flash of green and silver and blue in the twilight, which disappeared as soon as he looked. It was the lure of a passing fancy. A glimpse of flesh. Was everything really momentary and temporal? The fragility of things. Here was a world of rare, delicate things which needed softness and tenderness in a life where you needed to be hard and robust.

Fairies permitted you to be the person you couldn't be, touching female things. They broke the story. Made it possible to love things beyond what you were told. To achieve things beyond your capabilities. God, how weary he was of the slow daily grind. The wind, the constant rain, the storms. Of behaving the way he did, day after day, year after year, quiet, steady, sober. Waking, working, sleeping. Constantly driven down the same narrow furrow by convention and tradition. By Elizabeth and the children and the neighbours and the minister. As if you couldn't think for yourself all these unthinkable and unsayable thoughts. Inside, far deep down in the fairy knoll where the grass was silk and constant music lit up the silence. The fairy knoll stretched and condensed time: you entered as a young man and emerged a hundred years and a thousand adventures later still the same age as you were a century before. You could be forever young, and live forever.

Calum sat on a rock by the river. After a while in the dark you can see everything. Things begin to glow. The pinpricks of the stars become lamps hanging from the rafters, and then homes, and villages and great cities and constellations. Faraway places become as intimate as your own home. There's America: it's a shining place entirely made up of stars. What it would be to live in the Great Bear, all illuminated as you walked along herding your cows before you. They would need no flailing stick or barking dog, for the animals would follow these bright lights all the way home.

Would good dry potatoes grow on the moon? For they needed good soil – the sandy machair was best, though he didn't think they'd have that up there. And down there on the shoreline the will-o-the-wisp hovered: the souls of the living dead. The whole world was lit up. He stood aside to let a phantom funeral past, looking down so that he wouldn't have to bear the burden of knowing the future, where light and matter are interchangeable, where energy has been converted into time.

An alternative had been imagined. And once it vanished (it never of course vanished at all, for nothing ever disappears), that lightning sight of silver and green and blue remained with him and he knew for certain that she would come again, down there in the hollows, when the time was right. And he waited, for he was a man of patience. What is tasted once will be savoured forever.

About a month later, as he was walking home from the shore, with the sun beginning to set to the west, he glanced over towards the hollows, not allowing his eyes to rest, for that was to give too much away. That he was impatient. Keen. Passionate. Any signal had to be faint and distant, like moonlight on the horizon, which made shadows live. Too much consciousness would make the fairies hesitant. It was always better to be casual about it, so that it would look as if you'd just stumbled upon them, that you just happened to be there when they were out, frolicking and dancing in the evening light, and your unexpected appearance surprised and delighted them and they would then invite you to their party. They had to be given freedom to live and die. The secret was to give them power. They never took it against your will.

So he walked along slowly, casually. Whistling, for he knew they like a good tune. A pipe reel was best, for they are the finest pipers in the whole world, having given MacCrimmon himself the gift of music when music meant the pipes, and the pipes only. As he whistled, he thought he heard the refrain from the green mound to his left, so he varied the tune and sure enough the variation came back to him as the new tune. He stopped whistling and listened. There was a great silence. The more he listened to the silence the more he heard. Rustling and soft whispers and soughs of sweetness, as if the grass itself was bending into the earth to hear the secrets.

Moonlight was emerging now to the east. Those soft green knolls which were all around, and the liquid light of the moon cast soft shadows on the whole earth. Calum knew his birthplace like the back of his hand: down there the sea, and over by the river, and those seven standing stones a bit above them, then the small tattie field and the path to the glen where the ponies grazed, and on the other side, the old mill and the gravel path built by the estate workers down to the laird's big house. He had a name for everything. *Abhainn Dearg.* Red River. *Achadh na Coirce.* Barleyfield.

As the moonlight shone on that familiar world, Calum had to forget that where the moon shone and made a shape like a sickle on the path was really only the curve of the road, and that what looked like a cart was only the outline of the two large rocks, one dragging the other. Nothing was as it seemed during the day. The whole order was in peril at this time of night.

He heard the tinkling of glass, laughter, and music from the knoll above the river and when he walked over he saw her sitting by the trunk of the tree next to the river. There, playing a tiny silver whistle was the most beautiful creature he'd ever seen: long red hair, the bluest of eyes, wearing a green smock and a blue skirt above skin boots. She was luminous. A wooden quaich with a whitish liquid was by her side. She beckoned him to drink from it and it was the sweetest mead he'd ever tasted.

As he drank again, all the old stories he'd heard as a child stirred within him. How witches disguised themselves as birds, how music was always the first sign of danger, how the devil could disguise himself as the most beautiful woman on earth to tempt men to destruction. Nothing was ever as it seemed.

Calum took fright. He ran as fast as a hare through the shifting moonlight, jumping the streams, louping the stone walls, arriving home breathless to tell Elizabeth that he'd been chased by the famous grey hound of the moor which could leap rivers as wide as ten miles.

The addict begins small. At first, it's a rabbit taken in the moonlight. Then a salmon in the river, a deer on the hill, and before you know it you are forever on the alert for the sound of scurrying feet on the machair, the soft splash in the stream, the rustle of bracken on the mountain. You dream about hunting.

As he lay there that first night beside Elizabeth, he was ashamed of himself for having gone beyond the boundaries, opening himself to such danger and temptation, over by in the green moonlit hollows where all kinds of things were possible. He was fine where he was. This bed he'd made, and the stone walls and the rocks and the stream and the patch where they planted the tatties. The safe, settled globe.

Where the cabbage patch had been was now filled with carrots, and in the stream he had built a dam to make a pool where he caught fish. He had changed the world in his own little way. Things could alter. Change shape. Fallow fields could be planted. Calum knew that he too had changed shape when he'd seen that bonny lass. It had to do with patterns. He thought of the blankets Elizabeth had made that now covered them in bed. There was a brown square, a russet one, then a blue one and they made different shapes according to how you looked at them: brown, russet, blue, russet, brown, blue. If you squinted one eye shut, the world became blue, brown, blue, brown, russet.

Everything was different if you looked at it some other way. For when Angus had disappeared, there had been a whirlwind – which meant that the Airy Host had lifted him. Or maybe the Press Gang had taken him away as young Margaret said, claiming she'd seen the foreign men coming in by night by boat, but who would believe her, given her condition?

So Calum returned to where he'd seen the beautiful woman the night before. Everything was so different in the bare light of day. Nothing but the familiar. Sleepy green hollows, the running river, the old oak tree and the patch leading up the hill. Everything was as it had always been. Nothing had changed. Things hadn't moved. If they did, then nothing would ever again be as before. He knew that once something changed shape it could never again exactly recover its old shape. The ocean, for example, which in his young days used to reach only as far as the skerries, until one day they were breached by a massive tide and ever since that day the tide would now reach up to Bran's Rock high on the shore.

It was all to do with patterns. As with the bed blankets.

There were quarters. The true quarters of the year and the crooked quarters of the year, which differed so much. There was the brown cow, and the black cow. And there was the brindle cow. March boasted that he would take the skin off her, so she went into the woods for shelter. Then when March was over, the cow left the woods in the morning, and went skipping out into the open. She said, 'Goodbye to you, little, ugly, biting, grey March!'

But March asked April for the loan of a day and he gave it to her. And that day blew hard with snow, rain and cold. The Brindle was too far from home and had no shelter, and that day killed her. We don't know if April ever got the loaned day back since. The last two days of March and the first day of April have been called The Days of the Brindled Cow ever since. An Irish pedlar told Calum that when he was a child.

The pedlar carried two sacks. In one were pebbles which he would lay out in patterns on the ground. He insisted he was just playing a game though everyone knew he was staking claim to land and cows and children, for no sooner would he leave the area and move on than a child would fall ill, or a cow would die, or neighbours would quarrel over boundaries. So they would all give him extra milk and bread, buy trinkets from him, allow him to stay overnight and give him porridge in the morning. And as soon as they began doing that, no-one fell ill. The pedlar had told many stories which Calum now realised had shaped his world as much as the cliff edges had defined the limits of the eastern landscape.

How mice and rats and cats and pigs came into the world: they were made from St Martin's fat. One night St Martin came to a house where a man had just threshed a stack of oats and there was a lot of chaff and grain lying about the yard. At that time, there were only cattle; there were no pigs or piglets. St Martin asked if there was anything to eat the chaff and the grain. The man of the house replied, no, for there were only the cattle. St Martin said it was a great pity to have that much chaff going to waste. So at night when they were going to bed, he handed a piece of fat to the servant-girl, and told her to put it under a tub turned upside down, and not to look at it until he would give her the word next day. The girl did so, but she kept a little bit of the fat and put it under a keeler to find out what it would be. When St Martin rose the next day he asked her if she had looked under the tub, and she said she had not. He told her to go and lift up the tub. She lifted it up and there under it were a sow and twelve piglets. It was a great wonder, as they had never before seen pig or piglet. The girl then went to the keeler and it was full of mice and rats! As soon as the keeler was lifted, they went running about searching for any hole they could go into. St Martin pulled off one of his mittens and threw it at them – and made a cat with that throw. That is why the cat ever since goes after mice and rats.

Folk always asked the old pedlar what he carried in his other sack, but he never answered them until the day Calum was hit in the eye by the fairy's arrow and lost his sight. He'd been out on the moor when the wind blew up strong. It started raining heavily and as he took shelter behind a big rock the arrow came flying towards him, blinding him in the left eye. The strange thing was that there was no blood, except that he could not see anything from the eye. On the way home, he met the pedlar.

'Here,' he called to Calum, 'sit down here by the well and we'll see what we can do for you.'

And he took the secret sack from his pouch and asked Calum to dip his fore and middle fingers from the right hand into it, then put the liquid on to his blind eye. He told Calum to do it three times, and on the third brushing of the liquid against his eyelid he opened his eye to perfect vision.

'What is it?' Calum asked.

And the pedlar said, 'It's a bag of tears. Which only heal

when they are tears of laughter, not of sorrow.'

And then he laughed loud and long until the tears came, which he let fall into the bag, as he told Calum this story, as if it was funny.

'Three brothers they were who went to sea in a ship. They spent a long time at sea without meeting land, and they feared they would not meet any, but finally they came to an island which was wooded to the shore. They tied their ship to a tree and went inland. They saw no-one and met no-one. They set to work and worked for seven years. At the end of the seven years one of them said, "I hear the lowing of a cow." But no-one answered.

Seven more years passed.

The second man spoke then.

"Where?"

It went on like that for another seven years.

"If you don't keep quiet," said the third man, "we will be put out of this place".'

And the pedlar's big tears kept dropping into his sack as he walked off down the road, laughing.

Calum shrugged off these memories. For him the business in hand was to work out a way to see his fairy lover again, or he would pine away and die. It is said that fairies' hearts are soft to love and admire persistence. So every evening after supper he would make his way to the knoll where the oak tree was beside the river, and sit there for hours, watching.

He would sing, for he had heard that the fairies liked music. And he sang in Gaelic, for that would be the way of it and their native tongue, and what better than the love songs which would make the apples fall from the trees and the corn grow gold in the fields? *O chraobh an ubhal, Oh,* he sang, *Oh apple tree, apple tree, branch of the apple tree, Oh apple tree, know the tree that is mine, the tallest with the sweetest apples, its trunk strikes downwards, its top is bending, Apple tree, may God be with you, may east and west be with you, may every sun and moon be with you, may every element be with you, Oh apple tree, apple tree, branch of the apple tree, Oh apple tree.*

And she would always appear halfway through the song. As soon as he sung *east and west* he would hear her joining: *be with you.* The two of them would sing, *may every sun and moon be with you, may every element be with you,* and gravity dissolved and she would take him by the hand and lead him over the hollow to the far side of the knoll where the hill would open and he would see the lights and hear the music and laughter from deep inside the brugh.

Yet he was always careful to carry some bit of iron on him, in case he got stuck down there, never to come out again. He needed to be careful not to speak either, for to speak inside the mountain was to be trapped there forever. The more he was in the knoll, the lovelier she looked and the sweeter the music sounded and the better they danced and, after all, wouldn't it be as well just to forget the sliver of iron the next time and speak out his heart and to his heart's content? Which is exactly what happened.

It was the bonniest of summer evenings. On his way to the knoll Calum tossed the little iron knife aside and when he saw her, combing her auburn hair by the river, he deliberately forgot all taboos and took her hand and the side of the hill opened up and they descended into the fairy place which smelt of honey and apples. And because this time he had no iron and spoke and groaned, he was trapped there for a hundred years and never came out again until everyone he had ever known was dead and gone, and no-one recognised him and he recognised no-one. He was in a place where consequences didn't matter anymore.

She was tender with him, caressing the lobe of his ear as if that small lump of flesh was the most wondrous thing in the whole wide world; in return, he spent weeks running his fingers through her hair which was like gold ribbons flowing down from the skies. There was a curve between the river and the hill, then a perfumed hollow where you could lay your head down, and as soon as you had rested you could then climb the brae to where the apple trees were, and those small pots of honey secreted away in the bushes where the fauns played on silver whistles and time stood still. It was a place like those beds of silk brocade in the stories the black tinker used to tell. Rivers flowed, rushing uphill then cascading down the rocks like spurting waterfalls with each stream a different colour, and after you had run so fast you could rest forever in her arms which were as soft as summer.

Things had no weight. You could lift stones as if they were feathers, push mountains and they would open, visit the insides of things. There was no bending over to plant or lift potatoes, no climbing cliffs to find eggs. The cows didn't need to be fed or moved from pasture to pasture. The ground didn't need to be tilled. And this fairy woman loved him, even showing him her full naked body while it was still light. She was translucent, covered in oil, and glistened. As they lay by the river she dipped her hand into the water and dredged out a sparkling blue shell. She gave it to him. It was whorled and serrated and rough in the hand. So unlike her skin.

'It's got seven layers,' she said. 'The magic number. If you put it next to your left ear you will hear the future.'

He listened and heard her heart beating like the ocean and mermaids singing in the distance.

The more you listen to a sound the more familiar it becomes, until it signifies the thing itself. A single bee droning in the sun becomes a whole summer, the wind whistling in the eaves of the house an entire winter. Calum never thought he had much of a voice, but discovered that she loved the way he spoke, slowly and softly, and he even joined in her songs, at first merely singing the chorus but building up enough confidence and energy to sing on his own as she played the silver whistle. She made magic shoes for him out of rabbit skin to match her own, which meant that they could run as fast as the wind, and move silently from one river to the next in the curragh she'd made out of wicker and hide. They flew with the wind like seasonal birds from south to north and east to west and back again.

Rumours spread that Calum had been kidnapped. Stories circulated that he wandered on the headland on moonlit nights and that he had returned unshaven and bedraggled, frightening the children and begging for bread. Some said he'd become an old man, others said he'd become young again. But all said that he came back the same age as when he disappeared; that he came walking over the moor and asked a man if he knew where Elizabeth was, and the man said that he didn't know, but that he should ask his father, who was sitting inside by the fire. And so Calum went in and asked the old man by the fire if he knew where Elizabeth was, and the old man said he didn't, but that he should ask his father, who was down in bed. And when he asked the wizened old man in the bed if he knew where Elizabeth was, he said he didn't, but that he should ask his father, who was sitting inside a pouch at the end of the bed. And when he asked the little ancient man inside the pouch if he knew where Elizabeth was, he said he didn't, but that he should ask his father, who was hanging in the atom dust in the air. And when he asked the tiny little man inside the atom dust if he knew where Elizabeth was, he said he didn't, but that he should ask his father, who was out in the invisible sky. And the ones who told the story said that they saw Calum calling up into the sky and walking westwards, beyond the stone wall where the sun was setting red.

7

AFTER CALUM DISAPPEARED, Elizabeth and all the neighbours searched for him all over the place. Despite the claims that the fairies had taken him, Elizabeth was convinced that he had fallen off the high cliffs on the eastern edge and that his body had been swept out to sea. So she built a cairn on the cliff's edge to mark his passing, for no-one should be without a memorial stone.

The wailing women condemned her lack of tears. It wasn't strength. Just that she wept when alone, which was such a difficult place to find. In the house the children would see her, and around the village there were a dozen prying eyes, so she'd find reason to go out to the moor or down to the shore where she recalled that first time she saw Calum. On the way to the kirk, his dark curly hair cascading down beneath his bonnet. What a daftie he was, when she thought about it. As handsome as a summer's day and his head in the clouds. And that day they were supposed to plant the potatoes, but instead he took her by the hand down to the shore where they spent the morning building sandcastles.

'You make such beautiful ones,' he said.

And that day she did, a castle within a castle within a castle, surrounded by five wide moats which he dug deep with the potato-spade. She missed him terribly, for no-one else could make her smile simply for being alive. Daily, she chose to remember him for his best self, wishing he'd given himself the chance to be as good as he'd intended to be.

The pregnancy wasn't easy, but the child would be

fine, Elizabeth knew that. All her pregnancies had been so different. Looking back on them all she felt she could now trace their future from the past: those constant movements that Angus made in the womb, prophesying his travels in the Crimea and off to America; the way Iain kicked; the quiet, almost apologetic, ways in which Mary and Catrìona and Joan had been born, without a cry. This new life within was moving as if impatient to be out and about with her in this strange world.

Elizabeth considered herself a widow, though some of the other women around treated her like an abandoned woman whose husband had been taken by the Host, substituting an unborn child for a full-grown man. For hadn't Alasdair Mòr MacKintosh been lifted by the Airy Host on his way back from Strathfarrar, leaving a widow and ten young children to fend for themselves while Cumberland's army ravaged the country? And hadn't MacGillieChaluim himself been drowned by the coven of cat witches who had called up a storm out of nowhere, leaving a grieving family behind? Smaller gifts always replaced the bigger things that were destroyed. That was the way of it.

Two weeks after Calum's disappearance Elizabeth gave birth to their daughter, Anna, who was christened on the 26th of September 1876, according to the old church records. This Anna was the first and only child of theirs to go to school, the Education Act of 1872 having made the building of a school in every parish compulsory. It opened up a whole new world for every child in the country, who were now all forced by law to attend. The local whipper-in was a bushy-bearded former constable named Duncan MacKenzie.

Anna had to forsake her native Gaelic to enter this magic world of learning. The schoolmaster was Mr Johnstone, who combined standard rote learning with a passion for the Wild West of America, where he'd spent some years as an itinerant preacher during the years of the gold rush until drink almost killed him before he was shipped back to the family home in England. Although he still took an annual drinking bout, he was sober enough through the school year to survive as a teacher in various parishes before moving on. Further and further north he travelled – a season in Shropshire, then Cheshire, Lancashire, Westmoreland, and on to Cumberland and Northumberland; in Scotland, working his way through Dumfriesshire and Lanarkshire and Stirlingshire and Perthshire and Inverness-shire before arriving here on the edge of the known world with nowhere else to go to except the ocean.

He was an invigorating teacher. If you learned the three Rs from him you never forgot them as long as you lived. Along with all the others from the surrounding villages and glens, Anna worked her way through *The New Royal Primer* and never forgot the rhyme which opened the door to Mr Johnstone's marvellous new universe: *those children who would learned be, must first begin with ABC.*

Anna loved that her name began with the first letter of the alphabet. And how easy everything was for her to learn when it rhymed!

In Adam's fall
We sinned all.
Thy life to mend
God's Book attend.
The Cat doth play
And after slay.
A Dog will bite
A thief at night.
The Eagle's flight
Is out of sight.
The idle Fool
Is whipped at school.

Mr Johnstone spoke with a twang which affected Anna's speech pattern for the rest of her life, so that her *A*s were always slightly angled and the *O* sound always tended towards *ay*. Even in old age she carried hints of an Anglo-Bostonian-Scotch accent from an earlier century.

Anna would sit in her wicker chair in her old age and sing screeds of songs she'd learned from Mr Johnstone – 'Oh, Susanna', 'She'll be Coming Round the Mountains', 'The Battle Hymn of the Republic', 'I'm Going Home to Dixie'. He'd been a great lover of spoken-out poetry and taught young Anna to stand up when she was reciting from memory, so even in the nursing home she would stand on her frail legs and chant:

> By the shores of Gitche Gumee,
> By the shining Big-Sea-Water,
> Stood the wigwam of Nokomis,
> Daughter of the Moon, Nokomis...

Mr Johnstone was astonished at Anna's capacity to learn things on one hearing, whether a poem, a story, the multiplication table, the capitals of all the countries in Europe, or a list of all the native tribes he'd seen in America. *Apache, Blackfoot, Cherokee, Cheyenne, Chickasaw, Choctaw, Comanche, Cree, Crow, Navajo, Pawnee, Pequot, Shawnee, Shoshone*, Anna would recite, with no notion that there were hundreds of others which Mr Johnstone had never heard of.

London was the capital of Britain. The longest river in the world was the Amazon. 1314 was the Battle of Bannockburn. Latitude was the distance north or south of the equator, Longitude the distance east or west of the meridian, which, said Mr Johnstone, was an imaginary line running north and south through Greenwich, England. There were two places in Australia called Kalgoorlie and Coolgardie which sounded terribly like the teacher saying, '*Cailleach a' mùn air cùl gàrradh.*' ('An old woman pissing behind a wall.') So the pupils would ask Mr Johnstone to tell them about the recent gold rush in Australia so that they could secretly snigger at his mild innocent obscenity.

Somehow he'd managed to carry a great big sea-chest north with him and sometimes he would let the scholars rummage in it for a while and extract the marvels of the universe: maps and a globe; a telescope and a magnifying glass; a photographic camera which he set up under a dark blanket on a summer's morning to take a picture of them all standing in front of the school. He told them to stand still for ages and ages, but the very young ones moved and the photograph would therefore be useless, he said. For decades after that they would all sit stock still if anyone took their photograph in case a flutter ruined the moment.

What confused Anna at first was the exactitude of school. She was used to the uncertainty of home, where things depended on the weather and upon her mother's health and her neighbours' fortunes and the varieties of God's will. One day, all would be well and there would be food on the table and her mother would be singing; the next, there was scarcely a bite and her mother would hold her stomach and rock backwards and forwards by the fire, asking her to fetch a pail of water from the well, or go out and gather some sticks for the fire.

In school everything was so precise and clear. There was either a right answer or a wrong answer. One and one made two. Always and every time, without exception. But boundaries were very clear, same as at home. Mr Johnstone had a map of all the countries of Europe and it was easy to see where each country began or finished: France was all blue, but as soon as you stepped out of the blue you were in a green country called Spain; from there, if you jumped across a line you were in a red land called Portugal. Anna

ANGUS PETER CAMPBELL

thought how beautiful it would be to live in a place which had blue grass and what fun it would then be to hop from country to country across the colours on to green, red, blue, orange, yellow and purple grass.

And there were different colours of people too, Mr Johnstone said. Yellow ones and white ones and brown ones and black ones and multicoloured ones and maybe even purple ones out in space, though he wasn't sure about that. But he was sure about the others, for he had seen them himself, in America. And he had books in his big sea-chest to prove it, books of half-naked people with bones through their noses and jewellery hanging from their mouths and painted people with big feathers on their heads and spears in their hands.

Above all else, science was Mr Johnstone's great mantra. The earth and the sun and the moon and the stars, he said, were to be studied scientifically. When they dared to ask him what that meant, he asked them if they knew what a frog was? They all remained silent, except for young James MacDonald, the daftie who knew no better, who put his hand up and said, 'A king under a spell.'

His brother Donald MacDonald said he was wrong, that it was a witch, while Archie Mackay said that he had heard tell that all frogs were devils.

So Mr Johnstone took them all outside and led them down to the edge of the loch, where the frogs lived. He waded into the water and scooped one up from the sedge and led them all back to school, where he laid the poor terrified frog on his desk, took out a penknife and divided it in half, then into quarters and eighths, before asking them all to take a bit of the frog in their hands and then put that bit under the magnifying glass, where they could study it scientifically.

Anna got the frog's head, which she thought was beautiful under the microscope. Green skin, eyes of gold with blue streaks all around in the background. James was probably

90

right. Even though Mr Johnstone explained that the frog was just an animal which could be described by colour and texture and behaviour and could not be anything except what it was. Which he knew was nonsense even as he spoke it, for nothing was as it was, and would he himself not go on the drink again soon and become that beast which he wasn't, or maybe really was, beneath the sober external mask of the schoolmaster?

'The difference between a cow and a sheep,' he told them, 'is not just that one bellows and one bleats,' though he never went any further to explain what that difference was except to say the word 'species'.

'The origin of species, boys and girls. The origin of species!' As if that explained everything.

'Why don't we have four legs?' the Daftie asked, 'because I'd like to be a deer and run very fast over the hills.'

'You do,' Mr Johnstone said, and everyone looked at Daftie to see if he also had antlers growing out of his head.

Mr Johnstone tried to teach them the science of the sun and the moon and the stars, though they remained unconvinced, perhaps because he himself was unconvinced. For as he would tell them about the strength of the sun's rays and about how the moon was merely the reflection of the sun's light and how the stars were really big exploding balls of gas, he would diverge into stories about how Icarus flew into the sun and about how the moon came down to earth when she fell in love with her own reflection in the Atlantic, so that for the children it became one fantastic big story where anything was possible.

'We are a small island in an ocean of nescience,' he declared. 'Vasco da Gama and Columbus enlarged the earth, Copernicus enlarged the heavens. And remember that Savonarola and Leonardo were born in the same year.'

The marvellous names people had elsewhere, while here they were all called Angus and Donald and Peggy and Morag.

'Sir,' they asked, 'Is there a man on the moon?'

And though he instantly thought of telling them the truth he knew how partial that was, so he said, 'Of course there is,' and told them how the man on the moon got there, in the days when wishing was powerful.

'One Christmas Eve, a man went out and stole cabbages from his neighbour's garden. And when he was in the act of walking off with his load, he was seen by people, who wished him up to the moon. So there he stands till this day in the full moon, to be seen by everybody, carrying his load of cabbages to all eternity.'

James MacDonald said he saw a goat in the moon, while his brother Donald argued that it was a bull, though Anna knew fine it was a rabbit, so she put her hand up and asked Mr Johnstone how the rabbit had gotten to the moon, and he said, 'That also happened a long time ago, when wolves used to roam the whole country, and one day a big bad wolf spotted a little rabbit out of its burrow and chased her across the fields and hills and was just about to catch her and kill her and eat her when the rabbit, as a last chance of escape, made a desperate jump on to the face of the moon, where she remains safe and sound to this day.'

He took to telling them riddles, which they loved. *Little Nancy Etticoat, in a white petticoat, and a red nose, the longer she stands, the shorter she grows!*

Anna's hand was always first up.

A candle!

As round as an apple, as deep as a cup, and all the king's horses can't pull it up!

A well!

How is the lazy man's bed too short for him?

Because he is too long in it!

But Mr Johnstone was beginning to waver. He began speaking in Latin, which was his own warning signal to be off on the great Roman road north. Which he was, one late spring evening. The next morning there was no sign of him, the schoolhouse empty and the sea-chest gone. Bushy-bearded MacKenzie arrived to tell them that Mr Johnstone had gone north and that he himself would have to teach them for a while. They all quivered, for they knew what that meant, with that thick tawse belt hanging from his waist. So the stories ceased, except for the resurrected single story that the cat sat on the mat and that one plus one made two and – thwack, you stupid boy – did I not tell you to speak English in this class?

The scholars drifted off, stayed at home to milk the cow, or to fetch water from the well, or to gather the peats, and only the cruellest of parents forced their children to attend school to be beaten into submission. Elizabeth was not one of these, for she was horrified when Anna came home with dark bruises on her wrists and arms saying that Mr MacKenzie had given her twelve lashes of the tawse for getting an answer wrong. Finally her mother forced the issue out of her –

'He asked me to say "the cat sat on the mat" and I said "the cat shat on the mat", but I didn't mean to.'

Anna didn't even know what she'd done wrong, for she was unfamiliar with the word in English.

Her mother just said, 'Don't you worry. If he comes here to complain that you're not at school, I'll just ask him to repeat this fast one hundred times: she said she should sit so she sat.'

And they both said it, *she said she should shit so she shat*, until they fell down, exhausted.

So Anna stayed at home, learning other things. Her mother was not that well and her survival into the dawn of the twentieth century was entirely due to Anna's knowledge and use of herbs. There was a useless doctor over the hill in the adjoining glen, but who on earth had any money to use him? So Anna became expert in vulneraries, febrifuges, emetics, cathartics, irritants and tonics, everything from kidney-vetch to the petty spurge, which was wonderful for removing warts. Dog violet boiled in whey was good for allaying fevers, while house-leek mixed with cream got rid of earache.

But maybe it was simple touch that mattered. She noticed that the more she visited people to give them the remedies, the better they got if she herself rubbed the ointment on to them or fed the treatment to them rather than leaving it with them or watching them supping it themselves. And she just knew that medicine was as much social as biological, and that things worked better when people sensed they were loved. Which is why she eventually trained as a nurse. She would have been more than able to have been a doctor and maybe would have been, had not Mr Johnstone left that day to go further north in search of whisky.

At least Mr Johnstone had prepared the ground for alternatives: those who had been with him for the year he was there could all read and write. And papers began to arrive and to be read. From Wick, Iain occasionally sent a copy of *The Northern Ensign*, which was full of news about the herring fleets, while the girls down in Glasgow regularly sent copies of the *Glasgow Herald* and the *Weekly News*, which Anna read out loud for her mother and everyone else who gathered round to hear the great words.

They always insisted on everything being read, from front page news of the death of Grand Duke Louis IV to the advertisements for Carters Little Liver Pills, which also relieved *distress from Dyspepsia, Indigestion and Too Hearty Eating. A perfect remedy for Sick Headache, Dizziness, Nausea, Drowsiness, Bad Taste in the Mouth, Coated Tongue, Pain in the Side.* Anna read carefully and precisely. *They regulate the Bowels and prevent Constipation. Forty in a phial. Purely Vegetable and do not gripe or purge, but by their gentle action please all who use them. Established*

1856. In phials at 1s 1½d. Sent by post. Illustrated Pamphlet Free. British Depot: 46, Holborn Viaduct, London, E.C.

The old crones would listen carefully, as if they were listening to a story. Even though half of them didn't understand a word of English, they would nod their heads sagely or shake them in disbelief, imitating the few who understood. And wasn't it strange that there was so much crime out there when there was none here? All these wars and murders and assaults and robberies when none of that happened here.

So they heard that Gladstone was once again elected Prime Minister and that Edison had invented an electric lamp; and nearer home, from the *Northern Ensign*, that the sailing ship *The Copeland* of Leith had run aground at Langaton Point, Stroma, when homeward-bound with a full cargo of Iceland ponies. *Most of these were got ashore and fed*, Anna read, and everyone smiled and clapped their hands. And the ponies were then also all reshipped and the crew were all saved though the ship itself was hurled over the reef and sank in deep water. One of the passengers, the paper said, was Sir H. Rider Haggard, an author who had gone to Iceland to gather information for a book he was writing.

Some of the people listening realised that these were all just like their own stories, except that they were written. The news items and the advertisements and the deaths and births and marriages read out by Anna brought to mind so many things, and they would tell again of people long dead, and the children who had been born and the marriages that had taken place, or should have taken place, or could have taken place.

Most of it was information, but intricately laced with comment and moral judgement, so that it was difficult to work out what actually happened and what should have happened. Like that time Flora had a child, though it was obviously a changeling for it withered away and died within weeks of having been born looking as healthy as an autumn berry; or the time that Fiona was promised to George, who then disappeared on the evening of the wedding and was never seen again, and that very night a silver rainbow was seen hovering over Fiona's house before slowly moving westwards towards the sea. What would these fancy foreign papers make of that? Things happened to women and children which only those who guarded the secrets of the language understood.

Inevitably someone would allude to Calum, though one look from Elizabeth would silence them. So the ghost stories would begin instead, which made you shiver because you knew that out there in the dark all kinds of horrors waited for you unless you prayed in the name of the Father and the Son and the Holy Ghost, in the name of Mary, Bride, Peter, Paul, or unless you carried bits of iron or threads of coloured wool or the pearlwort; and even then they would get you if your time was due, despite every precaution and charm and rune. Such as poor Seonaidh, who carried every known incantation and amulet yet fell and drowned in the tiny hill pool one night, as predicted by Dòmhnall Mòr. There was hardly enough water there to drown a mouse, yet there he was face down, dead, in a few inches of mud in the morning.

And trying not to believe didn't help one little bit. You could walk along saying to yourself 'Ach, it's just the wind in the trees,' but the next thing you were lifted and taken to a strange place. The bogle's power wasn't extinguished by your atheism, for it was sustained by habit. Who were you to think you could erase belief overnight, by just thinking differently?

Anna had her mother's dark looks and her father's stature and as far as the neighbours could judge a mixture of their personalities. Though they didn't say that, for fear of tempting fate. And there were suitors – old Archie MacIntosh tried his hand, and the laird's factor, a pock-faced man called Souter, would leer at her at every opportunity, but Anna withered him with a look. It wasn't the evil eye, for evil is in the eye of the beholder. They said his balls shrivelled.

And then the water-horse got her. She was out on the moor one evening gathering herbs when he appeared out of the fog by the lochside, pale and sleek and neighing. She knew it was him and tried to run away, but it was boggy and difficult underfoot and he caught up with her by the time she reached the rocks west of the valley. She knew that if she managed to get hold of the bridle and keep it from him he would lose all his strength and power, but he was slippery and wet and strong and easily overcame her. It was only by the skin of her teeth that she managed to escape being drowned at the end as he tried to drag her with him into the loch where he disappeared with a splash, leaving her all covered from head to toe in slime and dirt and blood.

Elizabeth knew what had happened as soon as she arrived home, bruised and crying. She washed her and comforted her and said nothing, in the hope that Anna herself would acknowledge the truth. Surely it was hers to tell? And she did: how he had come at her out of the dark, and how she had fought, but the power he had – the strength of a horse – and how everything all blurred into one, of skin and slime and hair and dirt, and Elizabeth hugged her close, whispering, 'Sush, sush, sush, my dear child.' The two of them slept that night in each other's arms, mother and daughter.

How can anyone tell what happened? The afternoon was rainy and cold, though when the story was told later it was dry and sunny. And not because it wasn't dry and sunny, but that was how the miller recalled it – hadn't the sun shone brightly as he'd left the mill to go and gather the sheep? For no-one tells lies. And as he walked down by the loch it began to rain and a sort of fog descended, and maybe it was the echo of his boots, but he thought he heard voices and as he trudged through the sedge there she sat, bathing by the river, combing her long hair. Anna, whom he'd known since she was a child. The widow's daughter. And how she'd grown. Johnny the miller's head was full of voices. These stories he'd heard since he was born the miller's son: Johnny the miller's son, Johnny, son of Johnny the miller, son of Johnny the miller, son of Johnny the miller and back and back unto a thousand generations when the first Johnny had established the mill, right here by the tumbling river. She was already loosened like long hair, and given far and wide like fallen rain.

Some millers were good and some millers were bad. You should have heard the songs and tales that had been made about them, such as the story of the carpenter and his lovely wife and the two clerks who are eager to get her into bed.

And once there was a miller who was poor and had a beautiful daughter and the miller and the lass, a pretty little maid so neat and gay, to the mill she went one day, a sack of corn she had to grind, but there no miller could she find, tiddy fol, tiddy fol tiddy fol le day, rite fol lol lol tiddy fol le day! Oh!

At last the miller did come in, and unto him she did begin:

'Come, grind my corn so quick-e-ly, around your stones my corn must fly.'

'Come, sit you down,' the miller did say, 'For I can't grind your corn to-day; my stone is high and my water's low, and I can't grind for the mill won't go.'

So this couple sat down to chat, they talk'd of this, they talk'd of that, they talk'd of things which you do know, and she soon found out that the mill would go.

'Oh! it's now, I says, young miller-man, you grinds all flour and no bran.'

Then an easy up and an easy down – she could hardly tell that her corn was ground.

'Now I think I will make my best way home, if my mother asks me why I've been so long, I'll say I've been ground by a score or more, but I've never been ground so well before.'

And everything rose inside Johnny's head, like the tide rising on a wild winter's day. The way it surges over everything, sending spume flying, making you deaf in the wind and blind in the spray. The miller was a powerful man, and given extra strength by the force of the oncoming waves. A girl had no chance in these circumstances except to turn into flotsam on the surface of the tide. There was no name for it, unless her brothers found out and killed him, but they were away at work and war. He was nothing, but needed to be named as much more than nothing, so he was given the ancient name of *each-uisge*, water-horse, which came out of the dark sleek and wet, unearthly, devilish. You could know one truth and yet confess another, or a lie. For you were as innocent as the corn in the storm or the child before the man.

Elizabeth worked hard at erasing the poison that not to be conceived in love was to be under a curse, because love was not born, but given. So she sang to Anna, and told her about the nightingale who was given the voice of a crow but still sang like a nightingale, while the crow, when granted the voice of the nightingale, still croaked like a crow.

She was a white swan, as in the great song: *Guile, guile! Guile guile!* And the song took all the anguish and, as with all magic, transformed it into what had been there before the deception. For nothing emerges from the magician's cloak other than what is there before. No rabbit comes out of the hat that wasn't secretly placed there before. So she was pure and blameless and could not be punished.

They went down to the stream and filled a jar with water taken with the current. (It must never be taken against the current.) And in the water in the jar Anna placed seven bits of peat, and seven handfuls of meal and seven cloves of garlic while Elizabeth said the rhyme. And when the bairn was born he was as bonny and good as the May sun. Fair-haired with blue eyes, just like Johnny the miller's son, so no wonder folk said the fairies themselves had given him to Anna as a gift, for that was how the good people sometimes chose to work, for Johnny was such a good fine lad, with an inheritance coming his way too. At least it wasn't a changeling. And Elizabeth and Anna named the baby John, and they put a triple thread of white, rose and black round his wrist.

And maybe kindness matters. For despite things, this other bonny lad kept coming to the house. Andrew MacDonell, bringing meat and fish and laughter. He was invited inside and talked for hours on end in the evening with Anna and he listened to Elizabeth, and he loved Anna and she loved him. She loved him simply because he was fun to be with. He cared. It was that rare thing: tenderness.

He was a fisherman and said that of course he'd be pleased to bring up a fairy-bairn, for to do so was to bless the child and the new parents, and to do that was to bless the whole world. He was no simpleton. Just simply knew that to say something was to bring it into being. And despite all the prevailing taboos he asked her one morning to go out on the small boat with him to fish, for 'all that stuff about lassies on board was nonsense', and so they sailed round the point out towards the skerries where the fishing was best, and that day they took the best catch Andrew ever had. Saithe, herring, mackerel, cod and ling.

'Och, love grows,' he said as he threw back the smaller, living fish into the sea. And though it was nothing new, it moved her. For she too knew that the value of words is in the person who utters them, not in the words themselves.

And he told her a grand story about the first ever wedding, and said they too should also have a wedding like that.

'For the first wedding ever held,' he said, 'was on Little Christmas Eve. On the 5th of January. There was a big company gathered at the wedding, and they had plenty to eat and drink. And Our Saviour was there and his mother. The drink, you see, gave out as the night wore on, and the young couple were embarrassed that the drink hadn't held out till morning for the company. And the Glorious Virgin noticed, you see, that the young couple were unhappy about it, and she told her son to make more drink. So he gave an order then to fill the vessels with water, and every vessel in the house was filled with water, and he made wine of every drop of it, and as he did that from then till morning for the newly married pair, it is said that ever since the water becomes wine on Little Christmas Eve. The wedding was in Cana,' Andrew said. 'That is in Heaven, I suppose.'

He asked her to marry him. She said yes and asked if they'd have wine at their wedding and he said no, just water, which would then turn into wine. And she asked if it would be in a church, and he said no, it would be outside, for that was God's church, and she asked if there would be a minister, and he said, yes to sign papers for everyone needed papers now, but if she preferred they could just get married where they were, but they finally agreed to get married by the cairn up on the cliff where everyone could see them and celebrate with them, which is what happened.

And then they went by horse and cart over the hill to the kirk in the next valley where they were blessed and signed papers and returned afterwards to hold a ceilidh in the barn where everyone danced and sang and drank all the miraculous water they could find which tasted so sweet and heady while baby John slept in the straw.

Elizabeth permitted herself to die. She'd been fighting the illness for a while, and would have withered away had it not been for Anna. Consumption it was called then, when tuberculosis attacked the lungs, bringing coughs, fever, night sweats and weight loss. Mere willpower kept Elizabeth alive while she caressed Anna through the valleys, and that life was further extended when Andrew MacDonell starting coming about the house, for in Gaelic the disease she had was called 'Glacach nan Dòmhnallach' or 'the MacDonald's Disease', because it was believed that there were particular tribes of MacDonalds who could cure it with the charms of their touch and the use of a certain set of words. But there must be no fee given of any kind for the touch or for the words.

So Andrew, being of that tribe, came to her aid. Elizabeth lay down on the bed and Andrew took her flesh and bones and sinews and joints asunder and rubbed butter onto her body. He worked her arms in all directions, her knuckles meeting behind her back. Her shoulder-blades were pressed and worked to and fro and every fibre of the upper part of her body thoroughly massaged. Anna made the linaments out of heron oil and the powder of deer's antlers. She made Elizabeth drink milk warm from the cow from a clay crock.

After every massage Andrew would rinse his hands in cold water in the running stream, otherwise the disease would be transferred to the next thing he touched. Andrew also had the spoken charm which he chanted as he massaged his mother-in-law: *I trample on thee, evil wasting, as tramples swan on brine, thou wasting of back, thou wasting of body, thou foul wasting of chest. May Christ's own Gospel be to make thee whole, the Gospel of the Healer of healers, the Gospel of the God of grace, to remove from thee thy sickness in the pool of health from the crown of thy head to the base of thy two heels, from thy two loins thither to thy two loins thither, in reliance on the might of the God of love and of the whole Powers together – the love of grace.*

And whether it was the physical touch, or the spoken charm, or the need to stay alive until Anna and Andrew and John were settled didn't matter, for Elizabeth survived long enough to see the future and was buried on a clear winter's day in the ancient graveyard, surrounded by a trinity of love.

8

WHEN THE NEW century dawned, Anna and Andrew built a new house for themselves further down the glen, nearer the river and where the pasture was better. The passing of the Act of 1886 had given them all security of tenure, so bit by bit families began to improve their crofts, freed from the fear of eviction. It was, at long last, worthwhile building that new byre, extending the pasture land, draining and improving the soil. Progress was practical rather than visionary.

They spent a couple of years gathering enough stones to build a house and by the time the Boer War ceased they were in their new home. It had a bit of space – a fire-room, a closet-room for themselves, a sleeping-room for the children and a byre for the animals. The fishing was good and the market improved with the opening of the railway line to the south, allowing Andrew to send fish down as far as the London stalls. Billingsgate became a magic word. Anna had a loom and made tweeds which she also began posting south. At the school there was now a lady teacher, a Miss Tulloch, who was as gentle as a lamb and taught all manners of things, from sewing to science, with grace and wisdom and wit.

Anna and Andrew had four children of their own besides John. Three girls – Isobel, Mairead and Sandra, and a boy, Magnus. The best years are when the children are young and no-one dies or is ill. They learned and played, and afterwards Anna thought that the sun had shone for twenty years. They ran about barefoot and guddled the streams and imagined they were deep-sea sailors and brought shells home from the shore which were gold bullion from shipwrecks, and coloured pebbles from the streams, which they transformed into castles. The king or queen of the castle was always the person who could build the highest wall and all of them quickly learned that the best way to do that was to build thick from the bottom. It was no use just piling one stone on top of another. The first one always had to be long and flat and the others diminishing in size until the wall reached the sky. The child whose wall stood last and longest would shout out across the valley 'I'm the king of the castle, you're all dirty wee rascals', and order the beaten vassals to do chores for them. Lick their feet, or hand over all their pebbles as a forfeit, or promise to serve and obey them for the rest of their lives.

And perhaps the rest of their lives were shadows played out in that sharp sunshine. John was eighteen, Isobel sixteen, Mairead fourteen, Sandra twelve and Magnus seven when their father Andrew died in a fishing accident in 1910. No-one could explain why it happened – the old women who would have found a reason had all gone. Anna, herself just thirty-six, took the decision to leave the croft and go south to Inverness, for the sole reason that she believed her children would have better prospects there. They were good at school and Miss Tulloch helped to persuade her that they would all be better off in the town, where there was a very good Academy for the younger children and where there would be plenty of jobs available for John and Isobel, who were both very bright. Miss Tulloch had relatives in Inverness who were merchants and she said she would write letters of recommendation to them.

Which is how Anna came to be a children's nurse and chaperone in the home of the ironmonger Albert Fetlar and his wife Eunice, who had twin girls aged five. Fetlar also had a flat in the town which he gave to Anna in return for her domestic services, along with promises that John could start work any time as an indentured clerk in his business, for he was a bright, honest lad who could count well. Though John had no desire to be a clerk and made noises about joining the Army, which was based out in the splendid barracks nearby at Fort George. He'd seen them marching through the town on Saturdays and could hear their gunfire at night across the firth. So John signed up with the Seaforth Highlanders and was given training and their bonny uniform and then despatched to India with the 1st Battalion.

They sailed from Southampton on the *Kinellan* on the 1st of May via the South African route and arrived in Bombay two months later. His letters speak of the heat and the smell, and the initial marvel of such names as Agra and Dagshai and Ferozopre and Peshawar, which soon became as familiar to him as his native Gaelic names, *Achadh Garbh, Dail an t-Seilich, Fearann Oisein* and *Peighinn Iubhair*. One of his letters describes the sun as a furnace of flames and the smell of India like that of cooking herring on a peat fire. So many people just died, or went mad.

John's illegitimacy was never mentioned by his parents or siblings, but the shame of it drifted in the air outside like the smell of rotting tangle from the shore. As an infant he sensed difference, but he was seven before he first heard the word 'bastard', though he thought nothing of it because he didn't know what it meant. But he knew that the word was directed at him, and retained it like a small wound. Some years later he fell out with some of the bigger boys at school, who instantly used the word again when he knew what it meant.

'You bastard,' they shouted. 'Son of the horse.'

They would make clip-clopping noises as he passed, and neighed towards him, and some of the girls took to chanting the miller songs. God only knows how they all knew.

I don't suppose that joining the Seaforths had anything to do with all that, though the manly nature of war covered all kinds of scars. India was a melting pot of misfits, from the impoverished sons of Welsh miners to the gay sons of the squires of the shire, most of them dying to resist their fate. It was the survival of the fittest and it surprised John to learn that the race didn't always go to the strong. Often they were the ones who broke early, their outward brawn a mere mask for hurt and fragility. And yet the scrawniest and least likely survived and thrived and became heroes out in the east, commanding regiments, slaughtering natives, and establishing the great Empire upon which the sun never set. They all learnt the basic things out there, in the tented whorehouses and the wooden beer shacks, where they became men or sank. For John, as for all the other soldiers, the local people were invisible, apart from those who served the camps or died in battle.

There were so many ways to survive. To keep your head down and get on with it. To brazen it out. To hear nothing, see nothing, say nothing. To dodge and dive, to believe in it all and ascend. John kept his head down, though his subsequent history tells that if you keep your head under water for too long you run out of oxygen. At least he didn't get the clap or die of sunstroke. And then the Great War itself came and his battalion were brought back, this time via the Suez Canal on *The Lancaster* to Marseille.

They marched north in the sunshine towards the unknown mud, where he distinguished himself time and again in his service for king and country, at La Bassée, the First Battle of Messines, Armentieres and the Battle of Loos. From there, in December 1915, they were sent to Mesopotamia in the war against the Ottoman Empire, where he survived the battles at Sheikh Sa'ad, Wadi, Hanna, Dujailia and Sannaiyat, and earned his Gallipoli Star for his bravery in the fall of Kut and the subsequent capture of Baghdad.

The end of the war saw him serving in Egypt and Palestine, where he was finally wounded at the Battle of

Megiddo and invalided home. He learned that the only thing
that mattered, whether in the trenches or going over the top,
was doing your best for your comrades. Just get on with it.
And the worst of all things was to hide from whatever fate
had in store for you. Others then called the first heroism and
the second cowardice. You either got killed or you didn't,
for a shell would get you whether you were crouching and
hiding or standing and fighting.

He stayed with his sister Mairead, who was the
schoolmistress in one of the town's schools. John loved
Inverness in these glorious days after the war, when all was
peace and silence. Until quite recently, there were those who
remembered John, with his distinctive limp, walking in the
gardens down by the river where he would go twice daily to
feed the ducks and the wild swans. He'd been wounded by
shrapnel above the left hip, and though the army doctors had
done their best, the hip-bone was damaged and he would
forever walk with a limp. He would occasionally shadow
box by himself down by the river. He especially loved shinty,
and even though incapacitated was still able to play in goals
for the local team down at the Haugh, where he became
renowned for being able to stop any ball in the air from a
standing position simply by raising his stick in the air with
a single hand.

But he began to hear noises. Dull thuds which made
him jump and howling sounds which prevented him from
sleeping. After a while he began to hear voices. He was to
go down to the river every day and wash his handkerchief
in the Ness and after the fifth washing he would be given a
message written on the corner of the cloth. So every morning
he began to limp down to the river and crouch there washing
the handkerchief and reading the secret signs. It was from
Oliver Cromwell, telling him that he had been chosen to
set up the New Commonwealth and that the flag-raising
for the movement should take place on Mayday on the top

of Tomnahurich Hill. Meantime he was to go down to the river every morning to receive further instructions about this Second Commonwealth.

Voices tell you what to do. They cajole and persuade and tempt and instruct in the sweetest and harshest varieties known to man. Soft and low and high and shrill, male and female, young and old. They accuse. You bastard. They praise. There you go, my bonny lad. They question. Are you sure? They tempt. Go on. They encourage. You can do it. They lie. You can't. They flatter. All these things will I give thee, if thou wilt fall down and worship me.

The same low voice as his sergeant-major had at Fort George, and the same thin voice as his commanding officer at Agra. Instructions to stand, march, dig, run, sleep, dress, shoot, kill, die. Voices telling him about jiga-jig for a rupee, the voices of the loose-wallahs and the prayer-wallahs and the vegetable-wallahs and the beer-wallahs, shouting that they could cure cholera and enable him to have a permanent erection, and the voice of the Goat-Major pleading for them not to sacrifice the animal. Voices telling him that it would soon be all over, that justice and peace and righteousness would reign, that the desert would bloom like the rose, that poppies would grow in the mud, that there would be homes fit for heroes. And in the trenches he would sometimes remember the school lessons he had, about Oliver Cromwell and how he had beheaded the king and established a commonwealth, and an old woman he knew up north who advised her son not to go anywhere near Inverness 'because it's full of the dregs of Cromwell's Army'. And here he was now, the great man himself, giving him direct instructions to carry on his good work. And who better to carry out his instructions than he who had faithfully followed every instruction given to him by his superiors in India and France and Mesopotamia and survived?

His sister took him to see Doctor Russell, who wrote out

the official certificate which saw him admitted for the first time into the Northern Counties District Lunatic Asylum at Craig Dunain, two miles west of the town. It was a beautiful building with gorgeous gardens and like all asylums was filled with the mad, the grieving and the broken-hearted. Everyone from girls who'd had illegitimate children to homosexuals, from Napoleon Bonaparte MacKenzie to those who spent years rocking backwards and forwards in foetal positions in the lobbies or in the gardens.

John MacDonell's official medical diagnosis reads:

The patient has been behaving in an obsessive manner for a while. He is convinced he hears voices and consequently goes down to the River Ness every morning to wash his handkerchief and receive instructions from Oliver Cromwell. These voices and delusions may have been triggered by his war-time experiences. The patient was in India where he was of good conduct. His Army medical records show that he had malaria. He also took part in the campaign on the Western Front and then later in Mesopotamia, where he distinguished himself before being badly wounded by shrapnel. He shows no violent tendencies and is not a danger to anyone. His physical symptoms are also consistent with other patients who have suffered from shell-shock. He is of good intelligence and the prognosis is good.
Dr William T Russell, Academy Street, Inverness.

It was a beautiful summer's day. The rhododendrons and azaleas in the hospital gardens were in full bloom and the bees were dining on the clover. Every bird in God's universe was singing its little heart out, as if there was not enough time to celebrate the summer. They passed the pond where dozens of men and women were out feeding the ducks. Three men were rolling down the slope of grass in perfect unison. A lady with a parasol was dancing over by the fountain.

His mother Anna and his sister Mairead accompanied him to the hospital. They were all filled with fear. Not of the unknown, for that is nothing. But of the imagined unknown, or at least of the unknown about which they'd heard so many rumours and tales and stories. This place of horror and darkness. Of folk being chained up and locked in darkened rooms and being gagged and beaten and jumping out of windows. Everyone in Inverness had heard the howls when the moon was full and bright. But worse, the stigma of being labelled a lunatic, and all it meant: failure.

And indeed the building itself was a chilling place when they entered, with long clean corridors heading off into eternity. And it was quiet. So still. Which was a relief, for they had feared moaning and screaming, and none were to be heard. A lovely grandfather clock stood ticking loudly by the open fire. A white-bearded doctor met them and explained that John would be in the ward upstairs which had tremendous views over the valleys towards the town, and that they could visit him any time.

'We'll assess his progress daily,' Doctor Smith said, 'and it may very well be that he'll be back home with you in a month or so.'

They parted quietly from each other, for they were used to parting, and John was also used to going off to places.

They gave him some pills and he felt as calm as evening. He looked down on the wonderful green world far below. Since the windows were locked and barred it was completely silent, as if all the birds had gone mute, and he watched those three fools endlessly rolling in perfect unison down the slope. They'd stand at the bottom, and then holding hands would slowly climb back up the hill together to repeat the spinning voyage. The lady with the parasol continued to dance round the fountain. Then he heard a scream somewhere and the sound of running feet and some shouts before the silence resumed. A nurse came in to see him and looked into his eyes, asked him to open his mouth wide, checked his heart and his ears, took his temperature and wrote everything down in a book. She asked him how he felt and he said 'Fine.' She said morning tea was now being served downstairs and asked him to accompany her.

Hundreds of people shuffled along various corridors into the dining room for the morning tea, some muttering to themselves, some waving, some laughing and saluting. The tea was weak and tasteless, but the scones were lovely and creamy, with fresh strawberry jam. He ate three of them, sitting at a long wooden table. No-one spoke to him, though one man kept looking at him and winking. After morning tea there was an announcement that it was exercise time and immediately scores of them jumped up and leapt along the corridors to go outside, while others sat groaning and holding their stomachs, claiming that they were ill and unable to move.

Those who went outside worked through some basic drills, lifting their arms into the air, making circles, touching their knees. Those who could, hopped, first on one leg, then on the other, then on both, while some people laughed and cackled. Because of his gammy leg, John was allowed just to stand and watch. Afterwards he was told to go for a walk and the nurse who had earlier taken his notes joined him. She was called Mary and was from Lewis and asked him if he spoke Gaelic and he said of course he did. So they continued their walk in their own tongue. Mary's own brother had also been in the war and he too had suffered shell-shock and spent some time here, she said.

'And is he well now?' John asked.

'Yes. He was one of the lucky ones.'

For it was true that there were so many folks from the

far islands, who spoke another language, or lived a different way, who would be brought there in straitjackets and asked to explain themselves in an alien tongue which they could hardly understand or speak. Mary and some of the doctors were aware of that and went out of their way to make them feel at home, but it was a constant battle against a system and against certain nurses and doctors who believed that their strangeness was the problem, not the solution.

John realised that his illness was mild compared to many of those around him. Poor old James who would continually strip naked and then have to be restrained and carried away for yet another cold bath. Claire, who sat in the corner plucking out her beautiful dark hair until she was completely bald. They bound padding round her hands to prevent her, but she would chew through it and almost choke, so the staff decided that discretion was indeed the better part of valour. Many of the inmates were troubled by religious mania – the certainty that they had committed some awful sin which deserved continuous punishment, or the opposite certainty that they were Christ reborn with a special message to save the world.

There were so many secret – or at least unspoken – lives. Emma Christenson, a forty-three-year-old married woman who had been brought all the way down from Shetland in a straitjacket and spent all her time playing an imaginary fiddle and handing out cards inviting people to concerts at which the King himself would preside; and who, in her day, had indeed been one of the best fiddlers amongst thousands in these musical northern isles. Ernest Woodward, who went around saying he was the Emperor of Russia, the strongest and richest man in the world, the finest player of any game you could mention, that he walked two hundred miles every morning to get an appetite for breakfast, could run a mile in five seconds, that he grew four inches in height every day and that his wife, back home, was growing too; and that he knew everything there was to be known by inspiration alone and that whenever he went to a dance all the ladies would fall comatose at his charms. When asked by a nurse what he thought of his surroundings, he replied 'I never saw such a damned lot of idiots in one place in my life.' Mr Woodward had advanced syphilis and the doctor's official report stated: 'I am inclined to think that his mental derangement is due to excessive sexual intercourse.' Which made a change from several others whose diagnoses was 'excessive masturbation', which led to all kinds of mental health issues sometimes cured by iced baths.

One day it dawned on John that he was actually already in the secret commonwealth and that Oliver Cromwell had delivered on his promises. He was in the *Sithein*, the fairy knoll and all these strange, marvellous, people around him were not just citizens, but citizen members of this new, second commonwealth. They had been taken there by an imaginative leap which removed barriers, so that men could walk five hundred miles before breakfast, women could weep in public and anyone who felt like it could sing or dance or roll on the grass or scream or lie stock still for hours on end unless some earthly being came and wrapped them up in cloths or muffled them or carried them away to silence them with syringes. There were dangers and limits: violence could always be sensed before it happened, you could see it in the eyes of the men, but all you had to do was to be alert and ready for it when it erupted. Like the Reverend Kirk before him, John knew that fairyland was as constrained as the land above. Everywhere had its rituals and rules.

John found a copy of Kirk's book on a shelf in a cupboard and stored it away inside his jersey. He smuggled it out down to the disused beehives at the bottom of the garden where he read it while nurse Mary looked the other way pretending not to see. He knew Kirk had written this part especially for him. 'Some say that the continual sadness is because of their pendulous state and that these subterraneans have controversies, doubts, disputes, feuds and sidings of parties; there being some ignorance in all creatures and the vastest created intelligences not encompassing all things. For how much is written of pygmies, fairies, nymphs, sirens and apparitions, which though not the tenth part true, yet could not spring of nothing? For every age hath left some secrets of its discovery, as some men do to fishes, which are in another element, when we plunge and dive into the bottom of the seas, their native regions. And how long can one remain there, and still see? What is it to have the second-sight? The sight, you see, is of no long duration, only continuing as long as they can keep their eyes steady without twinkling. The hardy therefore fix their look that they may see the longest. But the timorous see only glances, their eyes always twinkle at the first sight of the object.' And in answer to the question 'Doth the acquiring of this second sight make any change on the acquirer's body, mind, or actions?', the Reverend Kirk reported 'All uncouth sights enfeebles the seer', and John twinkled, either saved from, or unable or unwilling to enter the hurricane. He was really only a shadow-boxer, not a proper one.

Those who would never be released from hospital were disappointed and angry with the world, which had frustrated their dreams. So they tried to adjust the world rather than their dreams. Who could forsake these hopes that infancy would return, that father would not die, that they had done no wrong? But they had, apparently. Mother had died. The corn fields were no more, and the old open field where the horses used to gallop had been sold and an ugly factory built on it which pumped out black smoke day and night, and that moment of half-wakening half-sleeping before dawn could never be recaptured. For when you woke, there you were again, back in the foul-smelling slum with a baby coughing, or alone, abandoned in the silence of your room.

You had every reason to be angry. So many disappointments. It was all very unfair. Mother should never have said these things. And father should never have done that. It hurt. It was beyond understanding. Things happened over which you had no control. That bastard with the white coat over there pretending he was a doctor when he was the one who had put the pillow over your mother's face and choked her, and the wicked police out there who spied on you day and night, and those newspaper people who peddled gossip and made the world what they wanted it to be. Why were they praised and rewarded for doing that while you were branded as 'mad' for doing the same? While they sat drinking in their clubs, men would come for you and certify you, sign papers in your name and bring you to this prison where they injected you with all kinds of drugs. But they wouldn't get you. Oh no. You were too smart for them, for when they came for you, you hid under the bed, or called for mother and – see – there she is coming running to save you, and if all else failed you could call on Christ Himself who would descend from the skies with wide open arms to save the righteous and even the damned, as long as they repented.

In the end, Mary saved him. One of her jobs was to give him hyoscine, but instead she would eject the bromide down the sink and just listen to him. For hours on end, both on duty and off, if such a distinction applied. He went back a long way: to that time his mother met the fairy lover that wasn't; and to the gentleness of his stepfather, Andrew MacDonell, who gave him his name and the move south; to the sergeant-major at Fort George, how he would walk along the inspection line as if he were inspecting flies; and then the long hot journey south, how the sea off the west coast of Africa bubbled and boiled.

The African campaign was the worst. To have survived it was like a secret triumph. John was in the Highland Brigade, which lost seven hundred men in the first seven minutes of firing. Not that the boys knew any of that, until the statisticians and historians wrote it down from the surviving officers' records much later.

What John remembered was the journey home. How blue the sea was. So blue that it was green and the sunsets so red that they were orange. There was hardly any room on the ship. You had to claim your spot early and hang on to it because your life depended on it. As soon as he boarded John found a shaded spot on the aft deck of the ship where he was protected from the mid-day sun by an awning. He made a deal with a fellow soldier, Tommy Griffiths, to share the space so that they could protect it from others. If either needed to go for food or to relieve himself the other would guard his space with his honour.

The only danger was from an English officer who was under medical supervision, but who was permitted to always carry a small stick. He believed himself to be the great W.G. Grace, and every morning and evening would come up on to deck and line himself up against the railings and hit imaginary fours and sixes high and wide into the Southern Ocean. John and Tommy took turns along with all the other time-served men to bowl for him, throwing invisible balls over and under arm for hours on end while the officer squinted into the sun to see where they'd landed. The danger was when he missed a ball and would come running at you with his stick, but the solution was to stand stock still and salute and say 'Mr Grace! Sir, your honour!' and he would immediately calm down and return to the wicket rails and take up position again.

The voyage to Southampton took fifteen days. As the officer was leaving the ship, with the doctor guiding him by the arm, he paused at the bottom of the gangway and turned to John and Tommy and all those watching him and solemnly said, 'In any case, you mustn't confuse a single failure with a final defeat.'

9

INVISIBILITY IS A magic thing. When John first left hospital, he believed no-one could see him. And because he believed it, no-one could. Though sometimes he thought it was the other way round: that he was actually invisible because no-one saw him. When he went for a walk, folk he'd once known would pass by without seeing him, and when he'd occasionally walk out in front of a horse, the horse would carry on trotting as if he wasn't there.

He remembered fakirs in India who would make things appear and disappear. And magic-men he'd seen in the Transvaal who could conjure up snakes and clouds and make the stone you were holding in your hand dissolve while you held it. They shouldn't have done it, but one night John and his pal Fred crept out of the camp and followed the drum-beats. Afterwards, vainly trying to avoid time in the guardhouse, they claimed they were hypnotised. In the clearing, scores of men and women and children were dancing and when they joined them they entered a world that was strangely familiar. In many ways it was like the war itself: the music of the pipes leading you through the dust, then flashes of light and the swirling thump of bodies as you moved. The women wore gorgeous coloured dresses and the men were painted blue and red and yellow, and in the very centre a man was on his knees beating the ground with the palms of his hands. Dust was everywhere.

The man in the centre then rose and swept round the company several times in silence. A young girl ran over and gave him a bird, which he plucked to the beat of the music. Everyone in the congregation moved forward and picked up a feather for themselves. The feathers were all bright blue. The five men who were beating the drums slowed down to a slow march and everyone sat. The man in the centre beckoned John forward. He motioned that John should give him his feather. As soon as he received the feather, the magic man twirled it three times round his head and gave John the live bird back in its place. John released the bird into the air and watched it fly into the darkness.

The magic man then gave him a small rounded stone. It was painted in seven circles. Purple. Blue. Red. Green. Yellow. White. Black. He indicated to John that he should look at the stone. All the colours disappeared, one after the other, until it was pure stone colour. As John held the stone, it began to weep. Little drops appeared in the centre of the stone until they made two eyes. Then more dripped out of the stone eyes, slowly, one by one. As the stone wept, John wept, until the stone completely dissolved, leaving John sitting there in an empty clearing, his face and hands soaking wet with tears. Fred was lying on the ground beside him, fast asleep. Everyone else had disappeared.

He wondered if he could make them disappear now. Here, in Inverness. But maybe he needed the right conditions. Dusk. Darkness. Drums beating. Blue-feathered birds and pounding dancing and an alien air. The fakir and the magic man had been so precise and certain, knowing what they were doing. Sure of themselves and their audience. But John was a bit unsure that he was truly invisible, for sometimes he suspected he caught folk glancing at him. Better to start small and work up towards complete invisibility.

It was like sin. Or love. There was no halfway house. You couldn't be selective about it. You were either invisible or you were not. Like invisibility itself, sin was an amazing thing. He knew the word. Knew it well, intimately, like a victim knows a crime. Had heard the word since he was a child. And when he was in Dunain, he heard a new word that he'd never heard before. It began with a K. What was it again? K. There was a woman there. Elsie was her name. And she stole things. Anything she could lay her hands on: gloves, bits of wood, bedding, thimbles, toys, coal. Any old rubbish she came across. Except she wasn't really stealing. Only gathering. Collecting things which had been left. Discarded. Abandoned. That folk didn't like or use or treasure or value. Or if they did, not enough. And the word came to him, was made flesh. Kleptomania. That was it: that word he'd heard amidst all the other manias that had been named in the corridors.

It meant taking things. And John wondered – if he was invisible – whether he could take things without anyone noticing. Without being seen. For if no-one saw the thing, maybe the thing didn't happen. Like when he was a child, and would shut his ears to the taunts of the other children, and shut his eyes when he passed the old mill and the loch where the water-horse lived. Shame didn't exist. Nothing existed.

It gnawed away at you however. Rotted you from the inside, like a rat eating the thatch. So. Better to start small. And he began picking up leaves from the ground and stuffing his pockets full of them. But no-one noticed. Or if they did, no-one bothered. And then he saw a trowel lying on a wall and he put it into his pocket, and again no-one noticed, or followed him, or chased him down the street. But he knew these were insignificant, trivial things. He sensed that the real test would come when he entered merchants' premises, where people bought and sold things, where money changed hands. Where things mattered. Had value.

Best to start small. The sweetie shop, where Gum Drops were in one jar, Peppermints in another. Nougats on the shelf. Toffees in wrappers. Black Jacks, the best of all. And

Barley Sugar Soldiers. He started with them. And no-one noticed. By the end of the week he had the whole collection – a Life Guard, a Grenadier Guard, a Royal Scot, a Scots Guard, a Dragoon Guard and a Hussar.

But being invisible also meant having no substance. No praise or condemnation. No-one seemed to take a blind bit of notice of him. For no-one knew that he had the Barley Sugar Soldiers. No-one acknowledged the craft and art behind the acquisitions – the careful planning it took to stake out the premises, to make sure that no-one was looking at the time, the sewing-in of extra hidden pockets into his coat, the quick sleight-of-hand it took to reach out and find the right sweet at just the right time when old Mr MacGregor was looking the other way or serving another customer.

John was unsure whether stealing was stealing unless the owner was aware that it was taking place. Maybe he didn't exist at all if no-one knew him. But they did know. They knew him as 'Poor John', and turned a blind eye to his weakness. They all knew he'd been to the big house up the hill and was mad, a daftie, a *truaghan*, a lunatic... whichever word came to mind. For each district had its caste. But he was harmless. More to be pitied than judged. Best ignored rather than challenged. So he was, truly, invisible because their pardon came from pity, not grace. All would be revealed one day and shouted from the rooftops.

John walked round the sanctified streets of Inverness as invisible as all the other poor souls condemned to this living death, this exclusion. Mad Meg whose conversation rambled from subject to object, from drivel to divine insight, sometimes laughing, sometimes crying. Who would lock herself up in any old room and rummage everything all about, pocketing all the rubbish she could – odd things, hairpins, matches, ornaments, rags, scraps, bits of food. William Clark, who told everyone that he was about to make millions of money by means of a patent for protecting ships of war by armour plating, and that such consisted of two excessively thin layers of steel containing powdered cork, and that this would cost about one-quarter of the present price of armour plating. And young Julia Scott, who went about telling people she had a divine mission to crush socialism. They were 'characters' to whom no-one listened, but to whom everyone was kind.

John knew that sweets weren't important enough. So he walked the streets of Inverness and made an inventory. Any obsessive always starts there: with a list, or lists. So, there were Aerated Water Manufacturers (Mackintosh & Co of Abban Street), and Agricultural Merchants (Ross, Duncan & Co of Baron Taylor's Lane), and Ashphalters, and a Blacksmith, and a Bookbinder and Boot and Shoemakers and all the way through his carefully annotated alphabet down to the Saddler in Queensgate (Donald Morrison), the Shipping Agent on Lombard Street (David Petrie), the Slater on Kenneth Street (John Reid), finishing where the letters ran out at Q with the Qualified Cash Chemists at 31 High Street, with their grand notice in the window declaring: The most desirable House in the District for the purchase of Pure Drugs, Proprietary Articles, Patent Medicines, Toilet Requisites; also Nursery and Sick-Room Appliances. W.G. MacDonald, Proprietor. John wanted to reach the end of the alphabet, so searched all the streets and markets and alleyways of Inverness to find a proprietor beginning with Z, but found none. There was a tailor, Zkajewski, but he had no sign up on his little back-street premises, so didn't count. He wasn't official, so John reckoned he didn't exist either. And anyway he was just known as Skat the Pole, which brought him back up the alphabet.

John eventually decided to steal a pair of boots. From JW MacKenzie and Co at 9 Church Street. Old MacKenzie himself still worked through the back, or at least supervised things there, while his two sons, James and Donald, made the boots. Good leather boots and shoes for men and fine leather brogues for women.

Old MacKenzie knew what it was to be without shoes and valued them all the more because of his own childhood deprivation. They were morally as well as financially valuable to him. They signified progress, development, education. Commerce brought with it a liberality of spirit. He minded fine his young days of walking barefoot through puddles and the laughter of the other children, and that mockery had given him an evangelical zeal for the best leather, the best shoes, the best value. He'd personally selected the leather for over fifty years from an old Sutherlandshire farming family he trusted, and had taught his sons the same loving care for materials and workmanship. It was a craft as well as a business. A vocation.

So when Limpy John came into his shop old MacKenzie wasn't surprised. Weren't old soldiers with gammy legs and one leg and no legs forever coming in expecting him to perform miracles? Which he invariably did, fitting a size ten on one leg and a size eight on the other, or a size seven on one leg and a false raised-heel shoe on the other Crimean foot. And he knew who John was, of course. Inverness wasn't that big. Hadn't he come down south from his own original native shires years ago? The illegitimate son of Anna. The son of the water-horse. And what if everyone talked, saying – and here they would whisper – that he'd been 'locked away up there in the big house'. No wonder.

Mr MacKenzie greeted John in Gaelic and asked if he could help, and John naturally said he'd like to be fitted for a pair of shoes. And while old MacKenzie himself went through the back to get the tape and the blocks, John scanned the shoes, deciding on a beautiful pair of oak-leather boots he'd seen in the window. He made no pretence of hiding his activities. He was tired of being invisible. So he put the new boots on and walked out of the shop with old MacKenzie standing in the door looking after him with some astonishment. And MacKenzie understood, for not only was he a Free Church elder blessed with the spirit of forgiveness, but he was also enough of a businessman to know that Limpy John would make a fine walking advert for him.

'There he goes,' he could hear the burghers cry, 'wearing MacKenzie's best. And what a fine sound they make!'

Ticketty-tack, clippity-clop, down the streets, like a great big Clydesdale horse.

Now that he was visible again, John went dancing that night. Mary was off-duty and they met for tea at Serafini's Café before walking over to the Caledonian Hall Ballroom. Everyone laughed, but who cared as they waltzed and moved in each other's arms, his oak-heeled boots setting sparks off the floor and her smile dazzling in return. They walked home by moonlight and stood for a while at Petrie's windows wondering whether to emigrate to Canada after all. Their eyes scanned the notice, though neither of them spoke out the words –

D Petrie, Cameron & Co, Passenger Agents. Book Passengers and Tourists to all parts of the world.
Agents for all the Lines to Canada, United States, Australia etc.
Agency for Women's Canadian Employment Bureau, Montreal. Employment found for Domestics & Farm Hands. Assisted passages to Approved Applicants.
Agents for CPR Farm Lands & Ready-Made Farms. Easy Terms of Payment. Apply Early. 2 Lombard Street, Inverness.

'I'd probably qualify for Assisted Passage,' he said.
'And I'd easily get a job as a nurse there,' she said.
They continued to study the words.

'Canada?' he asked.

She smiled.

'Australia?'

'Too hot.'

'New Zealand?'

'How about a farm?' he asked.

Instead, they returned to Mary's native village in Lewis, where John felt safe from all dangers. Temptations came, for they do always and everywhere, and maybe it was the wind and the rain and the open spaces, but he somehow felt less confined, less restricted. Less controlled in a way. Unlike India, there was a middle distance where you could see things in perspective. A cow standing in a field, but dwarfed by the hill behind. There's Donald-John and his youngest son, Murdo, out fishing in the wide Atlantic. Hawks hovered high over the cliffs.

He became one with the landscape and with the people who crofted and moved in slower tempo. Was visible when he wanted and invisible when required. And Mary loved him. For sometimes, when looking back at history we mistake care for love, or think that our grandparents loved less because they wore more clothes, or were more reticent, or religious or taboo-ridden. That they felt less lust than we do because they saw less flesh.

It seems that when he got to Lewis John forgot about his illness and about the war. Though 'forget' is such a big, impractical word. He just buried it, like dross or treasure, and concentrated instead on the visible and the manageable. Though that's not accurate either, for he became obsessed by the weather, which is as invisible and as unmanageable as any illness or war. The bare island was dominated by weather. You had to plan ahead. You had to be meteorologically wise. No use of thinking of planting seed if that howling gale was going to come in suddenly from the west. No point in going out herring fish if a storm was brewing. No sense in ploughing if a flood was on the way.

So he took to reading signs. If the clover is folded in, big rain will soon begin. If the swan is on the swim, warm showers are coming in. If the grass is dry at morning light, look for rain before the night. When clouds look like black smoke, a wise man puts on his cloak. Life had rhythm after all.

On May Day he would go out before sunrise and bring into the house a small green branch of whatever he could find – bog myrtle, perhaps – because it was right to bring in the summer on May Day. He would put the green thing under the thatch and leave it there till next May Day, to ensure a perpetual summer.

'Do you remember...' Mary would begin now and again, and he would immediately interrupt. For it is dangerous to remember.

'No. I don't. But what I do know is that the day after May Day was known in Ireland as Milking Sunday. You had the late-milking from then on. That is the day you start the late milking, Mary – you leave the cows in the field without being milked until nine in the morning.'

There was no escape from the webs he wove to replace memory. A black-handled knife: there is a great protection in it against ghosts. If you catch a lizard and lick its head, after that you can lick red-hot iron and it will not burn your tongue. If you hear a cuckoo with your right ear the first time you hear it in the year, that year will be a lucky one for you. And anything begun on a Saturday will take a long time to finish. Things long believed were safer than any new customs.

And Mary? She cared for the stock. A fine flock of Cheviot sheep and a good head of cattle which gave them milk and cheese and crowdie and cream, and mutton for the winter. She became known as Màiri Bhuachaille, Mary the Herdess, because she was constantly out on the moors or down by the shore herding the cattle. What she didn't know about cattle and sheep wasn't worth knowing about. All the diseases from Bluetongue and Foot Rot to the best way to take a cow's temperature. You disinfect a thermometer with alcohol and insert it into the rectum. The temperature should be around 101.5 degrees Fahrenheit. The pulse, meantime, should be between forty and seventy beats per minute. You locate the pulse of the cow at the angle of the lower jaw-bone where it can be felt by pressing the artery against the bone. It was nursing, really.

She built walls. Small stone dykes to separate the rams from the ewes, and larger ones to keep the bull from the heifers. She built hen houses and a pigsty and a larger byre which acted as a cow shelter and a place to keep everything dry, from peat-ploughs to ropes. And she learned by building them why some walls fall down and others don't. It's not because one wall is stronger than the other, but because it's more stable. It all had to do with stability. A long piece of rope was no stronger than a short piece of rope. A low unstable wall wouldn't stand any longer than a high shoogly wall. And once a wall was stable you could then decorate the top any way you liked, either with turf or flowers or shells.

Which is why John was now fine. He didn't need any strength. Everything was stable for him. Good strong walls were built all around him. Borders were clear, the horizon was always visible. If anyone walked the moor road he could see them, getting smaller as they walked away, or larger as they came near. Who's that? Ah – some holidaymaker going fishing on Loch Ruadh. He never went out in the twilight or in the dark, when things became hazy and obscure. Fog and mist were avoided. The sun rose in the east every morning and set in the west every evening. The ocean waves came no further higher than the shore. Spring followed winter, autumn followed summer. When he said something, Mary didn't contradict him with an alternative truth. No shrapnel flew about the place, no sudden orders were issued. If you put some of the clay round the threshold of the door to where the sharp pain was on your body, you would get relief. No-one stirred his past. Nothing shifted on the croft without his knowledge. If a gate fell, it stayed there. If a cow moved, it was for a reason: towards better grazing, or to drink from the water-trough. The sheep kept to familiar paths, without deviation.

Their own conversations were dislocated, though that didn't seem to matter much. Like swans swimming on a loch, it was sufficient to know that each other was there.

'What a day!' Mary would say. 'These sheep are obstinate buggers. You just can't control them. You know what they did today? As soon as I had put them into the grazing field, they jumped over the wall, one by one. And why? Just because one decided to do it.'

'In the old days,' John responded, 'there was a saying. *Wind from the star of spring, heat from the star of summer, rain from the star of autumn, frost from the star of winter.*'

They were like two different channels on the radio.

'The bee is under shelter, a storm and tempest will come,' he would say.

'I'll need to go and get the ram from Morag tomorrow,' Mary would reply.

They spoke like angels to each other, in tongues.

'I wonder why birds have feathers?' he asked.

And she replied, 'The cattle sales are a week Monday. I need to fatten them up for that,' although days or weeks later she might add, 'because otherwise they'd hurt themselves when they fly into bushes,' and he would know that the answer had arrived. Because things arrived. From elsewhere. From where things were made. In factories on the mainland. He would spend hours beachcombing every morning and find all kinds of treasures – not just the usual debris, but rare green indented bottles and nuts and stones and strange bits of wood brought in by the tides.

'Ash,' he'd say to himself. 'Or yew.'

Things that smelt and felt strange which had floated in from the Atlantic. Iron bolts on which shrimps grew. Keys that didn't fit any locks. A doll's ceramic head with dazzling blue eyes.

Those things brought in on the tide were gifts. *Faodail* the natives called them – goods found by chance, things found, stray treasure. There was a proverb – *chan e sealbh na faodalach a faotainn* – to find goods is not to own them. For nothing comes from nothing, and a big thing does not come from a smaller thing. A stone cannot come from a pebble, but the pebble must come from the stone. The doll's head must one time have had a ceramic body. This piece of ash wood must have come from an ash tree, John thought. Something bigger. Though that too would have been a tiny seed, once upon a time. Like himself. Everything was a gift or a curse. Iain Cuagach, Limpy John. Not a right. To find a long thick piece of wood on the shore which would make a doorpost. To have a cow or a wife or a patch of land, or to be crippled or poor or landless. To crouch for a cigarette in the trenches just before the bullets arrived which killed all your colleagues. You stumbled across things – once he'd found a gold watch inside a sealed box wedged between the stones by the lobster pool. While Mary knew that every drop of milk from the cow or every fleece from the sheep had to be earned, John believed that fate – or grace as he called it – would suffice.

They lived on the west side of the island, almost smack against the Atlantic, and John's songs bear witness not just to the power of nature but to the vein of grace which made things tolerable. The songs are hard to translate, not just because they were written in Gaelic, but because their sense depends as much on sound as upon meaning, from the days when sound mattered. In so far as anyone can ever separate the inseparable. For instance, there is the repeated use of the word *m'eudail*, which in its simplest form means my darling, but is derived from the word *feudail*, meaning treasure, cattle, prey, spoil, booty, since the most important thing once upon a time in every rural economy was your stock. Your treasure was your cow. So when grand-uncle John is calling Mary his darling, he is not of course calling her his cow, but neither is it a mere phrase, or cliché. He is saying that, like the cow in the old dispensation, she is the one who is the difference between life and death, who sustains him. And who is equal to such burden or praise?

There is a saying that a coin can take you to the mainland, but that a song can take you to the ends of the earth, and when you now read these songs that John composed, nothing is surer. Perhaps it is no surprise that the trenches are so seldom mentioned, though John made a splendid song about a little bird hopping from dead body to broken helmet across the wastes. Unfortunately, all the words have been washed out by damp except for this quatrain found in an old suitcase in the byre:

> 's an t-eun air iteig air a' ghaoith
> a' leum o cheann gu ceann
> gun fhios a bheil a' chas a' caoidh
> am fear tha marbh neo beò

> and the bird flying in the wind
> hopping from head to head
> not knowing whether his feet mourn
> the living or the dead

Other-ends-of-the-earth places are mentioned with more vigour – Afghanistan and Agra, and he also left a fine song about the Taj Mahal, seen on a clear moonlit night during the Indian Campaign:

Tha mise seo sna h-Innseachan
'S mo chridhe trom 's fo smàl,
'S gun sìon bheir togail cridhe dhomh
Ach gealach 's an Taj Mahal.
Ball beag cruinn air pàlais mòr
Geal air mullach òr,
Aon a' deàrrsadh air an aon.
Mar sgàthan air a' ghlòir.

Here I am in India
My heart heavy and burdened,
And nothing to raise my spirits
But the moon and the Taj Mahal.
A small round ball on a big palace
Whiteness shining on gold,
One reflecting the other
Like a mirror on glory.

10

MAGNUS – GRANDFATHER MAGNUS – looked after Anna as she approached old age. And in retrospect, that perfect thing, he was the one who entered modernity. He was the first to move. Really move, I mean. Of course the others had travelled, including John who had seen the Taj Mahal and the Somme, but in a sense they had never really left. Whether in India or in Inverness, they were still really elsewhere: back in the glen, amidst imagined eternal things.

Magnus was employed by the estate as a ghillie – helping the nobility on their fishing and deer-stalking adventures, though he was also a jack-of-all-trades on the property, able to put his hands to everything from building bothies to establishing the orchards. He was class-conscious, knowing from the first day he set foot on the estate that everything and everyone had its place, and though he knew that order was established by man, he also believed that it was ordained by God. Not that he couldn't see the nobility's folly and stupidity – for wasn't everyone in the world from the King down to the lowest commoner a sinner? However, that didn't extinguish the law.

Magnus himself was gentle, knowing that his job was neither to establish nor to abolish the law, but to see that it was obeyed. He was also the gamekeeper. One of his main tasks was to prevent poaching on the owner's lands and to control unwelcome natural predators, such as foxes and otters. He would trap and kill them with due care and efficiency. He was the guardian of things that could be caught and eaten: deer and salmon, pheasants and trout.

Gardening changed him. He then began to nourish and protect things for their beauty alone. For their colour and fragrance, not their taste or value. For the pure pleasure of smelling the jasmine, and seeing the primroses covering the river-banks. For the delights of the eye, the sounds of bees on the clover, the smell of wild garlic in the air, the soft touch of petals as he pruned the roses.

What colours each season brought! The white of winter and the purple of autumn, the bright yellow of spring and the thousand colours of summer. He learned that no colour existed on its own. The snowdrops were only white because they were on green grass. The roses were redder the greener the stalks. Everything was relative to its immediate neighbour, varied depending on what was around. Nothing was solid in its own ground. He became less certain of things. Of himself.

'For to be sure of yourself is to be sure of nothing,' old Joe the Master Mariner told him one evening. 'To be sure of himself is the last thing any man ought to be sure of.'

Maybe that's why Magnus liked rain. When the heavens opened and the streams overflowed, everything changed instantly. Solid rocks became wet, steam rose from the thatch. Like a parched horse at the trough, the earth drank in the rain. Things would, after all, grow.

His favourite season was winter, those crisp mornings when he'd leave his stamp on the frost like the first man who'd ever walked the earth. When he breathed out, a small globe of mist rose slowly into the air. And he especially liked the wind, whether coming lean and snell from the north or wild and fierce from the west. He would stand facing it, letting the full force of the gale and rain lash his face. The sting of the rain and the strength of the wind was life, life in all its fullness. Hailstones danced as they fell on water and grass and rock.

He'd done such a good job working in his spare time in the orchard that when Hamish the old Head Gardener retired, Major Fraser appointed Magnus in his place. Things grew. Slowly, gradually, one thing led to another. Things evolved. If you cut this bit from a plant and grafted another bit from a different plant, sometimes they would become a new plant – a hybrid – and Magnus discovered that if you nurtured and shaped and engineered things, all kinds of miracles could happen. A plant which wouldn't grow in sandy soil could be grafted onto a plant which did, and you then had a plant which would flower in all kinds of conditions. He developed roses which bloomed in the rockiest of soils, potatoes which grew in the wettest bogs, trees which flourished in the poorest of ground.

'Work changes destiny,' Joe told him.

Magnus turned what had been a sporting estate into one of the gardening wonders of the north, and his beautiful handwritten notebooks (which are now on display at Kew alongside the later ones from the south) bear witness to his meticulous ways. He had lovely round handwriting and the mixture of science and poetry in these notebooks makes fascinating reading.

His love of order is evident, not least in his drawings, which display a wonderful line and a delicate sense of architectural proportion. In the photographs that have survived – from the early ones of him lying in the heather with the gun firmly set on his shoulder, to the ones of him in his tweed suit and fore-and-aft taken in Kensington Gardens in the early 1970s. What a gorgeous moustache he had – neither military nor showy, but droopy, like the one Lloyd George had when Magnus himself was a child.

He worked alphabetically, much like his half-brother, John. His notebooks start with Annuals, then Bulbs, Climbers, Hedges, Herbaceous and Perennials, and on to Shrubs and Trees, and within these categories other sub-categories with the names of all the varieties he planted, from Asters to Zinnias. He put green circles round some of them. How luscious the bird of paradise must have sounded after the heather, and the japonica and the bougainvillea after the bracken.

Magnus moved south in 1933. For years, Lord Berkshire, who used to come fishing and shooting in Scotland every spring and autumn, had tried to persuade him to move south.

'There's such an amount of work to be done there,' Lord Berkshire would say, 'and you, Magnus MacDonell, are the very man to do it. In fact, the only man who can do it.' And he promised Magnus great things. 'Any plant or tree from anywhere in the whole world to decorate the gardens. From China, Mongolia, the Amazon. Money, you see, my dear Magnus, is no problem. And there's a lovely cottage on the estate which you can have for life.'

He was tempted, but his mother's ill health detained him. He still lived at home with Anna in their bothy and nursed her as well as he could when he came back after a hard day out on the moors or on the windswept lochs. The winter nights were best: she'd sit by the fire and tell him about Diarmuid of the Red Beard and the ring his great-great-grandmother lost on the floor of the loch seventeen hundred years before; or how to make a shirt out of bog-cotton gathered from the moor, carding it, then the spinning and the winding, and while making it you were not to speak a word to anyone, for if you speak everything falls apart; and how a grain of salt is always blessed and has a virtue against every enemy, and that if you had an itch in the palm of your right hand, a letter was coming to you.

During the day his sister Mairead would take care of Anna, before returning to her own home. Anna began to lose her memory with time and place dissolving and recognition becoming momentary and partial. She would sit in her wicker chair by the fire, reciting *Hiawatha*, and suddenly say, despite the surrounding wonder of electricity, 'Oh no. I must light the lamp, or I'll be late for school.' Mairead or Magnus would accommodate her delusion. They would light some candles and give her a book which she'd open carefully and then read out loud. She was still a beautiful reader with a lovely rounded Highland voice, so that in English her vowels were extended, with the emphasis always on the last word of any phrase or sentence.

'Once upon a time there were two brothers', she would read, with the emphasis on the word brothers; 'One was called True, and the other Untrue', and again the weight would go on the last noun.

Anna often spoke of things that were no more. Of Mr Johnstone the teacher and bushy-bearded MacKenzie and Miss Tulloch and the laird's factor.

'A pock-faced man called Souter, with the heart of a mouse,' she'd say, and ask when Andrew was due home. Andrew, who had the heart of a lion and the bonniest laugh this side of heaven. And she would always smile at the thought. And she would ask where John was:

'That special, special boy.'

Her mental wanderings became physical, and Magnus would sometimes wake at night to find her gone, and he'd go out with his lantern and search the woods and find her sitting in her gown down by the well or gathering sticks from the fallen trees and bring her back home, reassuring her that Andrew would be back soon. She was a danger to herself, lighting candles instead of turning on those alien switches, and the time came when they had to put her into a home where she was taken care of. Mairead and Magnus visited day about, with occasional visits from Isobel and Sandra and John when they'd manage up from Edinburgh and Glasgow or over from Stornoway.

The nursing home was situated by a river-bank. Anna's

favourite thing was to sit beneath the ancient oak tree in the centre of the garden. She'd close her eyes and listen, sometimes to what only she could hear: a cow bellowing, the sound of ploughing, a horse neighing, bells ringing, potatoes boiling in the pan, her mother singing.

And those stories about Calum, the father she'd never seen. He'd been a small man, they said. Dark skin and dark hair and one day, they said, when food was short because it had been raining and snowing forever and nothing had grown, he decided to go and tell the North Wind to stop being so cruel and starving them. So off he went but the way was long and he walked and walked, but at last he came to the North Wind's house and the North Wind said to him that it was impossible for him to stop blowing, because that was his nature, but that he would help him by giving him a cloth which would get him everything he wanted. All he had to do was to say: 'Cloth, spread yourself, and serve up all kinds of good dishes.'

The story was long and complicated and confused and involved rams and sticks and golden ducats, though everything worked out in the end, for nothing could be solved unless there was a puzzle in the first place, and in the sudden clarity that comes just before death Anna knew that this story was about power and poverty. The power of nature certainly, but also the power of people to scheme and steal and rob the poor. The story said that justice was magic. That the very things which brought shame were the same things which brought triumph. Justice was always in their own hands. She heard a tune and stood up and ran across the garden to the knoll by the river, where Andrew was waiting, looking ever so bonny in his kilt and tammy and playing the pipes – a wonderful dance reel called 'Anna's Welcome to the Fairy Knoll', which he had specially composed for her, for this moment. Andrew, being a fisherman, was standing in the river and once he finished the tune stretched out his hand, calling her over to himself.

'Be careful,' he shouted. 'Just walk steady, and here – here's my hand.'

Lord Arthur Berkshire increased the pressure on Magnus once his mother had gone. At the end of the following deer-stalking season he agreed to move south and join the gardening team at Cliffville, though his real work for Berkshire was much more diverse, from chauffeuring to stabling the horses. But the real reason Lord Arthur Berkshire wanted him was for the fishing. He knew that Magnus MacDonell was the finest fishing-ghillie in the land, with an instinctive knowledge of rivers and lochs and the ways in which salmon and trout moved in these waters.

Of course, that knowledge was no more 'instinctive' than any other knowledge; it had been acquired by long experience. Yet who can tell what primitive oceanography ran through his veins, for had not his father Andrew been a fisherman, and had his forebears not eked a grim living out of the sea, dependent on tides, winds and weather?

Magnus could read the rivers and the sea much as Lord Berkshire could read the FT Index. Just as stocks went up and shares went down, so did trout and salmon. They would spawn and migrate and return, and a keen and knowledgeable eye like Magnus's knew where the breeding grounds were and where they returned to and the times and pools they'd use on their voyages.

It was all dependent on conditions, as with the stock market itself. In the shade was always best, out of the glare of the full sun, early morning or late evening. High noon was best avoided, and everything depended on the flies used to deceive and attract the fish, so that they imagined, like the general public when it came to investment, that they were about to have a tasty meal when, in reality, a deadly hook was piercing their gills.

You had to have the right temperament – there was no point in taking an idiot fishing, for no matter how wise the ghillie was, the fool would always spoil things by splashing, or shouting, or flailing or the thousand and one other tiny things which would alert the salmon and trout to the fact that danger was present. Stealth and quiet were essential. And then too you had to have skill to reel in the fish – it was never a matter of brute force, but of gentleness and persuasion, making the fish believe that what was happening to him was all for the best, that resistance was ultimately futile. The sport of fishing made death reasonable.

Lord Arthur was a good fisherman. The best thing about him was that he took advice. He'd call Magnus into his smoking-room of an evening and give him a large dram and ask him to sit up by the fire and tell him again some of the old fishing yarns. The ones that got away, certainly, but also that time the Duke of Buccleuch caught the fifty pound salmon, and the other time when out sea-fishing with Sir Anthony Stokes and Lady Bracknell they caught the biggest skate ever, almost seven feet long and weighing in at seventeen stone. Berkshire always liked Magnus finishing that story with: 'a fish almost as big and heavy as Lady Bracknell herself!'

Lord Berkshire gave Magnus a car so that he could drive round England and make a private inventory of the best rivers and pools and lakes for fishing. All the famous ones are on Magnus's hand-drawn maps – the Trent and the Avon and the Wye and Ullswater and so on. The delights and jewels are the little secret ones which no-one else really fished, charted by Magnus on his travels. He did so by simply following his instinct and getting to know local people who would take him to out-of-the-way pools and streams where the best fish were. The informants were richly rewarded in kind, for Lord Berkshire was well aware that everything had a price – especially those things which were freely given.

And it has to be said that the exchange was mutual. For not

only did Magnus teach the Lord everything he knew about fishing, but Berkshire, in return, taught Magnus how to play the markets, which were as alien to him at first as England itself. Lord Arthur took him aside, showed him the *Sporting Life* and the *Financial Times*, and explained that horse racing and the stock market worked on the same principle – the race was to the strongest and the fastest, but there were ways of finding out, even fixing, which were the strongest and fastest. Though the word 'fixing' itself was never used. Facts were the thing. It was all down to 'information' and 'knowledge'. You never really profited from mere hunches, even though they gave you an occasional dose of adrenaline. Contacts mattered.

'It's very simple,' the Lord said to Magnus. 'You put a pound on a horse at five to one, and if the horse wins you get your pound and an extra five back. But if you put a pound on a company in the morning, you could have one hundred in your pocket that afternoon, depending on your friend within the company. And the more you put in, the more you can take out.'

But Magnus was a canny man and refused to stake big. Berkshire urged a portfolio of a thousand pounds on him – 'guaranteed to make ten thousand for you by the end of the month, man' – but Magnus refused the offer and said that a hundred pounds to play with would be more than enough. What his poor mother would have done with one hundred pounds, he thought. Or his brother John, stuck in his thatched hovel in Lewis, though he seemed happy enough out there on the edge of the world listening to the eternal surge of the sea.

So Magnus accepted the agreed sum from Lord Arthur and signed a covenant that as soon as he had reached his target from that initial investment, he would pay back double the original advance. Berkshire sat with him and circled the companies he should invest in – British American Tobacco,

British Petroleum, the Whyte and Mackay Whisky Company, Ford, Kellogg's and Uniliver. They all made a hundred per cent profit within the month and Magnus wondered whether Lord Berkshire had circled the companies for him before or after he knew their shares would rise. So he asked him.

'I know all these chaps,' was the reply, 'just as you know all the streams and rivers and pools. So I'll ask you a question – do you put the rod into the pool because you know the salmon is already there, or does that special fly you use attract the salmon into the pool and on to your hook?'

'Both.'

'Touché,' said Lord Arthur.

Magnus met Rachel in the Lake District. She served him breakfast one morning, and had the added distinction of not calling him 'Sir'. She was dark and pretty, the only daughter of an immigrant tailor from Lithuania and his seamstress wife. Born and brought up in Manchester, she had come to Ambleside for the summer to work in the Temperance Hotel, where the owners insisted on calling the guests Mr and Mrs rather than the usual sir or madam. She always learned the guests' names off by heart. Her own name was on a badge on her uniform – Miss Gilbank.

'Good morning, Mr MacDonell,' she said.

He looked up from the menu and smiled.

'Good morning, Miss Gilbank.'

She smiled back at the folly of it all.

'I don't suppose,' Magnus said, 'you would have porridge?'

'No, Mr MacDonell. I'm sorry. We don't.'

But what she served was excellent. Kippers, followed by bacon and egg and good strong tea with toasted home-made bread.

He asked her out on the third day and they went for a drive to the Lakes. They walked and talked and then sat by a waterfall for a picnic. Like Magnus, she spoke English as a foreign language, the accent falling in unexpected places, giving it precision and grace. They both had to really listen, because both dropped words into unexpected vacuums. Even in his old age, after more than half a century in England, Magnus would sometimes begin sentences with the verb, as in Gaelic, and catch me unawares. He'd speak in a roundabout way. So that if I was looking for *The Times*, instead of asking directly 'Do you want the paper?' he'd say 'Is it the paper you are after?' And Rachel would occasionally construct her sentences after the Yiddish fashion. *So what have you learned out from that, Magnus?* And like all of us, they constructed their own lingua franca, where the translated pauses and silences are as meaningful as the spoken words. It was a delight, in their old age, to watch their rhythm of speech.

Rachel persuaded him to confront things, even by silence. And she persuaded him by doing so herself, for it was part of her nature. Of her being.

She always remembered how shocked she'd been when her father told a lie right in front of her. They were at the park when they heard the sweet tinkling of 'Greensleeves' coming from an ice-cream cart which had stopped opposite the park. Immediately scores of children ran over to it.

'It's almost dinner time,' her dad said. Then he smiled, took her hand and joined the queue.

He bought four large cones.

'Two for you. And two for me,' he said.

'One for each hand,' she said.

They walked homewards, licking the ice-creams.

They could smell dinner as soon as they entered the garden gate. A stew. Her mum opened the door and looked at them. The speck of vanilla on Rachel's lips gave the game away.

'Have you been eating something?'

'No,' her dad answered. 'She hit herself on the swing and I put a bit of cream on it at the chemist's.'

And her mum had believed him. Or seemed to believe him. Or believed in him. Though bit by bit Rachel began to realise that he would sometimes say one thing and do another, or do one thing and say another. It was never anything major: just that he'd eaten something when he hadn't, that he hadn't put sugar in his tea when he had, that he'd taken the dog out for a walk when he hadn't. And she sensed that every little lie was like breaking a twig and that it diminished the forest. Trust. That was it, she supposed.

For herself, she decided to experiment by never telling a lie. Even to herself. She had no idea how difficult it would be, but she stayed with it. How much easier it was to say that you weren't tired and stay up an hour later, and how difficult it was to confess that you were exhausted and should go to bed, even though it was such a beautiful summer's evening with the sun streaming in through the window, the rays dancing on the bedcover. How painful it was to lie there trying to fall asleep and listen to the other children playing outside, *ring a ring o roses a pocket full of posies atishoo atishoo we all fall down. Horsey horsey don't you stop, just let your feet go clippety-clop.* And then it was suddenly morning, with the birds singing in the trees. But bit by bit she claimed the habit and it became second nature. The pain was always worth it, in the end. When the window was broken by a chuckie-stone at the school she confessed, though no-one had seen her flinging the stone. At a cat. Which moved so quickly that the stone hurtled through the void into the glass. So she was doubly punished by the Headteacher. First for flinging a stone at a poor defenceless cat, then for breaking a window.

The principle of truth-telling became so fundamental to her that she could sense untruth a mile away. For lies are always recognised by knowing the truth in the first place. She could hear a twig snap in the far distance. And Magnus was as error-prone as the next man.

'We'll meet at five o'clock then?' she'd ask, and he'd say, 'Aye,' and then turn up at quarter-past five and she'd look at him.

'Sorry – the bus was late,' he said.

But then he'd tell the truth.

'I just forgot. It was five o'clock when I remembered.'

And truth-telling became a delight to him too. Like putting on a better coat. Which could have been a chore. The constant pressure to conform, to align, to match the prevailing wind. What did five minutes here or there matter? What did it really matter if he'd come by train or by bus, walking or running? What did it matter that the salmon Lord Berkshire had caught was 8lb, not 28lb as he'd claimed? Except that it seeped, like water in the thatch, drip, drip, drip, and before you knew it the rafters under the thatch were rotten and the house leaking and everyone damp and coughing, and who had money to pay for a doctor?

And there were bigger things. He courted Rachel for two years before they were married, and during that time travelled between Berkshire and the Lake District when he could. They were glorious, snatched moments: out walking by Ambleside, hiring a small boat for the day and fishing on Windermere, going on an excursion out to the other market towns where they'd browse the shops. A beautiful little draper's shop in Keswick where they bought embroidered handkerchiefs for each other, with the tailor stitching their twined initials on the corner of each handkerchief: *MMDRSG*. Magnus MacDonell Rachel Sarah Gilbank.

He began to speak things to Rachel. Things that he didn't know he wanted to say, or could say. None of them were earth-shattering or shocking: just things that mattered because they'd been unspoken. It was fine to be tender. The softer weather helped, for it was less harsh and unyielding. You could risk saying that it might be a fine day tomorrow because even if it rained it wouldn't really matter, and it wouldn't last all day. It wouldn't be a gale force storm. You could be kind without fearing the consequences.

'What a beautiful scarf,' he'd say, not because it was the thing he ought to say, but because as she came walking up to him her chiffon scarf got caught in the wind and he could see the mauve and purple colours sailing in the breeze. He'd once seen a yacht in the Moray Firth with these colours on her sails. And as they kissed, 'What gorgeous perfume. What is it?'

Like Mrs Gould, he began to nurture delicate shades of self-forgetfulness and the suggestion of universal comprehension. He learned different quarters to the year: Lammas and St Peter's Day and Candlemas and St James's Day, rather than the old dispensations of Brighde and Beltane and Martinmas and Michaelmas. He learned to plant at different time. The appropriate time down here was St Barnabas's Day. The 22nd of June. He learned the old rhyme as a new guide: *Allus plant spuds on Barnaby-bright, longest of days and shortest of nights.*

They went to the pictures. Silent ones, black and white, but also the sung ones. They went to see *Anna Karenina* with Greta Garbo.

'Did you like it?' Rachel asked.

'She was too thin,' Magnus said.

'Not her. The film, I mean. The story.'

'I thought it was a bit long.'

'Don't tell me what you thought. Tell me what you felt.'

That came as a shock to Magnus, for he'd never made the distinction.

'What do you mean?'

'Feeling's what you really think, before you have time to mask it in words.'

And they kissed. Properly. For the first time as if they were falling in love.

Rachel forced him to choose between the past and the

future. To drive around England working for Lord Berkshire was one thing. To love was another. He could find and fish all the pools in the world, yet his heart would still be elsewhere, in the past. Love demanded undivided devotion to the present.

As he cleaned the stables in Berkshire he'd stop and smell the heather on the hills of Sutherland. As he drove through the Lake District in search of new fisheries what he saw were lochs: Loch Sheil, Loch Shin, Loch Migdale and all the other hundreds of little Highland lochs where the trout slept in the shade.

Like sound, place disappears. It is ephemeral. The place he grew up in was not an object like a stone, which you can leave in a secret place and return later to find it still there, unmoved, just as you left it.

Childhood does not remain in this world: it evaporates into silence. Magnus strove constantly to inhabit the silence. Sometimes he would stop at country churches and light votive candles against the dark. He would pray, speaking out the words so that he could hear the ancient rhythms filling the air.

'There is no going back,' Rachel said to him. 'Or if there is, you need to go back there physically and reinvent it all. But if you are staying here, stay here rather than there. Invent this rather than that. I'm not going to turn into a pillar of salt.'

That was all much later, well after the kippers.

In telling Rachel about John, Magnus discovered things that he'd never known. She in turn told him things that shocked and startled and surprised him, until one day they both knew that they were properly in love because nothing surprised them.

They were out cycling when he asked her to marry him. A windy day, a country lane, the hedgerows in full bloom on both sides.

'Will you marry me?' he shouted across. At first she thought he was asking her to carry him, so she laughed and said, 'Yes – I've got broad shoulders.'

They thought of returning to Scotland and getting married there.

'At least the wedding?' he asked, but she persuaded him that their future lay before them, not behind him; that to return to the Highlands to get married was a commitment to looking back, not forwards. So they discussed Windermere, but eventually took up Lord Berkshire's offer to marry in Christ Church Cathedral where all his own family had been baptised, married, and buried for centuries.

It was a grand occasion, right enough. Lord Berkshire lent them his coach-and-four for the day and the cathedral choir sounded heavenly. Though Rachel was no Orthodox Jew, a chuppah was erected inside the church for the wedding and the university Rabbi was present to do the Kiddushin. But the atmosphere was Anglican, with Lord Berkshire, resplendent in coat-tails, doing the great reading from Solomon's *Song of Songs – my beloved is unto me as a cluster of camphire in the vineyards of Engedi. Behold, thou art fair, my love; behold thou art fair; thou hast dove's eyes*. The vicar asked for a moment's silence after the vows and as they bowed their heads Magnus had a sudden yearning for the austere silence of Presbyterianism, but then the choir struck up with the Angelus and the moment was gone.

After their marriage they were set up in an estate cottage by Berkshire and Rachel worked as a personal maid to Lady Berkshire until the first child came along – a boy they named Angus. Two years later a sister, Miriam, was born.

Magnus was out working on the estate most of the week and Rachel agreed to Lady Berkshire's request to send the young children to the same preparatory school as her own grandchildren, which was, for the boys, a nursery for Eton and, for the girls, a feeder for St George's at Ascot. They had a wonderful education, boarding from the age of seven, and returning each end-term with new revelations about Cicero and Clive and cricket and hockey. Magnus would then remember some equally marvellous things his mother and John used to say about fairies and about India.

'Can you speak sing-song?' Miriam would ask, and Magnus would place Angus on one knee and Miriam on the other and say,

'Well, I suppose I can,' and his voice would rise and fall as he told his stories.

His mother said that when she was a little girl she and a group of children had been out on the road opposite the houses when day gives way to night and, at nightfall, they saw many horses coming towards them from the east, a rider on every horse. They went westward. His mother and all the children stood watching them. And after a while she said the riders returned from the west, and the moon was shining, it was a fine moonlit night. So she and the others stood and watched the procession going past to the east, and the horse which had been in front when they were going west was at the end when they came east – it was a white horse.

'Now,' said his mother, 'that was a year when the whooping-cough was widespread among the children. And we followed them east, and this is what we were saying to them, "Rider of the white horse, what cures whooping-cough?" And we followed them as far as the boundary of the townland.'

But Magnus could not remember if the children got any reply from the rider of the white horse.

The children were so different, inhabiting another universe. Angus was tall and dark-haired and athletic while Miriam acquired her father's fairness, and was blue-eyed and artistic. Angus had his mother's zeal for doing everything as well as he could, so it became less and less surprising as the years passed that he excelled at everything – science, rugby, rowing, and especially cricket where he became captain of every team all the way through the age ranges, from the Under-14s to the Under-18s. He also had the distinction of being the only player to have achieved four consecutive centuries for Eton in the great annual match against Harrow.

Miriam, although equally talented, preferred not to take any leadership roles at St George's, unless winning the Art Prize every year for six years in succession is counted. She also thrived in the Drama Department, invariably playing the leading lady in the yearly Shakespeare play which they performed at the end of the spring term. During school holidays she'd occasionally join her father out working in the estate gardens or setting the salmon nets on the river and recite the lines she was trying to learn to him as he snipped the hydrangeas or walked back from the river.

'There's rosemary, that's for remembrance,' she'd say. 'Pray you, love, remember. And there is pansies, that's for thought.'

She spoke with a beautiful accent. It was so pure that you thought of gold when you heard it and couldn't make out where in England she was from or what her background was, except that it was good. Angus was equally polished, speaking with such crystal clarity that any listener would have suspected royal pedigree. When home from Eton or St George's they would sometimes listen with wonder and no small sense of shame to their parents speaking in their strange regional registers. Some Mancunian Jewish words would slip into their mother's conversation and their father would answer with guttural imprecations before realising that the children were listening; then he'd switch to a fine lilting English that sounded like the stream at the back of the house trickling over the rocks on a summer's evening.

Dad became a diplomat. When he left Eton he went

to Oxford where he studied PPE at Christ Church, which opened up all the usual channels into politics. He told me that he was offered a safe Conservative seat in the Downs but that he yearned to go overseas, so instead joined the diplomatic service and took a junior posting in Ottawa when it was offered to him.

'There's a sign out in the bush in Australia,' he'd then say to me, 'which they put up after the rainy season. "Choose your route carefully" it reads, "you'll be in it for the next two hundred and fifty kilometres". Same with a career, old boy.'

I was never sure whether it was advice or a warning.

He met Signe in New York when he was on assignment there. She was a violinist with the Philharmonic, and they met at a reception hosted by the British Ambassador. Her father was Swedish and her mother from Ireland, but she too had gone to a private school in England when her parents moved to London to work at the Royal Academy of Music. That common interest brought them together at the party and they continued to meet up regularly, marrying in New Mexico in a hot summer of love. Aoife was born six months afterwards and two years later, just before their divorce, I was brought into the world.

11

I HAD AN itinerant, delightful childhood. Born in the Lower East Side on the 15th of May. 'Zodiac sign Taurus,' Mom always chanted. 'You'll bear a lot with ease.' After my parents separated, I would spend the weekdays at Mom's and the weekend at Dad's, or at least at wherever he happened to be any particular weekend. The one early constant was my Cuban nanny, Analena, who travelled with me everywhere and from whom I learned Spanish.

I think music gave me a good ear. I'd listen to mother playing. Note after note, in perfect sequences. She'd practise for hours in the front room while I played next door with toys. Analena helped me set up a perfect railway track which took me from New York all the way across the Rockies to the west coast, when the line then went underwater all the way over to Great Britain. We had twenty cardboard tunnels and to reach London I'd crawl under this blue plastic sheet shouting 'woo-hoo' every so often. And every time I'd emerge, the violin notes were still there hanging in the air next door. The practice was regular, monotonous, and consistent. I realise now there was no improvisation: none of the notes ever changed, because – I suppose – she was playing them exactly, with a sort of strict Puritanism, the way they had been written. There was no room for manoeuvre or interpretation. For nuance.

Like all kids, I had my own world in my room. These were early console days, but still we had the Atari versions of Space War and Sea Wolf, later moving on to the more sophisticated Avatar and Dungeons and Dragons. No doubt Analena saved me from the darkest recesses of nerdom, though I always envied those other cool kids who skateboarded past me every day with aviator glasses and Sony headphones to die for. We could easily afford them, but I wasn't allowed them.

My father was a keen fisherman and would take me out on fishing expeditions every weekend – sometimes sea-fishing, but more often up to our cabin in the Catskills. I loved spending time there with him. I loved everything about it. The anticipation of waiting for Friday, the adventure of leaving New York City and heading north, that adrenaline rush every time we set our eyes on the Hudson, the perpetual thrill it always was to turn off up into the mountains and climb in the wagon through the scree until we caught sight of the log cabin nestling between the stream and Aaron's Rock.

Aaron's Rock was our own private name for the high heap of stones on the far side of the river, ever since the weekend my friend Aaron came with us and scrambled up to the top in record time – in twenty-two seconds. Neither I nor my father could ever manage better than thirty, no matter how hard we tried. Or at least I did. Looking back on it now, Dad may never really have tried that hard.

Sometimes we didn't fish. When the weather was rough we'd just hang out inside the cabin, playing games. Dad would read to me – my favourite was The Legend of Sleepy Hollow. We would play backgammon or Ludo or sizzle sausages over the stove. There was no television, but there was a magic old wireless we'd spend ages tuning to get a station, as well as a beautiful old wind-up gramophone on which we'd play Dad's records – mostly classical stuff, though he also had some jazz and blues. Bill Evans was best. Things were invented there: you were never sure which note came next, and when it did, it was always surprising.

Our favourite time was on the Saturday evening after being out fishing all day. We'd have a barbecue and then I'd lie on the floor and he'd allow me to move the wireless dial fraction by fraction while he kept his eyes shut tight, and he had to guess which station I'd found. Hilversum! Radio Moscow! The BBC World Service. Call sign KAAY from Little Rock Arkansas! WUBC from Boston! And he was right every time.

We supported the Yankees. My favourite players back then were Thurman Munson and, after Thurman died in that air crash, Rick Cerone. Dad would always say that baseball had nothing on cricket, and later on when they sent Aoife and I over to England for our education I discovered how right he was. Watching the Yankees amidst all that noise was terrific, but those late summer afternoons sitting at Lord's and Trent Bridge listening to the sound of willow on leather was even finer. Beer in, the sun overhead, white figures moving like little birds on the green. I think the best I ever saw was Viv Richards' century against India at the Oval in 1983. It was like watching a majestic eagle swooping down on to its prey and veering off into the unknown.

Mom travelled a lot with the New York Philharmonic and took me with her when she could. Which, even with Analena to attend to me, was not that often, because increasingly she spent half the year on tour overseas. Twice, Analena took me to Cuba where I met her large extended family, who all seemed to sing and play music.

My memories are of banjos and guitars and dancing in the heat in the backyard of her Granma's. It was life eternal. Her uncle had a bright blue and yellow parrot which constantly whistled 'La Bayamesa' and who would only stop if someone else whistled 'The Star Spangled Banner'. We took it in turns to do that so as to shut him up, and whenever I hear either anthem on the telly I'm back in that mad, golden moment.

When I was twelve my parents must have come to some kind of post-marital agreement, because Aoife and I were sent off to England, to live with our grandparents, Magnus and Rachel, in Berkshire. We thought it was wonderful. We arrived on the Saturday and Granma and Grampa took us to church the next morning.

I can still remember how amazing it was for me to hear the great big cathedral organ filling the church with noise and then all of us standing up and singing in unison 'And did those feet in ancient times, walk upon England's mountains green?' It was as if the church building itself – the wooden rafters and the stained-glass windows and the stone pillars and the pews – were singing along with the congregation. And everything was green, and even now England to me is such a green and pleasant land despite the dissolution that has happened. It was the first time that I'd ever been in church, because my parents had no religion. And I remember after that first service standing out on the green cathedral lawn and looking up into the skies, where a flock of geese in the shape of a cross passed over the church. I have yearned for the safety of liturgy ever since.

Grampa enrolled us at the local independent school, and I recall as if it were yesterday the day he drove me there in his old Bentley.

'Lord Berkshire left it to me in his will,' he said. 'It's a lovely car, isn't it, Gav?'

And it was. Gorgeous red leather seats and this beautiful wooden dashboard with all these glorious dials. It even had a radio which was perpetually stationed to Radio 4 and when I recollect these days now the strongest memory is of driving that day through the leafy lanes and listening to *The Archers*. I could hardly make out what they were saying because their accents were so different and strong, but they moved with a measure of peace, and even then, at age twelve, I thought the sound of their voices was more important than anything they said. They made clear English shapes, like the sound that Grampa's crystal glass made when he clinked it with his pipe after dinner.

The school itself was fine, and I know now that so many folk scoff at it and consider that the pupils who were there were all posh and privileged. Maybe they were. But we were just children, doing what we could. My overall recollection is that few, if any, of us were consciously aware of advantage. We took it all for granted.

We had no idea that others didn't run under the same sun, for it surely shone everywhere. The perfectly manicured grounds were ours to use, and my clearest recollection of the place is lying on the grass towards the end of Lent Half cramming for the coming exams. *Shall I compare thee to a summer's day? Thou art more lovely and more temperate.* It was the time we were all in love with Annie Lennox.

It seems strange to me now that I actually specialised in the sciences, for I loved History and English and Art. But precision is attractive. I may have yearned for that finality because my parents were absent so often. So Freud claims. That we take the road we least like, as revenge. I remember once dating a girl not because I fancied her but because her best friend for whom I had the real hots rejected me.

Not that I despised science in any way. I loved the fantastic theories as well as the experimental practices. What was there not to love about Cosmology and Astronomy and Astrophysics, speculating on the origins and the evolutions of things? What was there not to love about dissecting a frog to see how the veins feed that little pumping heart, to see at close quarters how the tongue works, and the way in which the length of the frog's tongue has evolved, giving it a capacity to catch flies at what must – from the fly's viewpoint – seem a safe distance? You learn that distance itself never makes you totally safe.

And I had memories. Of a weekend in the Catskills with

Dad when we collected a whole heap of pans and bits of iron and wire from down by the stream and we made a bike together. It hurtled perfectly downhill, the two of us clinging to each other for dear life as steam poured from the boiled kettle that was supposed to turn the wheels. Science could be great impractical fun. I still dream of building a machine-free anti-gravity bike that will transport me through the air.

For a while in Upper Fifth and Sixth I veered between going on to study Biology or Medicine, but then towards the end of Michaelmas in Upper Fifth I became fascinated by the verbal truth of Mathematics and truly discovered the beauty of numbers and the fascination of problem-solving in algebra and geometry. I now know that the challenge was as much aesthetic as scientific, but then it was purely arithmetic in the sense that all these symbols were like a gigantic puzzle which somehow, somewhere, eventually all added up. Could I really have believed that at one time? That two and two make four, and not three or five, as Smith claimed? Great God, grant that twice two be not four.

At the time I became absorbed by it, I gave little or no thought to any of the philosophical issues hiding behind the numbers. Which may go part of the way to explaining why I became a banker when I graduated from Oxford. Banking then wasn't considered toxic and poisonous, but a noble enough profession. Which it was, with some branch managers still around who carried pocket watches and gold chains and a conscience, like Arthurian knights caught in the trenches.

Grampa Magnus had just retired from estate work when I arrived from New York City to stay with him and Granma. To me, aged twelve, he seemed to be beyond age. Grampa Magnus was very tall and had soft white hair, while Granma Rachel was smaller with genetically dark hair. I now apologise in retrospect to their departed spirits for being an arrogant child, a young Yankee who thought he knew it all. Forgive me, my dear, dead darlings.

Granma took me through to the cosy room at the back.

'You'll sleep here, Gavin,' she said to me. 'It's yours and nobody else's. Your private estate. Your castle. Your kingdom.'

My cabin, I thought.

She tended to speak in trinities.

Grampa then took me out for a walk around the place. 'To get your bearings,' he said to me, and led me quickly up the hill at the back of the house. 'It's called Paddock's Hill. Must have been toads here at one time.'

He raised his right hand and pointed.

'See that hilltop? That's North.'

He turned a quarter.

'That church-steeple. East.'

Another quarter.

'The windmill down there. South.'

And another turn.

'And that river over there is West. Try it yourself.'

And I faced towards the hilltop, stretched out my hand and said 'North.'

Did a quarter-turn, pointed towards the church-steeple and declared 'East.'

Another quarter-turn, pointed to the windmill and said 'South,' and a final turn, stretching my hand out towards the far distant river, 'West.'

'That', said Grampa, 'Is all you need to know!'

But he was smiling and I knew fine that he was really saying the opposite. That these directions were the least things I needed to know. The circle was both bigger and smaller than I imagined.

'Come on,' he said to me, and led me down the hill past the stream and over stiles towards the fields where the ponies were grazing. He whistled and a dappled grey pony came trotting over. He lifted me up on to the pony and asked me to hold on to the mane. He whispered into the pony's ear and off it trotted at a gentle pace round the edge of the field, stopping at every corner to look back at Grampa as if to ask for further instructions. Grampa whistled and the pony trotted on. He whistled again and the pony came to a halt. Within the hour I was riding him bareback as if we'd been born together to do this for the whole of our lives. It sort of perfectly sums up my relationship with my grandfather: he gave me a sense of direction, but the ride was mine.

I only knew them for eleven years, and it was only in retrospect that these years bore fruit. I was going to say made sense, but that would be untrue, for the eleven years I spent with them were full of sense. Aoife left for New York at the end of year five and later enrolled at the Rhode Island School of Design before moving to Mexico, where she met Raul. She constantly phones me, concerned about how I am.

'I'm fine,' I say to her. 'I'm fine. Just fine.'

She knows full well I'm not telling her the truth.

Above all else, Grampa Magnus and Granma Rachel were practical people. Grampa taught me how to ride horses, how to saw wood, how to catch trout, how to plant turnips and swedes and potatoes and radishes and onions, how to nurture rose bushes, how to view and manage the land – whether that land was a small square patch in the corner of the garden or a thousand acres or even a whole country.

They gave me a corner of their garden to nurture. Grampa showed me how to cultivate vegetables and herbs, and how to grow roses and azaleas and primroses.

'To sow an acre,' he'd say, 'is to reap a nation. Nature is the great economist.'

He had a hand-built log cabin down by the river where he did his carpentry work. Small water troughs and benches and stiles and other practical farm stuff. Also things that were purely aesthetic. He taught me how to use the lathe and once I made a model of the *Queen Mary* which I painted green and red and endlessly sailed down the stream, steering the ship with a long stick through the tall reeds. My favourite voyage was sailing her from New York to Singapore via the Cape. In the mornings, when the carpentry shop filled with sunshine, you could watch the sawdust dancing in the air. On Saturdays, Grampa would permit himself a strong coffee and sit on the bench with his legs dangling like a child, watching me with a smile as I jumped about trying to catch the dust with a sudden clap of my hands.

Granma taught me how to bake, cook, sow, and budget. Saturday afternoons we'd go into town together and wander around the market. Not really to buy anything, though she did have a sweet tooth and found it impossible to pass some of the food stalls without picking up some savoury croissants for the two of us, or one of those special cinnamon cakes that old Mrs Dowe always sold at her table. She loved auctions and would take me to the weekly one at Jowles's where all kinds of wondrous knick-knacks and unknown rubbish and treasures were scattered all over the place on benches and shelves and tables and floors. Granma had a particular fondness for cutlery, and would spend hours raking through knives and forks and spoons and old ladles to finally emerge triumphant with a wooden spatula made in Lithuania.

'Look at that beautiful carving,' she'd say, her thumb caressing the fading image of a troika rushing through the forest snow.

Grampa and Granma were both canny, to use that great old Scots word, which basically means to live within your means knowing that the future is uncertain. And yet I failed to apply that gospel. After school, I chose to go to Oxford and study Mathematics. These were the heady days when, in the wake of proving the Epsilon Conjecture, everyone was hell-bent on working out Fermat's Last Theorem. But by the time that particular problem was solved, I was on Wall Street. We sold dreams and made our fortunes. Folk sometimes wonder, and ask me if the Stock Market is any different from betting on the horses. It is. It's like being at the dogs. Those poor thin greyhounds, starved and drugged to make a paltry profit for their owners and a few coins for the gamblers who brave the snowy nights at empty racecourses.

New York in those days was fairyland. We all linked arms that snowy night we sang the song at Times Square as the Christmas bells rang out. I was merely a low caste priest of this new religion, though I realise that all movements depend upon silent operatives. Instead of black clerical suits and collars we all wore bright clothing and could be seen at twilight making music and singing and dancing until our heads were light and airy, just like the cook in Grampa's story who was as happy as the goldfinch in the glade. Many of us became genderless, for it was best not to have anything settled, but for all to be in flux. We moved in subterranean quarters, to the beat of ecstatic hip-hop which kept us flying for days on end.

I drifted into it. Graduated from Oxford (Mathematics, 1st Class), went down to the City, started as a good old-fashioned junior banker with Lloyds. Of course it was neither good nor old-fashioned. Nor was it really banking, if you define banking as looking after someone's money. Our job was to make as much profit as possible out of our customers' resources and needs. Selling insurance and mortgage and investment schemes. All those gullible people who believed our words. As Grampa said later, who really wants to confess in the middle of summer that a harsh winter is coming? We're not all Joseph. Instead, we surrendered to doom, which seemed at the time like triumph.

After a year in the City, I was transferred over to Wall Street as a reward. It was like getting to play in the MLB with

the Yankees. Even then I was conscious of the price I needed
to pay – turning a blind eye to this, a deaf ear to that. Better
men than I had traded their conscience for silver. I was no
Judas. Hadn't Galileo and Da Vinci hired themselves out to
the military to teach them the art of fortification? All men
need to live.

12

MY BOSS WAS Charlie Holroyd, who believed in investment as a fundamental article of faith. He'd sit in the window looking over to Staten Island.

'We're the engine of democracy,' he said. 'This great nation built on self-reliance, forging our own future, no matter the cost or consequence. Following in the footsteps of Daniel Boone in the land of the free. How else do we prevent poverty except by the creation of wealth? Some of it will drip down, like dewdrops of fat from the roast. As long as we avoid the twin evils of isolationism and patriotism. Remain global.'
He would point to Latin America.

'Revolutions will cease when folk have money. Then they'll have too much to lose.'

'Their chains?'

He laughed.

'Gav. At the moment they have nothing to lose. Look at China. Russia. Guatemala. Serbia. Croatia. Bosnia. Cuba. Economic development is always the road to democracy.'

And then I laughed.

'Really Mr Holroyd? Democracy receding by the day. The medium is the massage. And the Middle East?' I asked him. 'All that oil – all that 'economic development'? Oligarchs and executioners at every corner?'

'Don't pitch stereotypes at me,' he said. 'Even the USA has its false apostles. Once these people begin to value mobile phones like the rest of us, everything else will follow.'

I saw Mom and Dad again, though I didn't spend that

much time with them. Both had new partners, and had their own lives to live, so I suppose Wall Street itself became my surrogate family. It's all very well, in the perfect light of hindsight, to call it a dysfunctional family, but we were really only following trends. Wasn't everything a trend? America itself: the Pilgrim Fathers who followed their hearts to this New Jerusalem. Grampa once said to me, 'It's a pity you lot don't have a Statue of Responsibility instead of Liberty.'

'Have you forgotten,' I said to him, 'that this beautiful continent was built on these very pillars? The Protestant work ethic. Individual freedom and responsibility.'

'Gone with the wind,' he said.

But I wasn't dishonest. That is, if dishonesty has to do with being deliberately deceptive. I too believed in making money. Not for its own sake but for the simple reason that without money we'd all descend into poverty and chaos. But I didn't love it, and all things that are not done in love are dishonest.

It had its advantages. A beautiful warehouse flat on the Upper East Side with a view over the river from the bedroom window and our own company doctor. I volunteered on Saturday mornings at the homeless centre where poor wretches were kept going by the weekly contributions from our company. I befriended Gianluca who always sang 'God Bless America' before and after every grateful meal.

There are as many New Yorks as there are mountains. We rented a basement in Brooklyn where a bunch of us made music. Lou, Adriana, Serge, Lucie and I loved Cage's music and combined that with a rediscovered disco beat which became hugely popular at the weekends. And we formed a Bridges Running Club. If you managed to run across the Brooklyn Bridge in less than five minutes you earned the right to a free bagel every morning. I never qualified.

The sexy bit, though, was Artificial Intelligence. I knew some folk who worked there. It wasn't where the money was, but it was where the future lay. If you could separate money from the future. While Wall Street satisfied the present, these guys forged a future filled with limitless risks and possibilities. They could create a lover in their own image and likeness: any androgynous being you liked, from Athena to a slave.

Marina, for instance. I went out with her for a while, but it was like dating my phone. She was as slim and beautiful as my iPhone 6, though less obedient.

She was obsessed with the frontiers of intelligence. I was attracted by her beauty and repelled by her politics, as she was attracted by my humour and repelled by my indecisiveness.

'Machines will be no different from humans in that respect,' she said. 'It will be the survival of the fittest. They too will build a liberty tower. They will set goals, and achieve them. Simple.'

Granma's cancer brought me back to the UK. I phoned one evening and Grampa – and this was so unusual – answered the phone.

'We saw the doctor at the beginning of last week and tests have now confirmed it's terminal,' he said to me straight away.

I walked that night. All night. Across the Brooklyn Bridge to Manhattan. It was a beautiful night, and I knew that if I walked long enough, for days and nights, I would finally see all the stars twinkling once all the city lights had faded. To walk along the coastline past New Haven and Providence and on to Boston and up to Maine on to St John and maybe towards Nova Scotia. Surely I would see the stars then? I remembered them. All the symbols of greatness were still glittering here – the Empire State Building, the Statue of Liberty, the Chrysler Building, the Four World Financial Centre. A vertical city, reaching high into the heavens. New York was the Milky Way.

I thought mostly of Granma that night. And, through her, of Grampa and how he'd be hurting, and whether he'd cope. This dependency on one another, and our need to love and be loved. For none of us live alone, or die alone. The endless city anonymous in front of me. Eight million souls and counting. Where a couple of thousand Lenape native Americans had farmed until the Europeans arrived, one after the other. The Florentines and the Spaniards and the English and the Dutch and the French and the Portuguese. Then the African slaves and the refugees and the dreamers and the poor and visionaries from Russia and the ends of the earth. Until there were so many people that no-one could see the Lenape anymore.

Once upon a time people must have lived in small family groups. So small that they could hear each other. Depending on each other. In caves and under canvas. Hunting and fishing. Foraging. Huddling together for warmth and company. Looking at the moon, where the man with the hoe lived. Listening to the coyotes baying in the dark. Telling stories. Did I tell you what happened to me last night after I came back with the deer-skin? Singing little songs. *Bà bà mo leanabh*. On prairies and mountains and in woods and in meadows and villages and cities. Here. Now. Adam and Eve and their plump babies. And afterwards, how she warned 'Don't go out there in the dark. It's dangerous.'

New York is a single apartment tonight, partners lying quiet in each other's arms, a child sleeping in a cot. For after the party, when the crowd disperses, an old caretaker is always left, folding chairs and putting things away. Every morning and evening I travel by subway. We sit side by side, shoulders or thighs or feet touching, or stand crushed together breathing on one another. We live together, even if we die alone.

Granma used to read stories to me as I fell asleep. Once upon a time there was a little girl who lived in a village near the forest. The rest was a dream. Once upon a time a king and a queen reigned in a country a great way off. Once upon a time a mouse, a bird and a sausage entered into partnership and set up house together. In the beginning, God created the Heavens and the Earth. And here, right beneath my feet, native tribesmen and women and children set up camp by the river that flows two ways, the Muhheakantuck, before it became the Rio de Montaigne, the Rio de San Antonio and the North River before Hudson's great name reigned victorious over them all. As if it was a better story. It was Dante's moment of eternal fate and judgement, which is to end up forever as you are.

Granma Rachel was small. That's what prompted me to think of those things. The fragility of life. Of how tiny things grow. Things had simply gotten too big in my life, constantly living on the edge of gravity. On endless adrenaline, the perpetual search for profit, the next hit, the latest commodity. Living in a land which had no horizon. I found myself in a desert story, hallucinating about palm trees and freshwater wells where there was only burning sand.

I was being commanded to speak. In the middle of the journey of my life, I came to myself, in a dark wood, where the dark way was lost. I couldn't get Grampa's voice out of my head. The voice that had perfect grace and precision, rightly summed up as sing-song. He had taken me to archery lessons once upon a time, and his voice was like an arrow made from feathers, rising softly into the air and then descending in a perfect arc towards its destiny. There was a different story which could begin now and still finish on a long glassy road.

I had never taken a decision. Not a real proper one anyway – just drifted with the tide, accepting things as they were. School, university, the bank, Artificial Intelligence. Like a character in a story to whom things happen. I was neither Don Quixote nor Monsieur Hulot. I had never really loved, only consented. That night on Brooklyn Bridge I confessed that freedom was a choice made, not a circumstance accepted.

Back in the apartment, I looked at the old photographs. In one of them Grampa was cycling with Granma Rachel sitting on the handlebars and leaning back into his chest. She was barefoot and smoking a cigarette.

I resigned from Merrill Lynch in the morning, paid off my rental and booked a flight for London.

'Hi Grampa. It's me. I've booked the flight and I'll be in London tomorrow at six pm. I'll get to yours by eight.'

He looked older. Diminished. As was poor Granma, who had begun to yellow and wither. Though her mind was as bright as ever, and not once from then on till the end did I ever hear her complain about anything. She forever spoke words of encouragement.

'Gavin' she always called me, never the abbreviated 'Gav'. I like to think it was because she couldn't bear for anything in the world to be diminished. Though I was conscious that my middle name was never included, reserved for the sanctity of the written word.

'For Gavin John' old folk would write when giving me a book as a present.

'Gavin,' she said, 'how well you look.' Although I knew full well that drugs had taken their toll. 'Gavin, you're such a good lad,' she'd say, though I also knew my soul was frayed and my heart pumping with anxiety.

She loved the Psalms of David, so in these last days of hers I came to know them almost off by heart because she asked me to read them to her morning and night. *I waited patiently for the Lord; and he inclined unto me, and heard my cry. He brought me up also out of an horrible pit, out of the miry clay, and set my feet upon a rock, and established my goings. And he hath put a new song in my mouth, even praise unto our God: many shall see it, and fear, and shall trust in the* LORD. Texts begin to inhabit us.

She'd lie back on her multitude of pillows with her eyes closed and a smile on her lips, holding my hand, squeezing it with love any time the word Israel was mentioned. Israel as in God's chosen people, not as in the modern political construct which has caused so much anguish. Israel as a universal people set apart to worship the one true God. Behold, he that keepeth Israel shall neither slumber nor sleep. Truly God is good to Israel. Blessed be the Lord God of Israel from everlasting, and to everlasting. Amen, and amen.

And how offensive my liberal-hearted friends found these hundreds of verses I could quote about Israel's favour!

'What about the Holocaust?' one of them questioned me once upon a time on Twitter. 'Was that also God's favour?'

As if we can diminish love to preference, or pride to prejudice.

But I'm ahead of myself. These were Granma's portions and comforts in the valley of the shadow of death. Latterly, in between the nurse's regular visits, Grampa would sit on one side of the bed holding her hand, while I sat on the other doing likewise.

Most of the time we sat in silence, letting our presence speak. And, day after day, our trinity became more and more instinctive as if we all understood everything without saying anything. Granma had lost the power of speech and it was unfair to speak things to which she could not reply in words. Silence became the ideal language because it was composed of the the vocabulary of our memories.

During these days I thought of many things. I read Descartes and marvelled at the notion that nothing outside truly existed except that I thought it so. And to think it so was for it to exist. Whether myself or my Granma Rachel or my Grampa Magnus or the chair on which I sat or the tree

out in the orchard or the Brooklyn Bridge over which I'd
walked in the moonlight weeks before.

'For pray, whence can the effect derive its reality, if not
from its cause?'

And so on, backwards and backwards to the infinite,
which he called God. For something cannot proceed from
nothing.

'Were I myself the author of my being, I should doubt
nothing and desire nothing, and finally no perfection would
be lacking to me; for I should have bestowed on myself every
perfection of which I possessed any idea and should thus be
God.'

And I suppose it was the circumstances, with Granma
Rachel lying there between us, but I suddenly understood
what it is to love. That it is a matter of creation. That taking
care of Granma at this moment was not merely a matter of
looking after her and attending to her needs, but of creating
her existence moment by moment, affirming it, sometimes
by word, sometimes by touch, sometimes by silence, as we
sat there with her. We give each other life by assent, and
extinguish it by withdrawal. We sustain each other simply
by being there.

And who was I to reject what sustained them? Perhaps
that's what prayer is. But who prays to himself and who
creates from nothing? How could anyone argue that God
or a tree did not exist, when Granma and Grampa thought
so? As well to argue that none of their thoughts existed, that
none of their ideas had any value whatsoever.

'For though I assume that perhaps I have always existed
just as I am at present, neither can I escape the force of this
reasoning and imagine that the conclusion to be drawn
from this is, that I need not seek an author for my existence.
For all the course of my life may be divided into an infinite
number of parts, none of which is in any way dependent on
the other; and thus from the fact that I was in existence a

short time ago it does not follow that I must be in existence now, unless some cause at this instant, so to speak, produces me anew, that is to say, conserves me. For it is a matter of fact perfectly clear and evident to all those who consider with attention the nature of time, that, in order to be conserved in each moment in which it endures, a substance has need of the same power and action as would be necessary to produce and create it anew, supposing it did not yet exist, so that the light of nature shows us clearly that the distinction between creation and conservation is solely a distinction of the reason.'

We had to conserve each other, for if we didn't we would cease to exist. So I listened to Granma's breathing, extending her life by centuries by simply listening to it. And she magnified my life by smiling when I read the psalms to her, the pleasure in her eyes like fields rolling and extending towards the horizon, without walls or enclosures. And Grampa would bring in a mug of tea and a scone or sandwich and by that very act of kindness, we would live forever. For once we cease to love we die.

On the last morning Grampa brought in John Donne as the three us walked through the valley of the shadow. Who had known so well that everything was hanging by a thread and instantly soluble. As I read him out loud Grampa held Granma's frail hand.

Let me pour forth my tears before thy face, whilst I stay here, for thy face coins them, and thy stamp they bear, and by this mintage they are something worth, for thus they be pregnant of thee. On a round ball a workman hath copies by, can lay an Europe, Afric, and an Asia, and quickly make that, which was nothing, all. O Saviour, as thou hang'st upon the tree, I turne my backe to thee, but to receive corrections, till thy mercies bid thee leave. O thinke mee worth thine anger, punish mee, burne off my rusts, and my deformity, restore thine Image, so much, by thy grace, that thou may'st know mee, and I'll turn my face.

To read John Donne is to become John Donne.

We faced each other as Granma died. I offered to leave but Grampa bid me stay, so we sat there, each of us caressing a hand. Grampa spoke to her for hours, in his beautiful soft voice. He kept saying her name. Rachel. Raonaid. He talked of all those things I learnt then, and earlier, and later. He smiled.

'Ambleside, my darling. Do you remember?'

'And that time we borrowed the tandem and the brakes failed as we were coming down the hill.' 'Where was it again? That hill outside Cambridge, wasn't it? Wasn't it, Rachel?'

And she smiled.

She passed away in the early evening. We'd dozed for a while and when I opened my eyes I could see she had gone. I let Grampa sleep on until he too woke naturally. I left so that he would have that quiet moment of valediction.

13

'YOU WILL STAY on, won't you?'

'Of course, Grampa. Of course I will. Would love to.'

And so I stayed on after the funeral. To take care of Grampa, I was going to say, but it was really to take care of each other. I chummed him to church every Sunday morning. We knelt side by side to say our prayers.

We pottered about for a while. I offered to clear some things away but he said he'd prefer to do it himself, so while I bought and prepared and cooked food and looked after the garden and all the other household things, Grampa slowly worked through Granma's belongings, retaining and discarding. A time to keep and a time to cast away.

Grampa Magnus was a very neat and tidy man in every way. Fastidious. When I'd catch sight of him folding and putting things away I was seeing an older civilisation, like the ancient Greeks and Romans I'd studied once upon a time at school.

He kept himself fit merely by living. He had worked hard all his life and still, into his eighty-fifth year, moved well with the ease and balance and lightness of a young man. We went on long daily walks. I found it hard to keep up with him as he climbed stiles, jumped fences and ascended inclines which left me out of breath.

He arranged and packed Granma's things with natural care. An endless number of boxes marked 'Dresses', 'Jackets', 'Skirts', 'Gloves', 'Hats', 'Jewellery' and so forth. I didn't ask him what he planned to do with the boxes, but one morning he called me in from the garden and asked if I could take the clothes boxes to the East End Jewish Clothing Fund offices and the jewellery to the Feinstein Charitable Trust. He gave me a slip of paper with the addresses written out.

'I've already phoned them,' Grampa said. 'And they're very happy to take the items and sell them on for funds.'

I asked him if he wanted to go to London with me, but he declined.

'No. Best if you do that yourself. For me. And for Rachel.'

It was a privilege to do that for them, and so I drove to London and gave the various boxes to the folk at the Clothing Fund offices and at the Charitable Trust.

It was only years afterwards that I discovered the letter in Grampa's desk.

Dear Mr MacDonell,

We just wanted to formally thank you for your generous gift to our Trust. When you phoned us initially you of course made us aware of the fact that some pieces of your late wife's jewellery were very valuable, and you will remember that you insisted we should sell these items no matter the value, and let you know at some point how much we had raised. I am pleased to report that the diamond necklace and bracelets realised, by themselves, over half a million pounds, and that the Berkshire Brooch, as you marked it, realised a further half a million pounds. Altogether, you have generously donated over two million pounds to our Cancer Trust, and our thanks for that gift is immeasurable. We have no doubt that hundreds of sufferers will be greatly helped by your goodness and kindness.

With our very best wishes.
Shalom,
Esther Bergmann.

Grampa had mentioned the Berkshire Brooch to me in passing: a wedding gift to his wife from Lady Berkshire.

Grampa seemed sadder when I returned from London. I suppose it was the first opportunity he really had to grieve properly, to live with the absence. Dealing with Granma's stuff had kept him occupied. Everything he touched was filled with memories. And there was a fragrance, for any time we'd enter Granma's room her perfume lingered. Lilies and roses.

I suggested a journey. The old myth that you need to move away from loss. I don't know.

'France?' I suggested. 'We could get the train down to London then the Eurostar over to Paris...'

But it was obvious it was never going to happen. And of course I knew it. And perhaps I wouldn't have suggested it either had I not sensed the unspoken. The other absence. The north. I would leave it to him, and it almost took forever. It was almost too late. Though almost is such a stupid, superfluous, word. For almost never happened.

He began to drift. Forgot things. Would begin to put some toast on when he'd just had some toast. Would ask the same question a couple of times within the hour. Then one morning after breakfast he said, 'Gav, why don't the two of us go on a wee journey together? Up north.'

I acted nonchalant, as if it didn't matter. Though his use of the word 'wee' meant it was important. The ancient diminutive which masked affection, for anything more would almost be an indecency.

'Sure, Grampa. Sure. Anything you like.'

So we packed that day and the next and left on the Friday. Good Friday, it happened to be. Which was just about the worst day of the year to travel, holiday traffic already choking the M1. But I didn't want to endanger things by delaying and Grampa was by now impatient.

'Are you ready then, son?' he asked every few minutes until the car was finally packed and oiled and filled with diesel and ready.

'Where to?' I asked once we were on the M1.

'Ambleside,' he said, so I put the word into the sat nav and we drove on. He asked for some music and I played Bach's chorale cantatas, which I knew he loved. We bathed in the voices and in the music. Surely there is such a thing as sacred music, as opposed to music which is sacred? And the cantata brings you to that place. As soon as you hear that opening chord you are transported heavenwards, or at least upwards. Is there any culture whose heaven is downwards, in the bowels of the earth, where fire reigns rather than air?

'Do you have any pipe music on that thing?' Grampa asked. I touched the iPod, and Donald MacPherson showed up on the screen playing 'The Lament for the Children', that other music which makes you raise your head and defy death. Music which acknowledges death before it stamps on it. For without confession there is no resurrection.

'When were you last there?' I asked Grampa. 'In Ambleside?'

'Oh. I don't know. Let's see now. Fifty? Sixty? Maybe seventy years?

'That's a long day, sure enough,' I said.

He laughed.

'When you get to my age, son, it's not that long. Just a morning. Minutes really.'

The Temperance Hotel where he'd met Rachel was no more. In its place was a Premier Inn. We stopped and parked anyway and had coffee in a café down a cobbled alleyway. Home-made scones and jam. I idly wondered whether the waitress's name was Rachel. So I asked her. Not directly of course.

'Where are you from?' I asked.

'Liverpool,' she said.

'Ah,' I said.

Or maybe, 'Oh.'

'This is my Grampa,' I added. 'Magnus. He met a girl – my Granma – here many years ago.'

It was her turn to say 'Oh.'

'Lovely to meet you,' she added to Grampa, putting her hand out. 'My name's Zoe.'

We left it at that.

We drove on and stayed at Windermere for the night. And Grampa began to talk. Really talk. Bits of it were all jumbled up and now and again he veered from one topic to the next, but who doesn't live in a maze, working at clues, sorting out scattered jigsaws? And how come one bit is always missing at the end when you've spent weeks putting that enormous pale blue sky together?

And there was nothing maudlin or elegiac about his speech. Just a kind of running account, piecing things together like beads on an endless length of string. Unlike a rosary which is circular and confined.

'I loved this area,' he said. 'Ambleside, Windermere, Keswick – the whole Lake District. It became an alternative Highlands to me. Softer. More civilised.' He chuckled. 'Nearer hills and nearer rivers. You see, Gav, rivers run. Of course I'm stating the obvious, but the first time I ever saw a river I remember simply thinking: it runs. Moves and shifts and alters, unlike the mountains and the hills and the moors, which were there forever, still and solid and immovable. Water flows across borders, and even if other countries then give the river a different name, that doesn't matter. Our river was called *Abhainn Bheag* and though it became *Abhainn Mhòr* elsewhere, that's what it still is and always will be.'

'Forever and ever. Amen.'

He wasn't just talking about physical things. We both knew that. Or of things long ago. Our need to find metaphors, to put into pictures that for which we have no words, or for which words are inadequate. Those three magic words, 'I love you.'

We stumble into words as much as we stumble into anything else. There were thousands of things I'd never told anybody. I once begged on the streets for charity, and the only person who stopped to give me money was Dick Van Dyke.

'Chim, chiminey, Chim, chiminey, Chim, chim, cher-ee' he sang as he skipped down the street.

I was in love with a girl at school but never told her. She was in the same year as me, but not always in the same class because we'd chosen some different subjects. These periods of her absence were agony. Art was best, for we'd get the chance to stand next to each other at our easels and were officially allowed to talk and critique each other's work. I always praised hers. If I had my time again I would have praised her, not her work. I would be endlessly sending notes across the desks saying 'I love you'. I would have told her, face to face, looking deep into the Atlantic of her blue-grey eyes. She was called Lauren. We could have been Bogart and Bacall and run away to China to live happily ever after behind the city walls.

We stayed up late. In the empty snug at the back of the bar where Grampa sipped from a single glass of Pale Ale all night and I drank whisky. He talked about Lord and Lady Berkshire and how good and kind they'd been to himself and Rachel and how the old days, as he put it, were different because class was accepted.

'Except for the French Revolution and the Bolshevik Revolution and Red Clydeside and Joe Hill and all the rest,' I wanted to say, but kept quiet because I knew fine what he meant: that rebellion was always the exception rather than the rule. Who was I to talk anyway, whose only work had been to screw the thousands of folk who were foolish enough to believe in stockbrokers like myself high on ecstasy? Which was no exception at all, but the most shameful act of capitalist class complicity you could imagine.

I was desperate to ask him about Dad. What he'd been like as a child. If Dad had ever told me, I'd forgotten. I wanted to remember things at their best, when everything seemed as God intended. My interest was in fathoming how things came to be. Why everything was so fucked up. For nothing comes from nothing.

'Your dad was... taken from us,' Grampa said. 'Maybe that's the way to put it? Education made our children strangers to us. Though it's easy to blame someone else, or something else, for that. School, or Lord Berkshire himself, who insisted on us sending him there... but where do you stop? We blamed ourselves.'

He sipped his ale.

'For we all took decisions, and after a while we just thought it best to go along with things and not question anything. And he and Miriam came and went and came and went, and next thing they were all grown up and gone and Rachel and I just got on with our lives. It's not, after all, as if they did anything terrible. Or even wrong. It was just that... we never really knew each other. Properly, I mean. We became sort of... stitched-up. Stuck, like the zip in an old pair of trousers.'

And he laughed. When Grampa laughed, he became a child.

'Bet you had freckles,' I said to him, and he smiled again and said, 'I did. Everyone had freckles in those days. Being outside all the time in the sun and wind. You never see freckles nowadays. Do you think that's why the world's going to rack and ruin, Gav?'

I loved him then more than I ever loved anything else before or since. The certainty he gave me that a child running in the wind was worth more than all the stocks on Wall Street.

Grampa loved tea, and we shared three pots at breakfast. He preferred China tea made in a ceramic pot, and when breakfasting at home always insisted on the Yunnan variety, though in the evening he preferred green or Chun Mee tea. He loved the whole process of tea-making. Slowly boiling the kettle on the hob. Warming the teapot. Dropping the leaves in, mixing varieties when the fancy took him. Making sure the pot sat brewing for five minutes before any tea was poured, through the small silver sieve that Rachel had bought from old Jowles all these years before. Here in the Windermere Hotel we had no such choice or procedure. Earl Grey sufficed.

'As long as it's loose, not in bags,' he whispered to the waitress, then turned to me.

'At the Temperance Hotel where I met Rachel they served wonderful tea. Black and boiled in those days. Everything charred. The kind of tea that saved the working classes from the evils of strong drink, Gav. Always remember that! And what do we get nowadays? A crushed tea-bag flung into a cup and boiled water thrown over it! As if time was running short, or something.'

The smile was in his eyes.

We drove north again after breakfast. We travelled in silence, for Grampa dozed so I kept the radio off. Though silence is such an imperfect word. I could hear his breathing, light and steady. This old man slumbering beside me, my Grampa, a freckled child running barefoot through the heather.

'I love you, Grampa,' I said to him, knowing that he wouldn't hear me, for he'd be embarrassed.

And I? Who has never run barefoot through any heather, yet know how beautiful it is to feel the earth beneath my feet, without the barrier of leather. I remembered as a child walking barefoot through Central Park. The best was in the early morning in spring when the dew was still wet and you left impressive prints. Coney Island sand was the same. Heel first, then sole and five toes. But heather would be rough and would take a bit of getting used to.

'What was it like?' I asked him when he woke.

'Sore. Of course, we'd pretend it wasn't hurting. You didn't want the other boys to think you were a sissy. But you got used to it very quickly. You could then walk through fire if necessary. Then you softened up every winter when we were allowed shoes. But springtime always came round.'

'I miss her, Gav.'

Silence.

'My heart has gone. Even if I were to live now for another thousand years, I'll never see her again.'

Except that she was all around on this cloudless day as we drove up by Loch Lomond. Grampa was fully awake and singing. *By yon bonny banks, and by yon bonny braes*, a deep baritone voice. He laughed.

'You should see here on a normal day,' he said. 'Wind and rain and howling gale. Nothing bonny about it at all.'

We stopped in a lay-by. Grampa lit his pipe and I took a bonny photo of him puffing away. We sat on a wooden bench looking out at the water. Ducks waited for bread which we didn't have.

Then Grampa surprised me by suddenly asking, 'Gav, do you believe in God?'

'I dunno. Depends what you mean by God.'

'What kind of answer is that?' he said. 'None. When you get to my age the evidence is overwhelming. Every breath's a miracle, and the most innocent... the most childlike solution is best. I want to see my people again. I look forward to fishing with Augustine and Aquinas. We will talk about precision engineering. About exactitudes. How nothing can diverge from its destiny. If you cast a rod, a fish will be on the end of it. Every note in a symphony must fulfil its destiny. Order, not chaos, Gav.'

'Well...' I began, but knew that the words I was forming were abstractions which he'd despise – not because of belief or unbelief but because of their verbosity. Things about deism and existentialism and the relationship between reason and faith and science and religion, which would sound like so many evasions and justifications to him. It just goes to show how little you know anyone, for he said, 'You should read Descartes, Gav. He's kinder than Dante.'

Descartes? I thought.

'Really, Grampa?'

'He said lots of interesting things.'

I hedged. 'He sure did.'

'About the past and future, for example,' said Grampa. 'That the past only matters if it's a void. But if you fill it with the present, it ceases to exist as a past.'

'Meaning?'

He looked at me with some surprise, as if I were a child. He smiled and ruffled my hair.

'My dear Gav,' he said. 'My dear, dear Gav.'

I felt some tears coming, and resisted.

'Don't Gav. Let them roll. Be generous to yourself, so that you can be generous to others.'

He put his arm round me as I cried.

Afterwards, we sat in silence for a while.

'It's the eternal now, isn't it, Magnus?'

We were both surprised. I don't know why I used his first name that solitary time. Maybe I was asking for Granma.

'It is. Always. Like that loch in front of you, lapping backwards and forwards, backwards and forwards.'

He scruffled inside his jacket and brought out a yellow piece of paper on which was written: *'Above all else we should impress on our memory as an infallible rule that what God has revealed to us is incomparably more certain than anything else.' (R.D.)*

'Pah!' I thought. 'Pre-Newtonian.'

'You know very well that science has happened since, Grampa,' I said. 'Come on, let's go.'

I wasn't going to argue with an old man about something I wasn't even convinced of myself. For after solid wax melts and becomes liquid, is it not still wax? And even if I was convinced, that still didn't make it true. Folk are convinced of all kinds of astonishing things, from fascism to UFOs.

'Grampa – if I'd been born two hundred years ago I too would have believed in fairies.'

'No you wouldn't. You're too fearful. Metaphysics takes faith.'

It was the only conversation of its kind I ever had with him, for once we were back in the car, he fell asleep again and when he woke sometime later as we drove through Glen Dochart he glanced out the window and said something I didn't understand.

'What was that, Grampa?'

It was the first time I'd ever him heard speak his native language. Gaelic. I presumed instantly that's what it was. I don't think I'd even heard him refer to it, ever, but what else could it be now that we were here, back in his native Scotland? So I asked him.

'That Gaelic, Grampa?'

'I'm afraid so,' he said. 'The language of the peasants. I was so ashamed of it.'

'Go on.'

And he spoke and spoke in this tongue that sounded like water pouring over rocks. Like scotch on the rocks if you like. I didn't really listen. To the words, I mean, for I wouldn't understand any anyway. But the sound was pleasant enough, though drowsy. I was glad for Grampa, though, who seemed to be entering that reckless place of freedom where I'd been myself when under the influence of ecstasy. Out of your head. A place where you didn't give a damn about any external world, for all that mattered was the sound of your own voice. That sound which, despite everything, confirmed that you were alive.

'Are you hungry?' I asked.

'No,' he said. 'I'm fine. We can eat later.'

Grampa spoke on like pastures green.

'That hill,' he said, in his second language, 'is changed by my looking at it. In Gaelic, it's called Beinn Dòbhrain. It used to be covered in blaeberries and cowberries and garlic and cotton sedge. It's now denuded, as bare as death. In *ictu oculi*. It died of solitude.'

Emma, I will die of solitude. Speak to me, for I'm dying to hear your voice. Things turn to ashes when silence burns up the future. I have never really spoken to you. Never shared these things. I have never listened to you. And never really heard your voice. I am beginning to believe that all our voices echo the particular pulses of our hearts.

Grampa sang as we crossed Rannoch Moor and down into Glencoe. The Ave Maria at first, with its *hora mortis, mortis nostrae* for his slaughtered people long gone, and then a psalm so that we could lift our eyes unto the hills. Which was easy, given their beauty. Buachaille Èite Mhòr soaring above us in all her majesty and glory. Unlike New York this landscape was horizontal: you could see across the moors and lochs towards somewhere else.

We stayed in Fort Augustus that evening. Grampa went to bed and since my phone had no signal I walked round to the village shop to buy a newspaper. Lord only knows when I last read a newspaper in print. I only ever read them online, and even then tend just to scan the headlines. The most viewed. The most shared. The most commented. I am of the ten-second generation. Who on earth can be arsed reading all that stuff when you can gather it into your brain at a glance? Justin Bieber arrested. The FTSE 100 Index closes at 72.7 points down. Real Madrid triumph in Champions

League. What more could anyone want or need? So minus my iPhone I bought a paper. In fact I bought a few – *The Times*, *The Guardian*, *The Telegraph* and the local paper, The *Press and Journal*. Partially to have something to pass the time and partially to get an idea of what was going on. Even though most of the things that were going on wouldn't be in the press.

I went back to my room and lay on my back on the bed and read. I'd almost forgotten what astonishing things newspapers were – that old-fashioned mixture of photographs and print, news and gossip and adverts. And the always surprising things to be found in the for sale, wanted, births, marriages and death announcement columns. These were always the best things in a newspaper. I was very moved by this one: Mrs Katherine Lockhart. Died on 12th May aged ninety-two, peacefully, in her sleep. Widow of Fl. Lt. A.R.J. Lockhart R.A.F.V.R. Killed in action on September 18th 1944.

How gorgeous life really was. Full of all kinds of meaning for those who believed. And the letters:

Dear Sir, Spring must finally have arrived. I heard my first lawnmower this morning.
Yours sincerely, Dorothy Wellbank, Somerset.

It passed the evening.

The next morning we drove up Loch Ness on the way to Inverness. Grampa was right. The past is a fiction. We saw no monster, though we stopped by the loch and stood and looked for a while, then went on a lovely boat cruise and took photographs along with all the other tourists. We needed to capture what was in front of us because it would soon be gone. We captured the future, for even now I can touch a screen and the grey digital loch continues to appear. I think we were all secretly glad that we didn't see the monster. It belonged to the twentieth century.

I thought about one of Grampa's notes. That by 'vacuum' we do not mean a place or space in which there is absolutely nothing, but only a place in which there are none of these things which we expected to find. And what did we expect to find there? Nessie? Or just grey dull water which became electric blue when the sun burst through the clouds just there above Castle Urquhart? Instantly magical.

Imagine seeing a ball of fire rising in the east every morning and descending into the sea every evening. Would we not be astonished, as John Donne preached? A young woman stood by the loch-side with her child in a sling over her breast. She was pointing to the loch and smiling for the child.

'This is different,' Grampa said as we drove into Inverness. 'All these new houses there. These used to be fields when I was a child.'

Everything used to be fields when we were children.

'And there were no houses there – just cows grazing here in the fields and corn growing over there by the river. That car park used to be an orchard. If you stood on your tiptoes on top of the wall, you could pluck any amount. Lovely sweet red apples. Dangerous though. I fell plenty times, and once broke my ankle.'

He asked me to drive over the bridge and out westwards.

'It's up there,' Grampa said, 'The hospital. Where my brother John was a patient. I was always afraid to go there. The Sanatorium. I'd like to go there now.'

I turned the car up the hill towards the landscaped gardens. The sun was shining on a new building with signs stating Scottish Natural Heritage. Dualchas Nàdar na h-Alba in Gaelic. I took a photo to make sure I got the spelling right.

'There it is,' said Grampa pointing towards a derelict property. Workers with safety helmets were moving about.

'It's a new development,' one young lad told us. 'Private

flats. Wonderful view, eh?'

And indeed it was a wonderful view: looking down on the wooded glen beneath, and the city of Inverness itself spread out towards the horizon.

'Used to be a little town in my day,' Grampa said. 'A village really. Look at it now.'

We walked down towards the old gardens and sat side by side on a bench next to the pond.

'At least the ducks are still here,' Grampa laughed. 'I grew up in one world, and suddenly it's another.'

'He was older than me,' Grampa said. 'Eleven years older. A lifetime when you're a child. When I was seven, he was eighteen and already in the Army. He looked splendid in his uniform. I mind that. I mind that well. The regimental tartan of the Seaforths. Bonny blues and greens with a fine red stripe. I would have died to join him. But off he went. John. My brother John. My half-brother John. They took him up here after the war. And I only visited him once. The corridors were long. The wards were painted white. In our culture, we never said 'I love you' to one another. That was wrong.'

He hesitated.

'You can carry on in Gaelic if you like,' I said to him, and he began again and though I couldn't understand the words I could make out that his sentences were longer. He would rise and fall and rise and fall and pause after several minutes – not because there was a full stop, I sensed, but simply because he ran out of breath.

He was an old man running. Occasionally I would make words out. *Cogadh* was repeated often and the word *agus*, which seemed to link things together. The most prosaic things can seem marvellous.

I'd never seen Grampa cry. Even when Granma died. Perhaps that was still to come, or perhaps this was part of it, or perhaps they had been together for so long that not even physical death was able to separate them by grief. He cried now. Mourned. Wept like a child, and I held him close in just the same way as he'd held me close that time I fell down the gully and cut my head when I was a child when we were out fishing. He washed my wound in the river and put a plaster on it from his fishing bag, and I wished he now had a cut like that so that I could soothe and heal it with running water and a patch.

Afterwards we sat in silence on the bench. The wind was in the trees and enough heat in the sun to make things drowsy. Bees hovered on the nasturtiums and butterflies hovered over the geraniums. If you closed your eyes you could hear other things: a plane somewhere far off, a dog barking, someone shouting. Music leaked from a radio. Reggae, which neither Grampa or I would ever choose to listen to were it not discharging across the skies.

Grampa rested. An old tennis court lay far below us by the edge of the trees where a man and a woman parried the ball backwards and forwards, forehand and backhand. She would hit short and he would hit long. He would fling the ball high in the air when serving and thump it with a thwack; she would rock backwards and forwards on her toes and move quickly to flash it back. The ball hit the net and they both rested. Everything was still and silent.

Perhaps it was possible to be and not to be. For the ball to be served and returned. To be in the air and on the ground.

It was the moment I understood my job in Artificial Intelligence. Working out the arcs and angles of things so that the response to the ball thundering down at you would be perfect for the return. A high forehand required dexterity of feet, and the margins – those forehands or backhands down the lines, or those exquisite lobs just inside the base lines were, of course, where the games were won or lost. For a moment I saw everything as a grid. Little squares and you could step from one to the next. Circles which you could hop.

Here, in the gardens where Grand-uncle John had been healed once upon a time, was a grid to be calculated and fathomed. Not for its own sake, but so that the game could be played more marginally, more beautifully. Beauty lies at the edges. For who of us is not fascinated by those slices from Djokovic which whip down the chalk-lines with only millimetres to spare? The real game is played at the extremities of the court where only the most athletic and gifted players excel. Instinct is everything.

There are margins where knowledge is so acute, the fringes are the only place where what it is to be human can be properly played out. As with the fairies of old who lived on the edges of society and only appeared at twilight, in the margins of the day where unknown destinies lay. Federer and Murray and Nadal and all the rest of them play the game for us.

Here were Alexander MacKenzie's gaps between the commandments. The spaces where life was won. I began to realise that fairy-belief and the internet were one and the same thing: ways of filtering the universe. Making sense of strange things out there which were unfathomable and which could overwhelm you at any moment. So you created tunnels and codes and commands and strategies to enter that alien world, and before you knew it you were a regular visitor to the knoll, delighting in all its sudden joys and dangers. And sometimes you were trapped there forever, by accident or design. Algorithms were the new commandments to be decoded like the fairies.

My dream, born that day on the park bench in Dunain, was of labouring in a field where these possibilities could be examined; where the future could blend with the past; where all the knowledge and wisdom that Grampa and Granma had, and Grand-uncle John and Elizabeth and Calum and all the rest of them, from the Reverend Alexander MacKenzie to Mr Alfred Johnstone, could somehow be harnessed for the good of mankind; where I could feed this language that was hidden inside Grampa into a machine which could then not just analyse or understand or regurgitate or translate it, but transform it into a living tongue.

My concern wasn't really with language but with the wisdom of the ages. It was not just unfair, but immoral that the accumulated lessons of mankind would gradually disappear into so many graves and crematoriums. All their joys and sorrows, all the hard lessons earned, the crimes committed by Johnny the Miller's son and all the rest of them, all the tears shed in hospital beds and on benches in hospital gardens, all the errors made at Sevastopol and all the horrors done at Auschwitz. Dust to dust, ashes to ashes. This was more than Wikipedia, or a collective gathering of facts and information and knowledge, however comprehensive and transnational. Surely we could learn from the mistakes and triumphs of history?

'You won't,' Emma said, months later. 'Because you can't. They're two completely different things. Mathematics is not a reflection of anything. It's not a discovery, only a human invention. A game describing nothing. It's just an endless corridor.'

Grampa woke.

'Let's just stay here for the night, Grampa. You look exhausted. I can put you on a flight tomorrow.'

He was having none of it.

'No. No, Gav. We'll go on north. This is the time. But we can rest up here for a few days. That's no problem.'

We checked into a hotel by the river. Grampa had a front room with a balcony and a view of the water. And he asked for two radios, so that he didn't have to search between Radios 3 and 4.

'Terrible signal,' he said, 'you end up in no man's land.'

So I fixed one radio on 3 and the other on 4, which he could switch on an off as he pleased. 'Shostakovich and *The Archers*,' he said. 'Paradise.'

Grampa could be stubborn as an ox. Once he got an idea into his head it was harder to shift than any mountain. His politics, for instance, were a curious mixture of arch Toryism and socialism and – as with all beliefs – you could never convince him that his ideas were full of contradictions. A belief in meritocracy alongside a deep conviction that the old landed gentry knew best, and that if the running of the country had been left to the squires everyone would have been better off.

'They knew the difference between mutton and lamb,' he'd say, 'whereas those who own land these days wouldn't know the difference between a cow and a sheep since they both have four legs. The only use these people have for land is to sell it to developers for more houses and offices. And who are they anyway? Nameless profiteers. Offshore companies and Russian oligarchs and Arabs. We'll all rue the day when we'll have no more Lord Berkshires. Squires who knew their tenants by name.'

And when I'd argue that all land should be in common ownership anyway and that all Berkshire and his kind had done was to steal it in the first place and feed their own fat stomachs Grampa would look at me with disdain and shake his head.

'You don't know what you're talking about. Once you've farmed the land, tell me about it.'

'If my views are full of contradictions, so be it,' he said. 'The sun often shines when it rains, and I've seen the bravest men in the world cry.'

At heart he didn't believe that anyone had fixed views in the first place.

'See all these things people say? They're just saying them. But they do other things.'

And he'd explain how politicians who waxed lyrical about the rule of law all broke it when they could if it was to their own advantage.

'Look at all those duck ponds.'

'And all those vicars who preach about the sanctity of marriage who are forever jumping in and out of their lovers' beds.'

And the thing is he wasn't accusing any of them of hypocrisy – just of being human.

'For all our beliefs,' he suggested, 'are as flexible as the willow branch. It bends this way and that. Folk only state them to appear solid. Inwardly they are melting all over the place. Even iron melts in the furnace.'

I disagreed with him. Some people did believe what they said. That blacks and gays and women were inferior. That Snow White and the Seven Dwarves are alive and well and living in Trump Towers where there is no global warming.

'But people do believe all kinds of monstrosities,' I said to him. 'You watch television, don't you? Remember that school trip I took once to Paris to see the Louvre and all that?'

'Of course I do. I paid for it.'

'Did I tell you the most astonishing thing I saw there?'

'I don't know. I can't remember.'

'The Resistance Museum.'

'Oh?'

'There were four big screens there. One showed the occupation of Paris in 1940 by the German troops. The only thing I remember is how young they all were. Kids. Just young shaven-headed boys, their veins bulging with belief and certainty. The future was all theirs. Which ended in ruins in a filthy bunker in Berlin.'

'The folly of youth,' Grampa said. 'To think you know anything. The folly of old age too.'

I went up to Tom na h-Iùbhraich. The Hill of the Yew Trees. There, behind the modern cemetery, is the boat-shaped hill where the Fingalian heroes lie on their elbows, waiting for the horn to blow. And beside them lies the prophet Thomas who got his gift from sleeping with the Queen o' the Faeries herself. At one time this hill would have been all silent, before the canal was excavated and the bridges built and the traffic came. For environment is everything. You need to have green verdant mounds. Undisturbed places where you can experience things beyond the sound of traffic and human voices. Where you can hear things. Unexpected jazz or reggae spilling into the air. Sounds and noises which you can't quite fathom, which could be a spider dying or the voice of God. Perhaps no-one lives in isolation now, except the occasional scientist in her lab and the writer in his shed and maybe a lone forester or fisherman, though all of them now have wires in their ears or Mozart in the air as they create. But this silence is something else, where you can hear the beat of your heart, the pulse in your veins, the wind soughing through the trees, the polyglot birds singing in the air. Nature whispers things into existence.

And the light is crucial. Early morning or twilight is good, though moonlight is best. Only then do you see things which you never see at any other time. The veiling of the day illuminates things which are overshadowed by the sun. Gentle things emerge. Notions of the lost age of ploughing. Moths. Owls. Bats. Flimsy things shine and whirr. The sound of a twig snapping in the wind. That little rag flapping in the breeze. A farmer whistling in his field on the way home. The shadow of a rabbit in the moon. The moon as seen on Fifth Avenue. 'No wonder they landed on it, for it was so near,' Elizabeth told me.

'Electricity destroyed the little people,' Grampa said. 'The fairies used to dance in the evening light but they scattered and fled when beams shone on them.'

They were extinguished by the light in the way that silk burns in the flames. Replaced by brighter stars with smarter hokum here on my hand-held console.

'Twilight gave you a chance to prepare for the perils of the night. What happened to twilight?' Calum asked.

Quenched out like a candle by the shock of electricity. Though the smoke from the candle lasted a while before the whispering darkness was slowly silenced. There is no darkness any more. Even in the middle of the night a blue console bleeps somewhere. Folk here at Tomnahurich used to hear ghosts chattering in the night until they were crowded out by keener sounds. For sound and silence are like motion and gravity. Gravity always wins.

'Just look over the other side of town to Culloden Moor,' Ruairidh Bùidseach said to me.

That's where I went that afternoon. Walked the neat footpaths between the graves of the clans. Chisholms. Frasers. MacKenzies. The Memorial Cairn. The Field of the English. The Well of the Dead. The Cumberland Stone. Old Leanach Cottage. Wonderful audio-visuals in the exhibition centre. I went into the café for a coffee. I saw her in the mirror. She was reading a book. She had auburn hair, cropped short, and could have been the future, except her phone rang.

I texted Grampa to make sure he was fine. Of course I am, he texted back. Writing it out in full, the old fool. Not even a lol or a smiley. I caught a bus back to town and walked through the High Street back to the hotel. Bought some fries at McDonalds and while I walked eating them over the bridge I heard a small bell ringing. A man on a bicycle caught up with me and said something.

'You're a visitor,' he then said, 'because I know everyone here, and I go out of my way to introduce strangers to the delights of the capital of the Highlands.'

He jumped off his bike and walked with me over the bridge. Once I'd finished my fries he stretched out his hand

and said, 'I'm Seonaidh Treoncaidh – pleased to meet you.'

'Gav MacDonell,' I told him. 'Good to see you.'

He talked to me all the way back to the hotel, telling me that the Red Shoe Soul Shuffle was the real deal.

'Do you have a card?' he asked.

'No.'

'Email?'

'Sure.'

'It's only dictators who try to change the story,' he said.

Unfortunately I made a mistake and gave him my work email rather than my personal one, though it would have made no difference as I'm certain the company access all my electronic communication anyway. I should have just given him my earthly address.

Some weeks later I received an email from Jo, a new intern at HQ, thanking me for the new feed into the neural network. Under the Subject FW: 'The Northern Red Shoe Soul Shuffle' she wrote: 'Hi Gav. Hope you're well. Delighted to receive this memoir from your fieldwork. It will make Albert ever more human! J'.

'Here's hoping,' I replied.

A long time ago in Elgin, Morayshire – after Kennedy got shot and about the 'Rubber Soul' beat period – there lived a dance promoter called Albert Bonici who had a firm of ferocious but gentlemanly bouncers, a connect to the pop charts and substantial control over all the dance halls and 'variety!' events from Dundee in the south, to Wick and Thurso in the north.

This geezer-impresario had a little cafe in Park St, Elgin and the back of it was the Two Red Shoes Ballroom. Albert was known to enjoy Dolly Mixtures, American cars, and chicken legs as he negotiated with a string of visiting musicians fascinatingly from London, Texas, Leeds Sheffield and Manchester, as the music of Detroit blasted from the Juke Box in the background.

Mrs McBean's guest house was round the corner which was visited by many 'stars' including The Beatles, Roy Orbison, a very young Jimmy Page, The Hollies and Wayne Fontana & The Mindbenders.

A young Alan Mair (bass player) now 'Only One' and Jeff Allen (drums) now 'Mick Taylor' played in the 'Beat stalkers' and remember Albert's Chevrolet overturned on account of 'A Headless Badger' on the road to Rothes one dark night with the radio still playing 'Heat wave!' by Martha And The Vandellas!

Mrs McBean should not be confused with BABY FACE Beenz McBean, then bass player with fabulous Inverness combo, The Flock!

So here's the story – soulful, sad but true – about some fascinating faeries (people) I once knew, got 'nowhere to run!'. Later there was Liverpool Tommy and the other Swansea Pete and a Hidden place of Northern Archaeology, the Red Shoes Soul Shuffle.

Whether it was the first night I heard Johnny & The Copycats doing 'It's Alright' by Curtis Mayfield or the Nashville Teens doing 'Zip-a-Dee-Doo-Dah' in Craigellachie Town Hall... Those were the days when wearing 'Beatle Boots' could have got you beaten up. I and other musicians found solace in the 45s of Garnett Mims, Lee Dorsey – not to mention The Supremes – and The Four Tops. For us, the USA and the cities of Detroit and New York were millions and trillions of light years away. It was 1965 in the far north-east of Scotland – there wasn't even a motorway to Edinburgh then!

Intellectually opposed to the rule of thumb as a junior reporter with the Inverness Courier, the call of the wild took me away from my calculations for the lightening-up times and tides. I became more and more erratic as our music certainly got the girls excited. Some of the 45's we got in discarded sections of record stores cost as little as 20 pence (1 shilling sixpence). It was still a lot! – My wages were only about 13–14 quid!

At age 15 we created a quartet called Size 4. We won the Buckle Beat Contest, making sure one of the judges – Nigel 'Benson Beat' Benson – got drunk with us in our 15cwt Commer van on the way there. The prize was eight gigs from Albert and £40 guineas! A fortune in today's money. And we became part of the Northern Red Shoe Soul

Shuffle 'Vinyl North!' The 'Shuffle' involved travelling to the venue for 7.30pm, getting started for 9pm, break for tea at 11pm, back to work till 1am. Sometimes 2am! It was exhausting but the bouncers had your money and frequently told us to 'Screw it Doon! – Doon!'

Some of the best gigs were Sunday night at RNAS Lossiemouth and RAF Kinloss where the GIs and pilots were black dudes who seemed to like our White Boy Soul! – this would have been about 1966! – I remember The Impression's 'Big 16' album from then – I thought I'd died and gone to heaven when we 'heard it' – so then we played it! – Buckie lads, The Copycats – did great covers, and the incredible Pathfinders from Glasgow (who I'd later join as White Trash and Cody), did credible versions of 'Going to a Go Go!' and 'Sweet Talking' Guy'.

You needed many, many skills to survive the Shuffle – and when bands from Manchester and London came up we were very respectful and generous with each other. What did the Nashville Teens and The Pretty Things feel like in that Commer Van travelling through the snow'? Time travellers?

Some bird from Lossiemouth asked us to play 'Bend It!' one night, we told her to fuck off! We were warriors and cosmic spirits! My My Ma Ma MO town Fanatics! Musical intellectualists? The Who of the North! I used to smash an old VOX guitar up for sensational effect! The crowd loved it! – the crowd were Mods!

Inverness is such a strange! Place? The Beatles changed their name from 'Bee–' to 'Bea–' here, Gene Vincent played at the Northern Meeting Rooms in 1961, when I was 12. The queue went round the corner to Woolworths!

Time and Moment!

The Ghurkhas

It's worth noting here that my late father's imaginary vodka-induced wars were 'military and domestic!' – he was – particularly! Domestic with me! Do something! he'd say! What, dad?!"

He had an intense dislike of 'The Indian!' the 'Indian!' was ranted about all night sometimes! ... so up his own arse with his 'the Indian!'

Binges! It seemed to keep him alive a good... 'the Indian!' binge was stronger than Smirnoff!

Sikh! West Indian! Bengali! Native! He didn't care! They were coming to Dalneigh to get US!

Yet he started Crying Uncontrollably when the word 'Ghurkha!' was mentioned... 'Ghurkha! Ghurkha!' This made me very uneasy! So I took 3 blue valium instead of 1. Then a couple of mandrax – to help me over the shock of it all!

I'd been jamming with Sam Gopal a cosmic phschikdelic Sikh who I'd had an audition with in London courtesy of Lemmie the Rocking Vicar who gave me Hitler's methedrine! This made my father very very uneasy and ME very HIGH BABY! The Hitler's methedrine had me pinned to the roof for days! I thought I was choking to death when I came down! It was terrible! Between Hitler's methedrine and 'The Indian!' There was no escape! Except the great escape.

I was most relieved when I was diagnosed with a nervous breakdown!

Nice little nurse! Three meals a day! 60 mgs valium, 2 mandrax at night! These were the days you'd get a script for mandrax and valium for a sore back!

The British wanted rhythm... they always wanted rhythm! someone to march in step! So we could remember the 'fallen?' who were probably like the 'Indian!'

He never liked Germans either!

Father was like a 50s Sub Post Mistress! The type of frustrated Sub-postmistress who had a Bun in her hair and a Rage in her stomach!

Ghurkhas! Ghurkhas! I nearly vomited with the sincerity! How could you!' he wailed!

'The Indian! 'The Ghurkhas!'

'The Fallen!'

In fact he was nothing more than a Sub Post RACIST!

At least him and grand3ad were kind enough to take me to Ward 11 – the 'blue' room – Inverness District Asylum that sad day in 1969 I had my 'Break-down!'

Voila Cie Bonne!

Jeep Solid.

I smile, knowing that the original Albert would have loved the memoir.

Grampa was looking rested and relaxed when I got back from Culloden. We went for a meal and then for a stroll down by the river. Tomorrow we would head further north. It was a dark starry night. By which I mean that as Grampa and I walked over the wooden rickety bridge to the hotel we could see the stars twinkling in the dark sky. They looked tiny, like candles, even though we knew each twinkle was larger than the whole earth. Grampa and I looked up and we both smiled, and held hands as we walked slowly over the shaking bridge.

14

WE CONTINUED TO travel north.

Cold weather came from the north.

'When the wind is lost, seek it from the south,' said Grampa. 'And do you know how to curse someone? Wind without direction to you. Bad tidings for fishermen, Gav.'

I asked him about the wind as we drove north.

'The stuff about it is almost endless,' he said. 'South wind, heat and plenty. West wind, fish and milk. North wind, cold and tempest. East wind, fruit on branches. And it all depended on which direction the wind was coming from on the last night of the year – wind from the spring star; heat from the summer star; water from the autumn star; frost from the winter star.'

You learned everything about what sustained you and made it pretty with sounds.

'Weather is just weather. Rain, snow, sun, hail, wind. We need them all. Just that people have gone soft. Make such a fuss over it, with their brollies and shelters. They're all beautiful in their season. Except we've destroyed the seasons with our greed.'

Fire, Air, Water, Earth: the four elements. As we drove north, I asked him about them. What had he heard about them when growing up? He laughed.

'Nothing,' he said. 'I heard nothing. I just saw. Felt.'

'What did you see then?'

'Oh – the power of fire. Heat and food. The power of the sea.'

'All power then?'

'Aye. Till we tamed them.'

'And have we? Tamed the elements?'

He laughed again.

'Well just look out the window.'

I did. Hundreds of windmills adorned the hillsides.

'And the other side.'

I glanced to my right, down towards the sea. Five tankers moving south.

'After all,' he said, 'this car wouldn't move without fuel.'

'Do you know where they stayed?' I asked.

'Of course I know where they stayed!'

'How?'

'I was taken there. By my mother. It's on the other side of this hill. We'll need to park the car by the old church at the bottom of the hill, then walk the rest of the way up by the river. There's a path, but only for horse and cart. And where will you find these nowadays, except at posh weddings and funerals? The poor horses.'

The path led us through a green glen with low hills caressing each other on both sides. It was like walking through an old postcard. A stag, startled by our presence, leapt out of the bracken ahead and raced up the hill. Skylarks were singing high overhead. The streams were running, flies buzzed about our ears, I could hear Grampa breathing steadily a yard ahead of me. Three trees grew by the river. A birch, a hazel, a rowan.

Grampa paused, pointing into the sky.

'See!'

I couldn't see anything.

'There. Just above the cliffs.'

All was blue sky to me.

'An eagle!' Grampa said.

I cupped my eyes and caught sight of the great bird hovering high overhead.

'As well it's not lambing time, Gav. Though we all need food to survive.'

We walked on, with the smaller birds singing in our ears. Rabbits ran across the lower parts of the slope. Something stirred in the thick bracken and a roe deer stood, unafraid. Everything made a sound. The grass squeaked as we stood on it. Stones clacked as we stepped on them. Bees buzzed in the clover.

'Imagine it in the dark,' Grampa said as we sat down, 'on a winter's night with the wind howling. Everything grows bigger then. Every gust of wind brings a bòcan.'

'A bòcan?'

'A ghost, panting in the dark.'

'And during the day? On a beautiful summer's day like today?'

'Listen,' Grampa said.

And I listened, to the soft wind blowing across the stream. To the curlews crying overhead.

'Gav, the thing is – if you've no one else to talk to, you talk to the birds. To anything that will listen to you. And do you know the miraculous thing? They talk back to you. Even the rocks. See the marks on that stone? That might be your future. Three vertical lines and all will be well. Beware the horizontal lines though.'

We stopped and sat down by the river. I took my walking boots off and dipped my feet into the water. It was ice-cold. I stood on something gritty, bent down and picked up a blue shell. It was whorled and serrated and rough in my hand. Seven layers to it, ground together across time. I'd read that if you put a conch-shell to your ear you could hear the ocean. I listened and heard my heart and all of nature singing within the cavity of the shell.

I lay back in the grass and closed my eyes and listened to Grampa.

'I'm going to tell you my favourite story. This glen is

called Gleann na Beatha in Gaelic. Beatha means life. As in *uisge-beatha*, the water of life, which is whisky. They say that Adam and Eve lived here first. But if they had, they wouldn't be called Adam and Eve but Adhamh and Eubha. Or maybe Naoise and Deirdre. I don't know. Sometimes my mind gets all mixed up.

'This glen was a garden then, with trees of every sort and fruit growing on every tree. Apples, pears, oranges, lemons and hazelnuts and the older people used to say that on a warm spring day you could smell the orange blossom as far away as Inverness itself. This is where I come from. You too, Gav.' They were an old man's words. Forever going on about paradise lost. The eternal quest to regain his childhood.

After a while he got up.

'It's a terrible thing to be poor,' he said as we walked through the scree. 'Never believe the delusion. That to be poor is to be virtuous and to be rich is to be evil. There are poor bastards and rich bastards and rich saints and poor saints. It's what you do with what you have. Columba was a king and Francis a pauper.'

The old church was roofless. Grampa led the way, round the outside of the crumbling old cemetery stone walls. Uphill for a bit, then the path levelled as it crossed the moor below other ruins.

'That's where the mill was,' he said. 'The miller was always called Johnny.'

We followed the river inland, through heather and moss until we came to some old buildings in the shelter of the rocks.

'This is where the laird stored his fleeces,' Grampa said. 'The laird's mansion itself is in ruins over by the loch.'

The garden fountains with their bird-baths were cracked and broken and a chipped whisky decanter sparkled in the grass. We stood in the empty doorways and fallen halls and looked through the broken window frames where MacPherson had stood one hundred and fifty years earlier absorbed by the lady's long white fingers tinkling the piano keys. She always held the last note long and sustained, her fingers pressing down slowly as hard as they could.

We walked over small green hillocks.

'Fairy mounds,' Grampa said. 'The computers of their day. I suppose we all live inside a *sìthein* of one sort or another. Bankers, politicians, the media…'

We sat in the shade of an old stone dyke and shared tea and sandwiches from my rucksack.

'Tired?' I asked Grampa, but he shook his head and stood up.

'No. Not yet.'

We walked on, past other roofless bothies.

'Shielings,' Grampa explained. 'They used to take the animals up here for the summer pasture.'

He smelt the air.

'No cattle. The fragrance has gone.'

Something glinted in the sun over by the stream. I walked over and found a small oval mirror which you could hold in the palm of your hand. I brushed the dust and dirt away. A delicate carving of grapes on a vine ran round the edge. As I held it, it caught the sun which sprayed into a thousand splinters and I had that childish moment when I realised I could send its rays in every direction. I could set fire to the grass. I raised it up into the air and could see my tiny grandfather far off, lighting his pipe. I put the mirror in my pocket, then put it back where I found it. It wasn't mine to take.

I glanced at my watch. Midday. Grampa stopped and sat down on a stone. He plucked a blade of grass.

'You could travel to the other side of the world on a wisp of straw,' he said. 'Pop a bonnet on your head and shout "London" and you'd be there. It worked the other way round too. Murchadh Mòr from Kintail was held prisoner in the Tower. He took off his cap, shouted "Hurrah for Kintail", and there he was, back home.'

The magic of words.

'Are you returning home after this?' he asked.

I wanted to say 'I am home', but didn't.

'Yes,' I said. 'I'm going to see Emma.'

15

GRAMPA LIVED ANOTHER year. Though it was a quick decline in the end, the way primroses suddenly wilt, or the way in which the sun suddenly sets at the end of a long summer's day on the beach. Meantime you continue to sit there with the remains of the barbecue fire while the sea turns orange, then red, and softens and becomes a huge grey expanse fading to the horizon.

I miss his voice terribly.

'Ah!' he'd say. 'Ah!' breathing out the promise of a revelation. He told me a story about a place called The Parish of Nowhere. It was about a foreign girl who worked as a cook in a big house, but it was really just his way of telling me that he loved me. Miracles happened in the story: a little wizened old card-playing man came along, and if you beat him at cards he'd give you your wish. And if you closed your eyes and wished a thing, the thing was there when you opened them. And the old man gave this boy a ball and if he rolled the ball along the road in front of him the ball would lead him over rivers and mountains and oceans and give him the power to leap high over insurmountable walls to where his lover was kept captive. And they finally met and married and escaped wrathful parents and had a huge feast and lived happily ever after.

How else do you tell someone that you love them except by giving them your best story or singing them your best song?

Latterly his memory failed. He'd rise and make his own

breakfast and then walk for a while in the gardens. I set a wicker chair for him down by the orchard and he spent hours sitting safely in the shade.

He might cut some roses and then take them inside, fill a vase with water and place them in the conservatory. He would read *The Times*, which continued to be delivered to the house as it had been for the previous fifty years.

Nothing and everything had changed. I'd watch him reading the articles one by one, carefully, as if each word mattered. I loved the way his lips moved slightly as he read the words. Not because he wasn't completely literate, but because he remembered his mother reading that way. Words were like sweets to him, to be sucked and savoured, rather than chewed and swallowed. He'd frown or smile and laugh, put the paper down and stretch out his legs and have a snooze. The sun through the blinds washed him with light, but he seemed most at peace when it rained and he'd lie there oblivious to the great noise rattling against the roof and windows. He was already resting in God.

That day, after he told me the story, we walked down into the glen.

'There were two places,' Grampa said. 'The original village and the new settlement.'

We followed the sheep tracks and waded across a few burns and began to climb the moor. Grampa led, taking us round the edge, so that the walk was gentle enough. At the top he led me down the scree towards the cliffs on the far side. Knee-high bracken and silence. A few stones half-hidden in the grass.

'This is where the MacDonalds were. George and June.'

We walked towards a fuller ruin.

'The MacInnesses.'

And over in the shelter of the old temple mound we stood in the nettles where Calum and Elizabeth had lived, once upon a time. We walked the old drove road to the other settlement where Grampa's mother and father had been brought up. Andrew and Anna MacDonell. The ruins here were more substantial. Gable-ends and walls could still be seen and touched.

The lives led, the fires lit, the babies nursed, the stories told. The voices of those silenced by their time.

'It's freezing outside.'

'How's the bairn?'

'Are you feeling any better today.'

'Aye aye.'

'I'll need to kill the cow tomorrow.'

'He's just a wiffer-waffer o' a man.'

He too only knew scraps, fragments of the story.

'I just know that these were the settlements, and that these were the houses,' he said. 'She took me here once, when I was young. Much younger than you are now, Gav. So I don't really recall much, except the buildings themselves. They were in much better shape those days, most of them inhabited. The MacMillans over there. The MacIsaacs next to them. Old Geordie Cowan. Isabel Gowdie. The MacTavishes. Let's go home.'

He took me – whether deliberately or by accident – via the old manse where the Reverend Alexander MacKenzie had lived. Where, sometime later, I found his notes, perfectly preserved in a wooden box in the byre.

I always made coffee for him and one morning as I set down the tray he said, 'Gav, sit here beside me. Get yourself a cup too.'

Beethoven's Opus 133 was on the radio.

'Never trust a man in tartan trousers,' Grampa said to me. 'Too ostentatious. The only ones to trust are those who are unsure of anything. I'm leaving you this house and everything in it. But live your own life, not mine. Take care of it all.'

Afterwards, I understood what he meant.

In those last days, Grampa gave me traces, like the watermarks on old letters. I spent time with him. Sat beside him and listened to him and talked with him. He wanted me there. For whenever I'd move to go away he'd say, 'Stay, Gav, just stay for another wee while.'

And I did, and began to use the word 'wee' myself when I saw any small thing.

And he might ask, 'What's doing, Gav?'

And I might say, 'Och, nothing much Grampa,' and he'd smile.

Or I might say, 'I've just come back from the cricket, Grampa.'

And he'd ask what the score was, and because it didn't matter, I'd say, 'The West Indies were bowled out for 240 and England are already 150 for 1.' And he'd ask what the best shot was and I'd say the bowling was better, and that Leadbetter had taken five wickets in two overs just after tea and he'd say, 'There are times, Gavin, when no fact should be neglected as insignificant. Did I ever tell you about the time Lord Berkshire took me to see Don Bradman play at Headingly. He scored 212 that day. He was magnificent. And afterwards we had ice-creams, I remember that. Lord Berkshire and I sat in the car eating the ice-creams while Fred drove us south. Did you know Fred?'

'No,' I said, 'No – I didn't know Fred.' And he would tell me who Fred was.

And his mother would enter the conversation, and his half-brother John, and what mattered was the softness of his voice and his laughter as he told some disjointed story from a fragmented memory. What really mattered is that all these people were actually there as he talked about them. He didn't just talk about them, he talked with them and to them.

'Mother,' he'd say, 'do you think I could get a glass of

water?' And I would at that moment go and fetch him a glass of water and he'd take it and thank me and drink it and relax and then begin some other thread about a horse, or the finest field of turnips that he'd ever planted... or would, when Rachel came back from the shops.

'Who was that lady we met on the bus earlier?' he would ask. 'She was so kind, she spoke so well.'

And I'd be tempted to say, 'I don't know.' But I learned to say, 'I'm not sure. Did you know her?'

And of course he did, she was a retired teacher who lived up the hill. His comments about people were always decorous and respectful. 'And believe in Jesus,' he said to me. 'It's all that really matters.'

Dad and Aunt Miriam came home for the funeral. We buried Grampa beside Rachel at St Alban's, where hawthorn and rowan trees adorn the churchyard. Two rowan trees are intertwined and the hawthorn branches embrace in pairs. It is the communion of the saints. I go to High Mass there every Sunday to worship God.

I stayed on at Grampa and Granma's house for a good while. The only proviso in the will was that I would catalogue and archive the gardening and other estate materials he had gathered over the previous sixty years. It was a delight to do so.

I began with the garden notebooks, which were filled with grace. Cuttings of the loveliest species of plants carefully marked and labelled in all the greenhouses, with exquisite hand-written notes about their scientific and aesthetic properties. The loveliest things were Grampa's numerous side notes, which revealed a mind more interested in connections than in classifications. Beside Lonicera, for example, he wrote 'Leid is a temporary fireplace on which to set a pot'; and beside Galanthus, 'Every being quietens and stiffens when a foreboding of evil reaches him.'

What really interested my grandfather was how things

grow. Why these yellow petals are yellow, not green or brown. Working with hybrids taught him how fluid and liminal everything is – that just as easily, with a cell movement here and an adjustment there, it could be red or blue or orange or some other colour for which we have no vocabulary. He, like me, was interested in margins. When does a flower placed next to a flower become an arrangement? When does a tree become a wood, a wood a forest?

It was in his notebooks that I picked up a lot of this lore, stuff which signalled alternative ways of interpreting things.

The glow reflected from a buttercup when placed under your chin means that you will get married young.

If you have a hazel-stick in your hand when out walking at night you are in no danger from ghosts.

'When we were little boys', wrote Grampa, 'if we came upon a droning-beetle on the road, we would catch it and say to each other to throw it on high to see how the weather would be the next day, chanting "Droning-beetle, droning-beetle, will tomorrow be fine?" If it came down on its back, next day would be fine. If its back was upwards, next day would be wet.'

Grampa noted where one thing became another: one morning the roses would be bare, that afternoon they'd suddenly bud. One evening the fields would be empty, in the morning little green shoots appeared. He was marking the boundaries between evolution and creation.

He was a deft hand at making scarecrows. Wonderful scary ones. I remember pretending to be a scarecrow. I stood still, then moved an eyelid and a finger, then a hand and a leg, then let out a shriek which scattered all the birds into the air. Once Grampa planted the seeds, the job was to ensure things grew. To weed and water and fertilise, to guard from wind and rain and predators. Life had to be protected.

'Just stand there and flap your arms,' Grampa would say to me as he moved slowly about the fields doing the real work.

He was quite fond of 'X marks the spot'. All the farm maps are crossed with his danger marks. Mostly at the margins, at the edges of the fields where walls could crumble, or a gate could be left open, or where some animal could leap the dyke and trample through the seed.

It was clear from his notes that, despite the fact that he worked for Lord Berkshire, who owned thousands of acres of land, what Grampa really believed in was crop sharing and common ownership. He hated the ancient enclosures as if they'd happened yesterday.

'When every field was open, no-one would steal because they would just be stealing from themselves. Same with houses. The only point of stealing is to get what you don't have. The Garden of Eden had no walls.' For him, the enclosures were a sin. 'You should always be able to walk into someone's garden and take a nap,' he said.

Among his farm notes I came across a cutting from *The Times* about conserving the New Forest against housing developments. In the margin he'd written: 'These trees grew moment by moment across the centuries.'

What Grampa was saying was that Genesis is now. Every moment is the first moment. And nothing is dead, because at any moment you can create it anew. I learned from him that you can't tell someone you love them just the once: you have to tell them all the time.

It was raining heavily the day I left the house. As I was about to turn the key in the lock I realised my mistake. The past mattered more to me than the present. I'd taken enormous time and trouble to get to know Calum and Elizabeth and John and Mary and Anna and Magnus and Rachel, while ignoring the living. Emma.

'You prefer death to life,' I heard her say, 'because the past is safe. You can arrange and order it to your liking. Whereas I'm disorganised, changeable, human. You only love with your mind, not your heart. Like a robot. You've only ever heard the notes, not the music.'

I turned right and walked through the orchard down by the barn. Over the stile and across the meadow where the ponies used to graze. I was heading for Paddock's Hill, where I'd stood all those years ago mapping the compass. I deliberately kept the view hidden as I climbed, seeing only the grass beneath my feet as I ascended.

At the top I paused, closing my eyes. I raised my right hand and pointed. I was right. North. I turned a quarter. The church-steeple was still there, and the bells pealing through the rain. East. Another quarter. The windmill still there, now turning again after being restored. South. And another turn, to where the river ran, past the newly-built homes on either side. West. Music is not imagined but discovered. I stood and sang at the top of my voice to all four quarters of the compass as the rain poured down on England's green and pleasant land.

16

I RENTED GRAMPA and Granma's house out and returned to New York. It was really my house now, though I found that too hard to confess. It was to admit the finality of things: that all those years were gone. A local agency in Oxford dealt with the tenants and collected the rent so that I didn't have to see the property that had meant so much now inhabited by strangers. They were only passing through anyway.

Emma and I rented an apartment in Manhattan. 103rd Street. Later we bought the holiday place in Martha's Vineyard when the patent for the software our company developed for the early mask-bots was sold to the Chinese. It was either that or pay the profit in tax to the government, and who wouldn't choose a beautiful clapperboard house by the sea in those circumstances? It was our weekend escape: Enrique and the scallops, Jamie and the beach-chairs.

Artificial Intelligence was relatively new to all of us, though the most wisdom came from the old eccentrics from the '60s who'd once been hippies, but still nurtured the dream that technology was a friend, not an enemy. The best of them was Joe Hill, one of the original founders of the Santa Fe commune, who had pioneered off-grid living way back then and had developed an elementary form of Wi-Fi long before the term was invented.

In some ways the communications system he pioneered was just a logical extension of the rattling tin can.

'Basically I was inspired by the old comics,' he told me. 'Remember? You'd tie two empty tins together with a string, then one of you would crouch behind a rock while the other called into the tin. The sound was supposed to travel through the tin along the string. But it never did. It travelled through the air. So a bunch of us did airwave experiments. Shouting across the valleys to one another. And you know what? It all had to do with pitch and tone. The extremities worked, but nothing else. Singing was best. If you stood on top of the ridge and sang soprano you could only be heard down at the bottom of the ravine, whereas if you sang contralto it was the other way round – the guy sitting down in the ravine would not hear a sound, but every single note could be heard from the top of the ravine. It was as if high went low and low went high and I figured it was a bit like charging a car battery except in reverse – positive to negative and negative to positive. So from there we developed this inter-valley communication system based purely on pitch travelling through the air.'

He'd laugh. That hearty free and easy laugh of someone who believes that the worse has already happened and things can only get better.

'It meant there was a great demand for the guys and girls who could sing low or high. The sopranos and the contraltos. The countertenors and the basses. And you know what? You'd think the fattest would have the deepest voices, but they didn't. Invariably the thinnest travellers who came to the commune had the lowest voices and the highest voice projector we ever had was Big Bill Buffalo, thirty stone and growing who could sing like an angel at a regular pitch of 2,800 Hertz. They could hear him in California from Mexico.'

It was hard to tell what age Joe Hill was.

'Cannabis gave me eternal youth,' he joked, though he was now strictly teetotal, vegetarian and hadn't smoked a joint for decades.

'It kills you in the end,' he said. 'So you might as well stay clean and forever young.'

He was the lead apostle of transhumanism. Convinced that the emerging machine-being would usher in the millenial kingdom, giving us immortality though a postbiological future. The sort of heretic every young company needs. Someone who literally thought out of the box as a default position. Our young bosses were smart enough to realise that project managers and technicians and accountants and computing experts were essential for the business, but that the creative sparks could be provided by off-the-wall individuals who lived on the margins of orthodox thought. So there was a clear boardroom policy to occasionally balance the normal operative appointments with a wholly unexpected one – someone who had no formal technological or computer-orientated training, but who had crossed the desert or mountains to arrive at our base. All these appointments were under Joe Hill's jurisdiction, and the ones in his camp literally did their work under canvas, without the aid of any technology. All they produced were ideas.

I envied them. I'd been hired by the company basically because of my banking background. They needed someone who could do creative accounting, and once I returned from England I sent them my cv which contained the magic words Oxford, London Stock Exchange and Wall Street. And I was hired. Not merely on the strength of my cv. I hasten to add – the actual job interview itself was also practical. It was held in the gymnasium of a local hotel and once the verbal interview was over, I was asked to exercise on all the different weights and lifting and running machines and then I was given twenty minutes to design, on paper, a prototype robot who could do all the exercises more efficiently that the instructor who had demonstrated the equipment to me. I was so startled by the task that I retreated to some TV images I'd seen and designed a cross between Superwoman and Batman. Afterwards they confessed they gave me the job because it was clear that I couldn't think for myself and would do the simple operative jobs I was supposed to do.

The job was to turn Joe Hill's team ideas into reality. Every first Monday morning of each month we'd be called into his tent to sit cross-legged facing him as he streamed his latest revelations to us. Each of us would then take one of his ideas and try to develop it into some form of working digital reality over the next four weeks.

The ideas were terrific. Taking natural water and turning it into blood plasma for our robots by simply mixing it with sugar and natural juice: 'Folk always like to see what looks like real blood pumping through the veins when being served by a machine.' The same for other bodily functions. My colleague Linda was working on developing sweat glands, John-Pierre on urine and excrement substitutes, while Son-Lee spent all her time working on the complex breath patterns which different activities generated. I envied her greatly, for it was fascinating work, and accompanied her as often as I could on her research expeditions. Down to the docks to record the different breath registers the dockers used as they climbed ladders, descended into the hold, hauled boxes, cursed, swore and laughed. She spent inordinate times in the gym recording the different breath patterns the different genders and ages had as they ran, rowed, pumped weights and so on.

'The important thing,' Joe said to me 'are the faces. Old people want to see features that are familiar. The eyes, nose, ears, mouth – these things are easy. What we need is to fill in the spaces between, etch them with history. With life.'

'I'm not God,' I told him, but he merely said, 'Leave him out of it.'

So I spent time studying faces. My own. Emma's. The sharp contours of her cheeks, the dimple on the left side. The way she tilted her head back a fraction whenever she was anxious. I had a terrific time at the MOMA, where a special exhibition of Da Vinci's drawing were on display at the time. Every line of his was sparkling with life. I spent days and nights travelling the subway studying people's faces, discovering that light and shade made all the difference. A traveller standing on the platform reading a book would suddenly look different once inside the carriage where the artificial light was harsher. I realised that not a single face was fixed. Its life has to do with angle, light, perspective. The time of day or night. Joy or stress, the health or illness they were experiencing.

The design department I worked in was headed up by Hiroaki Nagano who was the best in the business. He balanced wonderful technical skills with a keen social conscience, always emphasising that the face masks we were creating were there to serve and not to rule. I was two years under his stewardship and learned everything there was to learn about machine emotional intelligence. We basically worked on algorithm-driven APIs using facial detection and semantic analysis to develop emotion recognition in our bots. The purpose was to develop highly sophisticated computer-generated human-like faces which were wired to instantly recognise and then replicate and develop the emotions human beings displayed or hid when exposed to different things.

Hiroaki and I specialised in the lucrative old-age market, so we would pay a demographically measured cross-section of the population to come into our facility where we would film them watching a whole range of events, from live country-and-western singing to television car adverts. Emotive analytics is based on charting human emotion into seven main categories: joy, sadness, anger, fear, surprise, contempt and disgust. Within those seven categories we developed other strata, for human beings are far more nuanced than those broad categories would suggest. We'd show a short film of an older lady, for example, whose only companion was her much loved dog. The dog became ill and died, and it was fascinating recording the emotions displayed by the cross-section of people we filmed watching the film. Interestingly, younger females showed more distress, while the algorithmic pattern of older women showed more fear than sadness. The dog food company who had funded that particular line of research found it really useful: they could concentrate on the daily health values of their dog food on the younger people, whilst emphasising canine longevity for the older women.

I loved coding. For the first time I felt superior to Emma. She could play Mozart backwards if she wanted, but here I was with my own secret cult language that only the initiated understood. It was like having magic powers: registering sequential codes into the software in the knowledge that at the end of the tunnels light and clarity would emerge, like fairies out of the knoll.

Hiroaki and I became good friends. He had a deeply ingrained Japanese sense of honour which I greatly admired. Everything he taught me he taught with clarity and precision, and would always make sure that I understood it thoroughly. He never taught coding in isolation. It was always framed in a social context. We went to several conferences where this aspect was stressed. I remember going with him to the First International Cultural Robotics Conference in Kobe, where I was particularly taken with the talk 'Towards Socializing Non-anthropomorphic Robots by Harnessing Dancer's Kinaesthetic Awareness'. The researchers were showing how dance movements could be used to develop body flexibility in the androids we were building.

The turning point came on our visit to Seoul. A small group of us were instructed to go over there to attend the parent company's seminar on Social Robotics. At the end of the week I was asked to go for dinner with Ban Hun-hyun, one of the major shareholders. For some reason

I thought he'd be a young entrepreneur. He was in fact a rather distinguished elderly gentleman. He wore a long white kaftan shirt over momohiki-style baggy trousers He had perfect manners and decorum. We met in the foyer of the Grand Hyatt and he was obviously well-regarded there. They led us through to an exquisite private garden room at the back. He had beautiful English, and approached technical issues with a poet's grace. Computers were like flower ponds, and coding was the modern version of haiku. He told me something of his family background – his father had been a rice farmer who'd lost his land in the great flood and was forced to move into the city where he began life again as a market-trader, selling vegetables. Mr Hun-hyun reminded me of my own Grampa. He had the same slow, roundabout way of saying things, yet always with a purpose.

Looking back on it, I suppose in fact that's why I was deceived. He was old and venerable, so I graced him with good intentions. He praised me immensely.

'Mr Nagano says you are the best,' he told me. 'The very best. And not just with the details of things. What do you call it? The software? But with the more important side of it. You know the story of the Holy Grail of course? Well, we have our own version of it. There was a man who grew very old – even older than I am,' and he smiled. 'And one day he knelt down by the pond to pick up a lily when he saw his own reflection in the water. And he was as young and beautiful as he had ever been. He had found the holy grail.'

His eyes were bright blue and shining.

'You know what people want, of course?'

I looked at him. I thought my eyes were playing tricks on me, for he appeared to be growing younger as he spoke.

'To live forever,' he said. 'To be forever young. Like me.'

And he was back as he had been at first, quiet and distinguished. His eyes had turned silver grey.

'I can offer you a share,' he said. 'What we want to do is

to develop a proper android who will be more human than any human. Who will laugh and cry, and fall in love and feel despair. That will be as beautiful as a wild flower in a field. And once we perfect the prototype, everyone over forty will want to be one. Those under that age think they already have that anyway,' he said, smiling.

So I sold my story. Handed over the rights to Mr Hun-hyun that evening in the perfumed garden room. I would develop the software from the information I had and send it to his people who would work on the physical engineering side. The percentage fee was substantial enough, though that's not why I did it. It would be fascinating to see what had gone given new life.

'We'll try and showcase the product at the Toronto Expo in eighteen months' time,' he said to me. 'The time it takes for bamboo grass to regenerate.'

I worked hard on slinging code. Over and above my own version of what I remembered, I had also taken photographs and video and had recorded Grampa singing and telling stories and Granma cutting the roses in the garden and all that visual and verbal data was critical in establishing the engineering platform for such mundane things as linguistic pattern, head position, tilt, eye tracking and so on for the APIs (the Application Programming Interfaces). The product itself was being assembled in Seoul.

Emma accompanied me to the Expo. It was a beautiful early spring week in Toronto. We arrived early on the Monday and after checking into the hotel took a walk up towards the river, which was adorned with daffodils on either side. I've never been back in that yellow city since. Mr Hun-hyun had sent a message saying that he couldn't be there for Friday's unveiling, but wished me well.

'It's been a tremendous success,' he said. 'I have no doubt you will be astonished at what we've produced.'

I went to some of the conference presentations which

took place from Tuesday to Thursday, while Emma visited the galleries. She was fascinated by the works of Gagnon, and especially Edwin Holgate, and later on I believe she managed to buy some of his finest smaller works. The AI workshops I found most useful were the ones titled 'Using Social Robots to Improve the Quality of Life in the Elderly', though the most enjoyable was the one on the effects of an impolite versus polite robot playing rock-paper-scissors. Oh, they have emotions, oh yes they do! Especially when trained not to lose.

The hall was darkened on Friday morning for the first public display of the 'MacDonell Android', as it was promoted. In the absence of Mr Hun-hyun the session was introduced by Hiroaki, who made a splendid short speech on the ethics of artificial intelligence.

'It's like a tree,' he said. 'It exists. It doesn't need to justify its existence. It just is.'

He then stood silent on the stage for a moment before calling out the two names that sent a shiver through me:

'Magnus. Rachel.'

And to my horror the two of them walked on to the stage, side by side, as if alive. Yet they had no life: all the features were right, and the walk and the sing-song voice of Grampa and the tender way Granma glanced at him were correct, but...

There was something obscene about it. They themselves were not there.

Life is more than mere motion and voice and gesture.

I shut my eyes tight, calling up other images to replace the dead ones on the stage. Grampa tying the silver-fly bait on to the hook. Granma polishing the brass on Saturday evening while listening to The King's Singers on the radio. I left the darkened auditorium. Living memories continue to heal the scars of the steel and plastic android images I saw momentarily on the stage.

Afterwards, I confronted Hiroaki.

'I never imagined for a moment it would cause offence,' he said. 'We thought you'd be pleased. It was Mr Hun-hyun's idea.'

'It would be.' I looked straight into Hiroaki's eyes. 'Is he...?'

'Yes. My grandfather.'

'Good God. You too, Hiroaki?'

I didn't tell Emma what had happened. When I got back to the hotel she'd just returned from the gallery and was so excited, wanting to show me the catalogue of all the works she'd viewed during the day.

'Look. 'The Mother and Daughter'. Isn't that gorgeous? And here – Lismer's work. 'Rain in the North Country', 1920.'

They were lovely – the nude mother, with the clothed daughter looking down on the open book in her mother's hand.

I began packing the following evening as soon as we got back to Manhattan. Emma was in the bath. Schubert's Impromptu in G Major on the iPod. The old recording of Kempff. Either she'd ask or I'd tell her. She called through.

'Going on a journey?'

'Aye.'

'Anywhere special?'

'Home.'

The long piano notes hung in the air, as Kempff waited for the right moment to distil the next one. He was long finished by the time Emma came out in her bathrobe.

'Home?' she said.

'Yes. To Oxford. I can't bear the work any longer. It's... it's all wrong.'

'So what happened today?'

'Maybe I saw the future and became afraid.'

'Of?'

'Myself.

She stood near me.

'I'm afraid too,' she said. 'Which is why I'm staying here. At home. To work my own way through things. But I'll come and see you. Promise.'

17

I HAD TO give the tenants in Oxford a month's notice, so meantime I rented an apartment in London. The New York office were in touch with me, either angry or distressed about my attitude. I wasn't sure which. Perhaps they regretted the money and time they'd invested in training me, or perhaps they were genuinely surprised that I had completely misunderstood their intentions.

To their credit, they didn't let go that easily. The main marketing director, Richard 'Rick' Steele and his assistant Sue emailed me to say they were passing through London on their way to Tokyo. They had five hours to spare at Heathrow. Would I meet them? We met at The Three Bells pub at Terminal 3.

'So. How are you?' Rick asked.

'Fine. Just fine.'

'We're sorry...'

I waved their concern away.

'It's okay. It... it's what happens.'

'Yes. Still...'

We ordered drinks. Wine for them, tea for me.

'Organic of course?' Rick asked as he went up to order.

'Of course.'

'I apologise for what happened,' Rick said. 'I thought it was what we all wanted.'

'"We" may have wanted it, Richard. But I didn't.'

'It's the future, Gavin. You know that as well as I do. You should not fear the future. People always feared the future. Cave people feared the wheel. Horsemen feared the engine. Men feared the emancipation of women. The future is always fearful unless you control it.'

I laughed.

'Rick! Really? You know where it's all heading, Mr Steele. A future controlled by algorithms. By multinationals. Despite your best ethics, commerce will rule and steer you down pathways that even you will reject sooner or later. That's what I saw on the stage under the control of Hiroaki. Or was it his grandfather? Mr Ban Hun-hyun. A beautiful name. I fully understand that Artificial Intelligence will do beautiful things as well. The problem is not what computers can do. It's what humans do.'

He was silent, maybe conceding the point. Who knows?

'It's a terrible pity that all your knowledge – all your research – will go to waste,' Sue said.

'Oh, I don't think it will, 'I said. 'There are other... perhaps more basic ways to use it.'

'Such as?'

'Such as this. Simply sitting here waiting in Terminal 3 talking and telling stories.'

'Well, it's one old-fashioned ways of doing it. But we wanted to get final value out of your researches so...'

'The last pound of flesh?' I interrupted.

'...have you learned anything that would be of lasting use to us?'

'Only that the happiest people live in a blessèd state of stupidity.'

'We know that,' Rick said. 'That's how we make money. By making sure they continue to live there. Anything else?'

The most useful thing I'd learnt was that everyone had a story. A mythology into which they retreated when the going got tough. Calum to his fairies. Mr Johnstone to his drink. Rick and Sue to their bright future in AI. Myself to... for the spirit is willing but the flesh is weak. But I didn't say any of that.

'No,' I said. 'Nothing that would be "useful", as you put it.'

I knew very well that all such information would be passed on to the machine makers, to improve performance. I also understood that what was not said would equally be reported back.

'He didn't answer,' they'd write, 'meaning he was hiding something.'

The tannoy called the flight for Hanoi. Then announced that their flight to Tokyo was delayed for an hour. We ordered some food. A chicken salad for me, and sushi for them.

'Might as well get some practice in,' they said.

'So. That's it. The end for you then?' Rick asked.

'No. Just the beginning. No more executive orders. No more corporate planning. Just one day at a time.'

'Sweet Jesus?' said Rick.

They ordered another bottle of wine.

'Do you really believe in it, Rick? Or you, Sue? In the ethics of the thing.'

They laughed.

'Which ones are these, Gav? Those involved in developing a technology that will help people in their old age?'

'No, Rick. The ethics which take every human trait and mechanise it for commercial purposes.'

They laughed.

'Oh, not that hoary old chestnut, Gav. Isn't everything commercial? Sex, war, leisure. To be bought and sold. What do you think prostitution and soccer are? Hobbies? Don't you have a mobile there in your hand? Cars, planes, computers, x-ray machines...? Good God, let's not exalt the Luddites again.'

They had a point. There is no rational argument against progress.

'Too much collateral damage, though. Millions unemployed. The sea ice melting. Algorithms steering our lives.

Drones killing children. But then, you know all that already. Profit from it.'

'It was always like that. Except in a more primitive way. Stones, then spears and bombs. At least social media has democratised the world.'

'Nonsense. It's just given the mob a voice. Handed them the twenty-first century equivalent of medieval pickaxes to hack their way into the White House.'

'It's called democracy. We walked in there with Donald in broad daylight. Same as Nixon and Kennedy and all the rest of them. None of it was hidden.'

'Except for the Putin bit?' I asked.

'That too was known, Gav. If it wasn't Trump, it would be someone else. Puppets are a dime a dozen. The thing is, we've earned the trust of the poor,' Sue said, smiling. 'The future is ours. What's the phrase? The post-truth generation. You could be the bright light in our darkness if you want to salve your conscience?'

'Not if it means selling my soul.'

'For what doth it profit and all that?'

'Something like that.'

They were friends as well as colleagues.

'We'll be sorry to lose you, Gav. You bring a certain kind of... humanity to the table. And we'll miss that. It would have been useful.'

'Don't undersell yourselves,' I said. 'Despite appearances, both of you are all too human! It's what makes us different from machines – our hopes and lusts. Our flesh.'

They were lovers as well as friends and colleagues.

'So. What do you plan to do with yourself?' Rick asked.

'Oh, I don't know. This and that. Become an ornithologist. Base myself at Grampa's farm and nurture things. Plough the land. Rear pigs. Keep hens. Guard the sea lavender of the salt marshes. All those little things which remind me I'm made of dust.'

They laughed.

'The great escape, is it? Back to nature and all that. Shall we call you Adam?'

'No. The very opposite. The great commitment.'

'Don't get all holy on us, Gav. You're not going to save the world. You're as dependent on technology as all the rest of us.'

'It's not about technology. It's about values. Big, global and corporate or small, local and organic. I'm learning how to use a spade and pencil again.'

'Listen to Mr Pious,' Sue said. 'You honestly think you'll be able to save yourself from the coming storm? After all, you're equally responsible. Equally guilty.'

'Of?'

'Compromise. Collusion – you didn't walk to London, did you?'

Silence.

'Not any more. I've done with it. Repented, if you will.'

I think they pitied me rather than believed me.

'Back to the future?'

'No. That was Trump's call. The one you voted for. The alternative fact.'

'And your choice, Gav? Just to drop out?'

'No. The very opposite. To drop in. To live as a human being, not as an extension of a machine. To sow and plant and reap and grow. I'll travel by mule if I need to, and dig the earth by hand. You'll remember those old-fashioned things I was supposed to feed into the robots we were working on? Stories and fables and songs and religious beliefs and traditions and customs and all that stuff? Things that were intended to humanise the machine. That were meant to inject empathy and understanding and a sense of justice and a common cause into the neural network. All that stuff I digitised for you. Until I realised that none of it could be programmed without flesh. That a song not sung by a fragile

227

human being is no song at all.'

'Quite a speech,' Rick said.

'No, Rick. It's not a speech, it's a story. My story. Jung predicted it all more than a century ago when he said that the reason for evil in the world is that people are not able to tell their stories.'

'They have told their story,' Sue said. 'Your problem is that you don't like their story because it's not yours. It's just a different story now, and you'd better believe it, Gav. What you're really shying away from is the coming story. The machine's story. The new humans that will emerge from beneath the silicone surfaces. It's not Hansel and Gretel, but it will do just fine because it will fit the day.'

'I've met them,' I said. 'I still prefer the old ones. The ones with souls.'

'That's a matter of opinion,' she said. 'Who's to say that our new machine beings won't have "souls", as you put it? What makes you so special? They too will have a history, relationships, personalities. They too will sing and dance and tell stories and believe some things and not others. None of the things you're concerned about are the problem. Amazon, Google, Trump. These are just the Gutenberg and the Caxton and the Nero of their day. Poor Donald is not the disease, just the symptom.'

'Of?'

'Change and decay,' said Rick. 'The decline of the Roman Empire.'

'Or the start of the brave new world,' said Sue. 'The mob always execute or impeach their dear leaders in the end. History outlasts its fools and tyrants as well as its heroes.'

They were getting drunk, began touching and kissing each other. It was obvious they wanted me to leave.

'You can afford to have a conscience,' Rick said to me as I left. 'You're lucky. You have land and money. Make good use of it. Cattle and horses would be a good investment.

You should also buy yourself a bolt-hole in California. Great weather, as you know, even though it might be a bit too close to Silcon Valley for comfort. Or New Zealand. Where all the millenials are heading.'

'Thanks,' I said. 'I'll keep in touch.'

He gave me a pencil from the inside pocket of his jacket.

'You do that,' he said. 'It's a Staedtler Lumograph. Writes beautifully.'

The next day the estate agents phoned to confirm that the tenants had vacated Granma and Grampa's farm and had left the keys under the white stone by the orchard gate. I remembered the day Aoife and I painted the stone.
'It will then always shine like a light in the darkness,' Grampa had said. It would be the first thing I'd do when I got back. I knew he always kept a good supply of sealed paint tins in the garden shed, and the years would not have damaged them. He'd have sealed them with angelic care.

I caught the last train north to Oxford. A few stragglers in fancy-dress costume were still making their way home. It was a clear starry night as we travelled through the Chilterns. A crescent moon was visible to the west. The one on which Calum had hung his jacket. I hadn't rejected Rick and Sue at all. I was in exactly the same business as them, of making masks. When the moon was full, Neil Armstrong jumped on to it. Otherwise, he'd have fallen off the edge of it.

'Aye, but they'll never land on the sun,' Mary had said.

'Of course they will, darling,' John replied. 'During the night, when the light's out.'

Whether in words and images or in plastic and bots didn't matter. All of us were in the business of bringing things to life. Rick and Sue would do it through a screen or console, just as I might with a pencil, as Calum had done with a spade, and Elizabeth with a mirror.

I started by making a drawing of Calum, for the picture always comes first. He would have been a small man. Dark haired, with grey-blue eyes and a stubbly beard. Large but delicate hands. Intelligent, and looking out at the world as if at a mystery. I gave him a spade and hoe for digging the earth. He'd get up before dawn and go outside to urinate and defecate, and as he crouched there would look up at the moon and talk to the man who walked there with a scythe over his shoulder. For the most distant planets have the best inhabitants. Then they spoke, for speech always comes after vision.

'How's the weather up there?' Calum asked as he crouched by the river, and the man in the moon replied, 'Och – the usual. Sun when you need rain, and a downpour when you're drying the corn.'

'And how was the crop this year?'

'Excellent. I rotated the patches better. Planted the turnips over by the lake and the tatties over there at the foot of the hill. At the dark spot there, see?'

And Calum could. The dark spot on the moon down to the bottom right next to the clouds. By the big star whose name he couldn't remember. Betelgeuse. That was it. And as he strained he promised to himself that he'd also do that next year. Plant the turnips over by the loch and the tatties in that small patch next to the trees at the bottom of the ravine.

And what a decent woman Elizabeth was. Gallus. I came to know her with increasing awe. Feeding and clothing and washing and educating all the children while that wayward husband of hers talked to the moon and had his fabulous affair with his fairy lover. Though she too had her conversations, and I sat humbled when I heard her groans and prayers. If there was no other proof for the existence of God, she was proof enough. The streams whispered Amen and the mountains shouted Hallelujah as she breathed.

Then there was Angus. Big brave Angus who single-handedly killed twelve Turks in one day at Sevastopol. You should have seen him, decades later, on his homestead near Calgary, sitting on the veranda in his panama hat, like a man who'd spent his entire life sowing and hoeing and ploughing and reaping. Like a man who had never done anything except watch the corn grow, which is enough in itself. He pretended to folk he was Irish and called himself Óengus.

There were no ghosts but Grampa and Granma's empty house was full of voices when I got back there at one o'clock in the morning.

18

WORDS WERE NEVER her forte. She preferred silence to noise, and as a young girl learned that silence was also a powerful note. You could often get your way with it. As the family quarrelled endlessly about what to have for dinner or where to go on holiday, Emma would stay quiet, knowing she wouldn't be noticed in the storm. And then when things settled down she would make a suggestion, and her sudden quiet voice sounded so angelic that her advice was taken. She would have her way.

She realised that words were both insignificant and dangerous. They could not only mean anything, but – more importantly – be made to mean something completely different than intended. She remembered her father saying to her mother each morning as he left for work, 'See you at five thirty, darling,' and once he'd gone, her mother would say to her, 'That'll be seven o'clock, then, Emma.'

There were bigger examples. Once, at college, she praised one of the lecturer's talks, and he immediately interpreted it as a come-on, asking her if she'd come to the pub with him that evening. He was ugly and middle-aged and she said to him, 'No. I admire how donkeys bray, but I don't go out with them.'

Music was always a comfort and a strength. The best way she could express herself really. She remembered the first time she heard the CD of Jacqueline du Pré playing the Elgar Cello Concerto. Every nerve end in her body stirred, and it was as if the whole universe had stopped, waiting to hear what the next note promised.

Like every other teenager, Emma also went through the phase where song lyrics spoke for her. She listened to anything and everything, from medieval madrigals to Beyoncé. The things that she couldn't say they said. 'Did you ever stop to notice the crying earth, the weeping shores?' Michael Jackson sang for her.

She always knew, however, that music was superior to words, because it articulated silence as well as speech. The trick was to create the void. The listener would then inhabit and nurture that space. Notes themselves were not just signals, but symbols. For things she'd felt and desired. She knew this: that she'd always wanted to sing. All the time, like a child, before the world tells that child that singing is inappropriate.

'Sush! Your father is speaking now.'

'Hush! I'm watching this programme just now.'

'Be quiet, so that I can hear myself thinking.'

'You don't need to make a song and dance about it, Emma!'

What else should you do except make a song and dance about it? Like a baby, rocking backwards and forwards. Like a child singing to her cat. Emma remembered asking her mother one day,

'Mum. Why do we not sing instead of speak?'

'Don't be daft,' her mum had said. 'Singing is only for special times. At concerts or in church. Places like that.'

Emma knew she was wrong. Singing and dancing had come first. And all speech and music had come from that. Singing was for all places at all times. She sang to the trees as she walked to school. The trees sang back, as they moved in the wind.

While I discovered my past, she explored the future. She spent those months on a work called 'The Moving of a Pencil.' It was a piece speaking of the joy of stillness and of movement, and of how the movement of anything, from the tip of a pencil to tribes crossing continents become constantly shifting spacetime.

Her father was from Belfast and her mother from Cork. Love had bridged the religious divide, though that hadn't stopped endless arguments about nationalism and independence. The fieriest times were when they disagreed about the so-called 'border songs'. Once he'd taken a few drinks her father would begin singing some Orange songs, which her mother claimed were traditional Gaeilge tunes.

'These are just Protestant unionist words laid on top of old Catholic tunes,' she'd say.

'Sure enough, the best thing to do with Catholic tunes is to bury them,' her father said, smiling.

It was lovely to receive a letter. I'd forgotten the pleasure of seeing the postman delivering an airmail envelope. I hadn't seen one since my mother sent me one decades ago, before electronics made them obsolete. I may have imagined there was an extra spring in the postman's step that morning as he walked up to the house with the letter. Certainly he was whistling.

I recognised Emma's handwriting. I made myself a coffee and went out into the conservatory to read the letter. It was a page of music. On the back she'd written,

I bet you looked at the notes and said to yourself 'Music'! But you'd be wrong. That's not music on the other side of this page – just lines and dots and signals and symbols. The music doesn't happen until you sing through and round and between the marks.

All my love,
Emma x.

I looked at the staves, the treble and bass clefs, the key and time signatures, all the dots, the quavers and semiquavers. This strange language which most folk couldn't read, but could hear if played. Just like my Grandfather's Gaelic. Everything meant something. I sang the tune, and even now, after all that has happened, the music means everything to me.

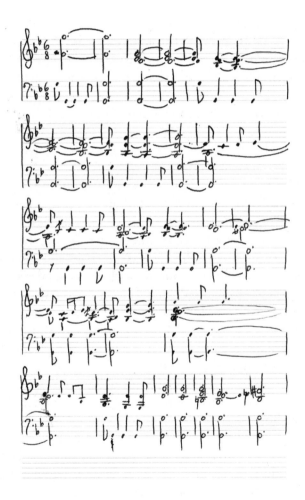

19

IT WAS SPRINGTIME. The time of year when the ground needed to be prepared. Fortunately old Bill Ashby still ran the neighbouring farm and offered all the advice and help he could give. He tried to persuade me to buy a tractor and a harvester, but I refused.

'I want to do it the old-fashioned way,' I said. 'Everything by hand.'

'It'll kill you,' he said, but was gracious enough to add, 'Mind you, so will everything else.'

So he took me in hand and showed me how the old potato drills worked, and where I should plant the turnips and cabbages and carrots, and which varieties I should plant, and we spent February and March getting the ground prepared as best we could. He was a hoarder too and though his children – and by now his grandchildren – had taken over his farm and mechanised everything, he had hardly thrown any of his own traditional implements away.

'Better to see them used than gathering dust and rust in my barns,' he said as he gave me a whole pile of old things, from hoes to hand-held ploughs.

'Of course,' he added, 'it's all a lifetime's work. Plant nothing this year. Just prepare. You've plenty time. Nature can't be hurried.'

Which was just as well, for I was waiting an Easter call from Emma, and I knew full well – or at least hoped – that would take up take up the whole of the planting and growing season. We'd made an agreement some nine months beforehand not to contact each other except in an emergency.

'I need time and space,' she'd said. 'To work. Six months at least. No texts. No emails. Nothing. I'll phone you on Easter Sunday. Promise.'

A few weeks before Easter old Bill called in.

'The Fair's next week,' he said. 'At Aikley. Still the best horse fair in England. We should go there.'

I wasn't sure I was ready.

'You need to start sometime,' he said. 'And I won't be around forever. So if you'd like me to help we'll go down there on Monday. Monday's always the best day. If you leave it till later in the week you'll only get the dregs.'

He spotted the horse for me almost the moment we got there.

'There. What a beauty. Look at her, Gav.'

A sturdy looking dappled grey horse.

'A Percheron,' Bill told me. 'Of course, in time, you'll need a whole team of them, but best to start small and learn, eh?'

'Of course,' I said. 'It's the only way.'

The seller delivered the horse at the end of the week and Bill then spent the next few days with me teaching me how to feed and care for the horse and how to harness it ready for work. I was a slow learner, but as Bill kept saying, 'Keep at it. Practice makes perfect. And for goodness sake, give the horse a name so that you can talk to her! And make sure you listen when she talks back to you!'

I called her Maggie. By Easter Saturday we were like old friends.

I woke early on the Sunday morning. At six. I made coffee and sat out in the porch to watch the sun rise. Magnus always claimed that the sun danced on Easter day in celebration of the Resurrection. It was shimmering somewhere to the east, rising over Europe. The phone rang. I let it ring seven times, as agreed.

'Gav! How are you?'

Her voice was warm, friendly.

'Emma! I'm good. You? Goodness, it must be early – I mean late – over there.'

'It is. One o'clock in the morning.'

'How are you?'

'Fine, just fine. Guess what?'

'You've finished the symphony?'

'No, not quite. It didn't work out. The first two movements are okay, but then I found myself in a cul-de-sac. A theme, but no music. And you?'

'The other way round. Music but no theme. And guess what.'

'What?'

'I've bought a horse. And I'm not going back to the office.'

She laughed.

'I presume the two are related?'

'Indeed. I've traded in Albert for Maggie, as it were.'

'I like the gender balance, Gav. Listen, I've also got some news.'

'Yeah?'

'I've been given a commission to write the score for a film. In Rome. They're giving me an apartment there for a year.'

'Must be a big budget.'

'It is.'

'So what's the film?'

'Chaplin in Europe.'

'Hasn't that been done?'

'Not this century.'

'I see.'

'I'm flying in via Dublin next Monday. I plan to spend a week to ten days in each European country – sort of researching, getting the feel of places – before settling down to write in Rome. Maybe you could join me for the latter part of the journey, once I get to Amsterdam?

I hesitated. There was the horse and the farm to think about. No – it would be fine. I was sure Bill would look after things for me till I got back. After all, he did say to do things nice and slow. That this year was just preparation. Next year was planting.

'Of course,' I said. 'With pleasure.'

'I'm keeping an electronic log of the trip. I could message you.'

' That would be good. A kind of last technological hurrah. I'm going completely off-grid next year.'

'Like Saint Augustine? "Lord, give me chastity, but not yet"?'

I still miss her sense of humour.

I'd check Facebook every few days. Most of the messages were cryptic, but embossed now and again with a photograph or a video link. Emma, descending the aircraft stairs at Dublin. Hair cropped short and dyed blonde. She looked tanned and relaxed. Wearing a light raincoat, like Bardot in the late 1950s.

'Chic,' I messaged.

'Not the rage,' she messaged back. 'Bouffants and trouser suits are terribly in just now, wouldn't you know?'

'You sound Irish.'

'Remember, my mother was from here. A corker from Cork, my father used to say.'

Emma was extra communicative over Facebook, as if writing things in absentia gave her freedom.

She stayed in a small hotel off St Stephen's Green. She sent me a photo of the ivy-covered door with a bell ringer in the image of the Virgin Mary.

'Emma's not my proper name,' she told me one day. 'I was christened Natasha. After the heroine in *War and Peace*. It was also my grandmother's name on my father's side. She was Natasha Semyonovna Petrovich. She married an Armenian Jew called Moses Garegin Geusugeutchugian.

When they emigrated to New York nobody could say their names right, that's why we became Getz. Then I read Jane Austen, and since our name had been changed over the centuries, I figured I'd call myself Emma.'

She was physically elegant. Every morning she'd alternate between yoga and ballet exercises and meditated for an hour every evening, saying 'Ohm' when she breathed out, and 'Yid' when she breathed in. The breaths were as regular as clockwork: a great stillness for five minutes, then an 'Ohm' as she breathed out. Then another great stillness for five minutes and a 'Yid' as she breathed in.

'Six Ohms and Six Yids' she called the whole thing.

Her yoga and ballet had the same kind of artistic discipline. When she made those movements which stretched her body to extremes she did it in slow motion as it were, as if placing your heel on top of your head whilst sitting straight-backed and motionless and upright was the most natural thing in the world.

'Which it is,' she'd say afterwards, 'once you understand it's all about muscle memory. Teaching your body to conform to your will. Just look at you, Gavin, hunched there as if you were born to crouch in a cave.'

And I would sit up straight for a while before slouching back down again.

She travelled for three months. Took the train south from Dublin to Cork and then on to Kerry where she spent a sunny week walking and cycling, before travelling north to Derry and to Belfast. The next message was from Paris. A selfie standing at the Atelier Brancusi.

'Have you seen Hemingway?' I texted.

'They say he passed this way a hundred years ago,' she texted back.

I was already beginning to regret my decision to go off-grid. All this would go too. This easy communication that was not spoilt by the physical presence of each other. By the look in the eyes which betrayed the words spoken, by the body language which contradicted what was being said. Here in this electronic world, everything was much safer. Emma chose when to speak and when not to speak. I chose when to hear and when not to hear. Nothing except the words themselves could contradict the brief messages we sent to one another. And when it came to the crunch, a lol always covered a multitude of sins.

I loved the photos she sent from Spain. Looking ever so healthy in her walking boots and shorts as she stood on the Camino Primitivo, and equally relaxed and at ease from the beach in Portugal.

' I will be in Amsterdam on Sunday afternoon,' she said. 'Are you still able to join me for the final stage?'

I almost sent a smiley, but decided words were better.

'Yes. Time? Location?'

'The Van Gogh Museum. At four.'

We hired bikes in Amsterdam and cycled through the lowlands of Holland and Belgium.

'Suits me perfectly,' I said to Emma, 'as a fully-paid up member of the Flat Earth Cycling Society.'

Even then, she still beat me, cycling away ahead of me at speed whenever the fancy took her. From Brussels we got the train to Berlin, where one morning we caught the wrong bus and ended up in this beautiful little Vietnamese café. Like Grampa, we drank loose-leaf tea from a proper china pot in delicate china cups before getting the bus back to our original stop.

'The best things happen by accident,' Emma said.

Once we got off the bus we walked in the opposite direction and wandered into one of those old second-hand bookshops where everything is accidental. It was run by a bereted lady called Hannah Raegenwelt, who told us she had escaped to freedom from the GDR by swimming the River Spree under cover of darkness. Emma found a book of Schoenberg's writings and, standing between the stacks, read to me, 'Everything we do not understand we take for an error.' As we were buying it, I accidentally dropped it on the floor and broke the binding. Hannah gave us the book as a free gift.

We went into a bar where a quartet were playing jazz. Vocals, bass, sax and piano. Now and again someone from the audience would saunter up to the mic and take over from the main vocalist. Some of the young people around us explained that it wasn't karaoke but a form of 'democratic improvisation' as one young woman put it. Emma went up to the mic and sang 'Autumn in New York'. It made us so nostalgic for something neither of us greatly cared for any more. Afterwards we went out into the park and made love under the maple trees.

Towards midnight we walked through the Tiergarten to the Reichstag. In reality, the building was even more impressive than we'd imagined. All these famous buildings throughout the world have now been professionally lit, so that once you've seen one you've seen them all. Every major attraction from the Taj Mahal to Eilean Donan Castle shimmer at you in computer-timed glows of blue and red and green and white. Nevertheless, the iconic steel and glass Reichstag Dome was something special. The two materials sustained each other in perfect unity. It made you believe that transparency was everything.

We sat in the darkened Tiergarten looking across at the illuminated Reichstag.

Emma said, 'Your proper work should really be this. To make a story out of glass and steel, not memory and straw. You need to deal with things as they are, not how they were.'

'Even if I prefer how they were?'

'Even if you prefer how they were. Nothing can be as it was. It has to be newly minted. Every day. Look at that building – redeemed for the future.'

The following morning we caught the train to Warsaw, then south the day after to Krakow. Emma had her laptop and began her Chaplin composition. She called it 'Glass and Steel'. She slipped a DVD into her laptop.

'When was the last time you watched this?' she asked.

Chaplin. *The Great Dictator*. 'Years ago,' I answered.

We watched it together as the flat Polish countryside swept by outside. I'd forgotten how funny and moving the picture was. How accurate Chaplin was with every gesture and movement and delivery. We were both in tears at the end, when Hynkel makes the great speech.

'Now that's glass and steel,' she said. 'Making fun of pomposity. Ridiculing fascism. Ignorance you can forgive. Stupidity you condemn.'

We visited Auschwitz and then travelled on by bus to Slovakia and on down through Hungary, Romania and Bulgaria. I liked Eastern Europe. There was less glass and steel. More concrete and dilapidated wood, and here and there through the rural areas you'd still see a lone herdsman steering goats up a hillside and men and women bent double working in the fields.

'It's why half the population are working over in Berlin and Paris and London,' Emma said.

We arrived in Rome from Greece on a beautiful August day. A berth on the overnight ferry from Patras to Bari, and then the early morning train north to the eternal city. I half-wished Bill was with me so that he could admire the sloping vineyards we passed. I took loads of photographs to show him when I got back home. Rome itself was hot and packed with tourists, but we got a taxi to take us to our apartment. It was in an elegant building on the top floor at the back off the Piazza San Paolo alla Regola, with a wonderful view of the city. From the roof terrace you could see across to St Peter's on one side and over towards Ostia and the Mediterranean on the other.

The film company installed a Steinway in the apartment to help Emma compose the score. She woke at five every morning and did her ballet or yoga and then I'd join her for tea and fruit at six. She'd then open the shutters and sit at the piano and play. She insisted I listen, which was a pleasure to do. She asked me to take notes, to tell her when I thought the music 'worked' and when it didn't. I protested that I was unqualified, but she said

'That's exactly why I'm asking you to listen. This is not music for critics, but for a cinema audience.'

So I listened with my ordinary ears. Sort of like a one-man focus group.

'Pompy,' I'd say to her if I felt the music was getting too affected.

'A bit more of that melody,' I'd suggest, or 'Maybe a bit less of that da-da-da-da, whatever it is.'

She always finished that 'consultation' part of the composition by about ten am. and I was then free to go about my own business while she spent the rest of the day honing up what she'd worked on, and playing it again and again alongside various Chaplin movies which she projected on to the cinema-size screen in the viewing room. And, day by day, everything surrounding her became part of the destiny of the music. The pigeons, cooing on the window ledges. The children calling and playing in the street far below. The church bells as they pealed for matins and mid-day and vespers. The scooters and hooting cars in the Piazza. And my presence, and silence too, in the room.

In the afternoons I walked the city. We had a hire car on permanent call from the film company and I took to driving out into the country. Not just to escape the heat and noise of the city, but to see for myself those vineyards and olive groves I promised to Bill. I got to know the Grazioni family in Casperia, who graciously agreed to show me the way they tilled and farmed the arid land that was theirs. The secret had mostly to do with irrigation, though that was just 'la evidencia visible' as Paolo put it. We conversed in Spanish which he spoke fluently, his mother being from Sevilla. But he had good broken English too, and when I asked him where all his knowledge came from he simply said, 'Experience.'

Rome is such a mythic place, so hard to leave. Who would want to depart from Raphael and Bernini and Caravaggio and Michelangelo? They made men out of marble and angels out of plaster, much as one might make music out of notes or fairies out of thin air.

The Chaplin film was a huge success. Millions flocked to see in cinemas throughout the world, and a good portion of them purchased the disc featuring Emma's music. It achieved everything she aimed for: melody and lyricism along with precision and clarity. Every note proved that time was fluid. After the premiere, we could hear the audience whistling and humming her theme tune as they left the theatre.

Here in Oxfordshire the earth has been prepared for seeding. Next year will be for planting, and I have even set aside a field for harvesting straw. There's an increasing specialist market in it for insulation and thatching. And just to balance things out, I've spent a good deal of time visiting the local scrapyards and architectural salvage centres, rescuing old school windows and sinks which I've reconstructed into a steel and glass dome which serves as a miniature greenhouse down by the orchard. It reminds me daily that the past is not the future.

Acknowledgments

I owe some of the architecture of this novel to the Reverend Robert Kirk whose remarkable work *The Secret Commonwealth of Elves, Fauns and Fairies* was published in 1691.

My thanks to Jennie Renton for her generous advice and guidance while editing and typesetting this book, to Ruairidh MacKenzie of Inverness for his permission to use part of his unpublished memoir as part of my text, and to my daughter Brìghde for composing the piece of music which is part of the story. My wife Liondsaidh Chaimbeul read drafts of the work and I thank her for her love and encouragement, as well as for designing the cover, based on photographs we took in New York and Uist. My thanks to Anna McEvinney and Imogen Clarke for their insight and help during the final edit, and to Françoise Latour of France who read various versions of the work-in-progress, and to my publisher, Gavin MacDougall.

I am particularly grateful to Janice Galloway and Stewart Conn for their generous words about the novel on the cover, and to Eireann Leverett who advised me about Artificial Intelligence.

I was awarded the Dr Gavin Wallace Fellowship at the National Library of Scotland through Creative Scotland in 2016, which gave me valuable time to work on this novel and other writings. My thanks to Dr Gavin's family and the library staff for their support and encouragement. The works of Descartes, Janácek, Barenboim, Stravinsky, Schoenberg, Donne and Richards have been direct inspirations throughout the composition of this book.

Copyright Acknowledgements

I want to thank Colin Gale and Robert Howard for their kind permission to use extracts from the wonderful book they edited: *Presumed Curable – An illustrated casebook of Victorian psychiatric patients in Bethlem Hospital*, edited by Colin Gale and Robert Howard (Wrightson Biomedical Publishing Ltd, 2003). The case excerpts from that book are on pages 114, 115, 122 and 123. My thanks also to Comhairle Bhéaloideas Éireann for their gracious permission to use extracts from *Sean Ó Conaill's Book – Stories and Traditions from Iveragh*, recorded and edited by Séamus Ó Duilearga and published by the Comhairle in 1981. *Go raibh mìle maith agaibh*. The folktales themselves were collected from Seán between 1923 and 1931, and I hope he'd be pleased that Grampa Magnus and others get the chance to retell some of them here.

Some other books published by **LUATH PRESS**

Archie and the North Wind
Angus Peter Campbell
ISBN 978-1906817-38-1 PBK £8.99

The old story has it that
Archie, tired of the north wind,
sought to extinguish it.

Archie genuinely believes
the old legends he was told
as a child. Growing up on a
small island off the Scottish
coast and sheltered from the
rest of the world, despite all
the knowledge he gains as
an adult, he still believes in
the underlying truth of these
stories. To escape his mundane
life, Archie leaves home to find the hole where the North Wind
originates, to stop it blowing so harshly in winter.

Funny, original and very moving, *Archie and the North Wind*
demonstrates the raw power of storytelling.

The tale is complex, but told in confident style. Although every
page is marked with some unquiet reflection, these are off-set by
amusing observations which give the novel a sparkle.
SCOTTISH REVIEW OF BOOKS

The Girl on the Ferryboat

Angus Peter Campbell
ISBN 978-191002-118-7 PBK £7.99

Maybe it had just been a matter of time: had we had more time, what we would or could have achieved, together. Had we actually met that first time round, how different things might have been. The world we would have painted. Had we really loved each other, we would never have separated.

It was a long hot summer... A chance encounter on a ferry leads to a lifetime of regret for misplaced opportunities.

Beautifully written and vividly evoked, *The Girl on the Ferryboat* is a mirage of recollections looking back to the haze of one final prelapsarian summer on the Isle of Mull.

Transcendentally beautiful. THE SCOTSMAN

An exceptionally good novel. This is among the best pieces of narrative literary fiction to have emerged from Scotland in the 21st century, in any language. WEST HIGHLAND FREE PRESS

Despite its gentle tone, the questions it raises about fate, chance, and love persist after the book is closed.
THE HERALD

Transcendently beautiful... a delight in any language.
SCOTLAND ON SUNDAY

A memorable love story. THE DAILY MAIL

Details of books published by Luath Press can be found at:

www.luath.co.uk

Extract

Chapter 1 from *The Girl on the Ferryboat*
by Angus Peter Campbell

IT WAS A LONG hot summer: one of those which stays in the memory forever. I can still hear the hum of the bees, and the call of the rock pigeons far away, and then I heard them coming down from the hill.

Though it wasn't quite like that either, for first I heard the squeaking and creaking in the distance, as if the dry earth itself was yawning before cracking. Don't you remember – how the thin fissures would appear in the old peat bogs towards the middle of spring?

A gate opened, and we heard the clip-clop of the horse on the stones which covered The Old Man's Ditch, just out of sight. An Irishman, O'Riagan, was the Old Man – some poor old tinker who'd once taken a dram too many and fell into the ditch, never to rise.

Then they appeared – Alasdair and Kate, sitting gaily on top of the peat bags in the cart. He wearing a small brown bunnet, with a clay pipe stuck in his mouth, while she sat knitting beside him, singing. The world could never be improved. Adam and Eve never ate that apple, after all.

They were building their first boat, though neither of them were young.

At the time, I myself was very young, though I didn't know it then. The university behind me and the world before me, though I had no notion what to do with it. I had forever, with the daylight pouring out on every side from dawn till dusk, every day without end, without beginning.

I saw her first on the ferry as we sailed up through the Sound of Mull. Dark curly hair and freckles and a smile as bonny as the machair. Her eyes were blue: we looked at each other as she climbed and I descended the stairs between the deck and the restaurant. 'Sorry,' I said to her, trying to stand to one side, and she smiled and said, 'O, don't worry – I'll get by.'

I wanted to touch her arm as she passed, but I stayed my hand and she left. My sense is that she disembarked at Tobermory, though it could have been at Tiree or Coll. For in those days the boat called at all these different places which have now melted into one. Did the boat tie up alongside the quay, or was that the time they used a small fender with the travellers ascending or descending on iron ropes?

Maybe that was another pier somewhere else, some other time.

Algeciras to Tangier: I think that was the best voyage I ever made, that time I caught a train down through Spain, the ferry across to Tangier, and another train from there through the red desert down to Casablanca. Everything shimmered in the haze: I recall music and an old man playing draughts at a disused station and the gold minarets of Granada shining as we passed through.

The windows were folded down as we travelled through Morocco, with men in long white kaftans bent over the fields. I ran out of money and a young Berber boy who was also travelling paid my fare before disappearing into the crowd. That was in my third year at university, a while before time existed.

I walked over to where Alasdair and Kate and the horse and cart had now come into sight. 'There you are, Eochaidh,' I said to the pony, stroking the mane.

'Aye aye,' the old man said as we walked over to the

stream to water the horse.

While Eochaidh drank his world, Alasdair and Kate and I carried the peat bags to the stack. They would shape her later. Kate made the lunch and the four of us sat round the table eating ham and egg and slices of cheese and pickle.

Big Roderick they called my boss – the best boatmaker in the district when he was sober, who would occasionally go astray before returning to work with renewed vigour, as if the whole world needed to be created afresh. At this time we were at the beginning of creation: all revelation still lay ahead.

I was just a labourer. Big Roderick's servant.

'The tenon saw,' he'd shout now and again, and I'd run and get hold of that particular kind. The one with the thin rip-files for cutting across the grain. That was for the early, rough part of the work before the finesse set in and his ancient oak box with the polished chisels emerged to frame and bevel and pare and dovetail.

'How are you getting on?' Alasdair asked.

'O,' said Roderick, 'no reason to complain. You'll be launched by midsummer.'

'Blessings,' said Alasdair. 'Didn't I tell them there was no one like you this side of the Clyde?'

'Isn't truth lovely?' said Kate.

She was called Katell at the beginning. Katell Pelan from Becherel in Brittany, but who had now travelled the world with this little man she'd married nearly fifty years ago. Since they'd first met in a house in Edinburgh where she'd been a student but working in Bruntsfield as a servant girl and he cleaning the windows before starting his apprenticeship. A while then in Leith when he worked at Henry Robb's shipyards, and Clydebank after that under the shadow of John Brown's, before they went to Belfast and Harland & Wolff and the long years when he was at deep sea and the children came. First the bits of Breton and Gaelic then their mutual English and at last, here they were at the end of the journey, which had come so suddenly.

Big Roderick and I were caulking the carvel planks with oakum, fitted between the seams and the hull. How simple building a boat was: like a jigsaw. You only had to use common sense. Put one part next to another.

'Logic, boy,' Big Roderick would say, 'you just add bit to bit and before you know it you have a boat.'

Though we both knew fine that nothing was that simple. The difficulty of course was in knowing which bits fitted where, which bits made sense.

We rested a while by the unfinished stern, looking out west towards the Atlantic. A large vessel of some kind was sailing north.

'So,' he said then. 'And did you learn anything of worth at that university of yours?'

Well, what would I say? That I hadn't? – the great lie. Or that I had? – the bigger lie. Sartre and Marx and Hegel and all the rest.

'Yes,' I said, 'though I'm not very sure what use it'll do me.'

He lifted the gouge from his apron. 'Never tell me that a thing is of no use. You got a chance I never had. With this gouge I can shape wood. But with your education…'

He stood up, pointing to the vessel which was far out at sea.

'The day will come,' he said, 'when there will be no day like this. When we'll all be strangers and we won't believe a thing. Keep your education for that day.'

And we continued shaping the wood for the rest of the day.

Luath Press Limited

committed to publishing well written books worth reading

LUATH PRESS takes its name from Robert Burns, whose little collie Luath (*Gael.*, swift or nimble) tripped up Jean Armour at a wedding and gave him the chance to speak to the woman who was to be his wife and the abiding love of his life. Burns called one of the 'Twa Dogs' Luath after Cuchullin's hunting dog in Ossian's *Fingal*. Luath Press was established in 1981 in the heart of Burns country, and is now based a few steps up the road from Burns' first lodgings on Edinburgh's Royal Mile. Luath offers you distinctive writing with a hint of unexpected pleasures.

Most bookshops in the UK, the US, Canada, Australia, New Zealand and parts of Europe, either carry our books in stock or can order them for you. To order direct from us, please send a £sterling cheque, postal order, international money order or your credit card details (number, address of cardholder and expiry date) to us at the address below. Please add post and packing as follows: UK – £1.00 per delivery address; overseas surface mail – £2.50 per delivery address; overseas airmail – £3.50 for the first book to each delivery address, plus £1.00 for each additional book by airmail to the same address. If your order is a gift, we will happily enclose your card or message at no extra charge.

Luath Press Limited
543/2 Castlehill
The Royal Mile
Edinburgh EH1 2ND
Scotland
Telephone: +44 (0)131 225 4326 (24 hours)
email: sales@luath. co.uk
Website: www. luath.co.uk